Readers love the Fabric Hearts stories by KC Burn

Tartan Candy

"…a captivating read with characters I really enjoyed, steamy sex, interesting secondary characters and a sweet love story."
—Open Skye Book Reviews

"Sweet, romantic love story you will enjoy very much if you like hot men, kilts, and true emotions."
—Three Books Over the Rainbow

Plaid versus Paisley

"KC Burns gave us two lovable characters with flaws and struggles that not only endeared me to them but I cheered for on the sidelines."
—Diverse Reader

"*Plaid Versus Paisley* proved to be a satisfying, worthwhile read…"
—Just Love: Queer Book Reviews

Just Add Argyle

"I can't recommend *Just Add Argyle* enough!! The story is intense, the depth of emotion behind the writing is just, WOW!"
—Love Bytes

"This was an amazing read and definitely on my recommended list."
—Gay Book Reviews

By KC BURN

Grand Adventures (Dreamspinner Anthology)
One Pulse (Dreamspinner Anthology)
Pen Name – Doctor Chicken
Rainbow Blues
Tea or Consequences

FABRIC HEARTS
Tartan Candy
Plaid versus Paisley
Just Add Argyle

TORONTO TALES
Cop Out
Cover Up
Cast Off

Published by DREAMSPINNER PRESS
www.dreamspinnerpress.com

TEA *or* CONSEQUENCES

KC Burn

REAMSPINNER
PRESS

Published by
DREAMSPINNER PRESS

5032 Capital Circle SW, Suite 2, PMB# 279, Tallahassee, FL 32305-7886 USA
www.dreamspinnerpress.com

ISBN: 978-1-63533-894-2
Digital ISBN: 978-1-63533-895-9
Library of Congress Control Number: 2017906668
Published September 2017
v. 1.0

Printed in the United States of America
∞
This paper meets the requirements of
ANSI/NISO Z39.48-1992 (Permanence of Paper).

Chapter ONE

FUCKING CLIMATE change. Riley Parker scowled at his reflection in the mirrored interior of the elevator. A furious sneezing fit had woken him up before his alarm and started everything on the wrong foot. An unseasonably warm April had unleashed a torrent of pollen, and Riley had been forced to break open the antihistamines. Even with the pharmaceutical assistance, congestion filled his head with cotton balls and he'd managed to miss his usual streetcar. He wasn't late yet, but it was a near thing.

The elevator rocked to a stop. He strode into the lobby of Gautier Cosmetics and dredged up a half smile for Alisha, the receptionist.

"Good morning, Riley." As always, Alisha was so cheery not even Riley's bad mood was immune.

"Morning, Alisha. How was your weekend?"

"So-so." Alisha rolled her eyes. "I had a blind date."

Riley grimaced. He'd been set up enough times to know that odds were the date had been a total shitfest.

Alisha correctly read his expression. "Yeah, it was that awful. Free for lunch? I can tell you all about it. I swear, I could write a book."

"You could. Although it might put the rest of us off dating for life."

"Hey, if something good comes out of it...."

Riley laughed. "Not sure about lunch. Mondays can be a bit of a nightmare." Likely it would be even busier than normal since his boss, Gabrielle Gautier, president of Gautier Cosmetics, had been away since Wednesday and the inmates would be champing at the bit for a piece of her.

"C'mon. Surely you can get away for even half an hour."

Riley let himself be persuaded. "I'll do my best."

As he was a temp, nobody gave a shit who he had lunch with. He didn't have to worry about political landmines or petty interpersonal wars. No one cared who socialized with him, and that was a great perk of his career choice. On the other hand, some people pretended the temp didn't exist, or underhanded employees thought a temp at Riley's level might know something useful, but Riley had been dealing with two-faced bastards since high school, and he could spot them a mile away.

Alisha wasn't like that.

Due to his late start, Riley didn't have time to chat. With a minute to spare, he made it to his desk. Or at least the desk of Gabrielle Gautier's customary assistant, Aaron Brown.

Just like every other morning since he'd started his contract at Gautier Cosmetics, Gabrielle was already in her office. After booting up his computer and scanning the shared calendars, Riley knocked and poked his head in.

"Good morning."

"Bonjour, Riley."

"How was your long weekend?" Without a husband or young children to pressure her into it, Riley had been surprised Gabrielle had taken time off so close to the launch of their new product.

"Perfection. Las Vegas is so stimulating."

Las Vegas? Never in a million years would he have guessed.

"I haven't been in a long time, but I liked it." The week after graduation, he and his best friend, Shaun, had flown down and celebrated. They were lucky neither of them ended up getting alcohol poisoning, gay bashed, or arrested.

"Riley, *chéri*, what does my schedule look like today?"

"Busy as usual. You're booked solid starting in about an hour until quitting time." Riley's quitting time, that was. Gabrielle got to the office before Riley and left after him. Yet another reason Riley much preferred his own career path.

Gabrielle stood and paced by her desk before pausing in front of one of the floor-to-ceiling windows. As high up as they were, the view was fantastic, and Riley didn't know how she ignored it for hours on end. He might bitch sometimes about how many people Toronto held, but the city looked vibrant and beautiful, and he wasn't sure he'd ever want to live anywhere else.

"Do you believe in love at first sight?"

Riley blinked. They'd occasionally spoken about personal topics like the difficulties of being a woman in her position, and the challenges of employing her extremely competitive children, but he'd never heard her speak about something quite so frivolous.

"I certainly haven't experienced it." Hell, he hadn't experienced love at all, but there'd been a boy in high school. A boy who'd turned Riley's guts inside out whenever he was around. A boy who'd made Riley wave his gayness around like a beacon, trying to get a reaction. But that was hardly love. "I don't know if I'd discredit it out of hand, though."

"Perhaps I am just a foolish old woman."

"Definitely not." Gabrielle's employees might use a number of unflattering adjectives to describe her, but *foolish* and *old* were not ones Riley had heard, nor would he ever be tempted to use them.

Gabrielle sighed again before sitting down. Something wasn't right. Gabrielle was a sophisticated, glamorous woman in her midfifties who'd built a thriving company while raising two children as a divorced single mother. She'd certainly earned the right to be tired, but this was the first time Riley had seen her look anything besides perfect.

"Are you feeling well? Perhaps you should take the day off." There would be screams of anguish from many departments, but Riley excelled at creating barriers to prevent access to his employers.

Gabrielle answered with a half smile that did nothing to brighten the tinge of gray in her face. "*Merci, mais non.* I may have indulged too much this weekend. But it will pass."

Admitting weakness of any sort was out of character for a woman like Gabrielle, but there was something about being a temp with a nondisclosure agreement that made some people drop their walls.

"Is there anything I can do? Run out for something special to eat?"

This time Gabrielle's smile was stronger. "You're just a treasure, Riley. What would you think about staying on with me after your contract is up?"

Riley respected the hell out of what she'd done with her company, she never asked for anything ridiculous or illegal, and he loved the direct commute on the King streetcar, but he doubted he'd accept her offer. He wasn't about to refuse outright, though. Despite the French endearments, Gabrielle was every bit as ruthless as any CEO he'd come across, often harsh even when she took her vice president of

Finance and vice president of Development to task, who were her son and daughter, respectively.

"You'll feel differently once Aaron is back on his feet." This wasn't the first time Riley had said that, and he suspected he'd be saying it a few more times.

"Perhaps. Perhaps not. Should Aaron return, I can always find a position for him."

Riley wasn't about to argue. "Anything else I need to know about today?"

"I've got an appointment with my lawyer at eleven. We'll be going to lunch afterward. Please rearrange my schedule to allow for that."

Shit. Between the short notice and the looming launch, rescheduling around three hours of meetings was going to be a nightmare. He'd faced worse, though.

"Of course. I should get to work on your new schedule right away."

"Surely, *chéri*, you do not need to rush off *immédiatement*. Have a cup of tea with me. I think I'm going to need the fortification."

Riley desperately wanted to know what the meeting with the lawyer was about—not the first time his professionalism warred with insatiable curiosity.

Metaphorically biting his tongue, Riley leaped to his feet to prepare tea. It had taken all of a day for him to realize Gabrielle's "suggestions" were nothing less than cashmere-wrapped orders.

Gabrielle might not have much time outside of the office to enjoy the finer things, but she hadn't skimped on the tea tray in her office. Hidden in a cabinet made of the same mahogany as her desk and other furniture, Gabrielle's tea caddy would make a barista swoon. Or... was there another name for tea aficionados? Riley didn't mind tea, but tea preparation was almost an art where Gabrielle was concerned.

Vendors, clients, associates—anyone who wanted to get or stay in Gabrielle's good graces sent her teas from all over the world. To give Gabrielle her due, she sampled everything and quickly dispatched a thank-you note. She definitely had her favorites, which Riley wouldn't use to wash dog shit off his shoes, but some of them he'd taken a liking to.

As they relaxed back in their chairs, steaming cups by their sides, the dainty teacups terrifying in their delicateness, Riley waited for further instructions, but Gabrielle merely sipped at her tea, lost in thought.

Riley cleared his throat. "I'm sorry if this isn't any of my business, but is it weird owning a company with your ex-husband's name on it?"

Gabrielle stared at him for a moment before laughing. "*Mais non, mon petit*. Gautier is my name."

But that didn't make sense.

"Oh. Since François and Floriana are both Gautiers, I assumed that was your married name."

He could see Gabrielle returning to her maiden name after her divorce, but had she never been married at all?

Gabrielle waved a hand. "In Quebec, it's not permitted for women to take their husband's name when they marry."

"Really?"

"Yes. It was a new law when I got married, but it made things a lot easier for me. My husband's name was Hall. David Hall." Her accent disappeared completely as she spoke her ex's name in flat, nasally tones. She was clearly imitating an English speaker, but he didn't know if that was just her standard anglophone accent or if she was mocking the man himself.

"What's wrong with that?"

Gabrielle lifted a shoulder and took another sip of tea. "There is no music in that name. As for the children... *mon Dieu*, Gautier-Hall sounds like a horrific boarding school with delusions of pretentiousness. David allowed them to take my name, and it worked out perfectly for the business."

Riley took a giant mouthful of tea—almost draining the tiny cup—because he wasn't quite sure how to respond. It was the twenty-first century, and the need for women to take their husband's name as though they were some sort of chattel seemed unnecessary and old-fashioned, but he wondered if the unlyrically named David Hall had taken the naming of his children passively. Riley also wondered how François and Floriana felt about their mother's dismissive attitude toward their father.

"Do you think Floriana will keep her name if she marries?"

In anyone else, the noise Gabrielle made would have been termed a snort, but her elegance tempered the sound into something equally disdainful and yet somehow still refined. "She will if she wants my approval."

Interesting. Gabrielle had a hint of an archaic tyrant in her. Riley glanced at his watch. It was about time for him to return to work if he was going to give her subordinates appropriate notice for changed meeting times.

"Thank you for the tea, Gabrielle. Can I fix you another cup before I get back to my desk?" He'd learned early on that Gabrielle didn't like the phrase *get back to work*. She didn't see tea breaks as frivolous and claimed she did some of her best thinking with a cup of tea in her hand.

"Non, merci."

Riley rose and made a move to take her teacup to bring it out to the kitchen for washing, but she moved her hand over it.

"I may make another cup." She drank far more tea than Riley fixed for her, and although he didn't mind making tea when she had meetings— all part and parcel of being an assistant—he might be annoyed if she called him into her office every time she wanted a cup.

Without another word, Riley left her office and ignored all the messages and emails in favor of getting Gabrielle's calendar in order. She'd already blocked time for her meeting with Mr. Hanover, her lawyer, and it was merely a case of shifting all her conflicting meetings to other days and times. Then he shot a quick message to Alisha. With Gabrielle going out for lunch, Riley would be free to do the same.

RILEY WAS back at his desk well before Gabrielle was scheduled to return from her lunch. The well-dressed older gentleman who'd proven to be Mr. Hanover had been quite attractive. Perhaps there was more going on than just business. Riley smiled to himself. He'd seen enough of Gabrielle's volatile children to wonder how they'd deal with their mother having a romantic life.

Taking advantage of Gabrielle's absence, Riley slid into her office to check for dirty teacups. He gathered up three, the last one from her desk. Normally Gabrielle kept her desk tidy, so the stack of folders with pages partly hanging out was unusual. Also out of the norm—they were older files she'd apparently retrieved herself. If they were on her desk, though, they weren't ready for filing, so he set the cups down and straightened out the pages. Peculiar wording on one caught his eye, and he flipped open the folder.

Gabrielle's will. Riley sucked in a breath and pressed a fist into his stomach. This explained the visit from the lawyer. Was she ill?

The will had been signed over ten years ago. Riley slapped the folder shut. Without checking the terms—even he had to admit that was nosiness beyond the realm of decency—if he had to guess, it had been revised around the same time Gabrielle's youngest, Floriana, had been hired by Gautier Cosmetics. Was she cutting one of her children out? Had Floriana actually ended up with an unsuitable boyfriend as he'd heard once or twice in the halls?

It didn't have to be bad. Maybe François's wife was pregnant. Given Gabrielle's extensive wealth and holdings, the arrival of a grandchild— her first—could easily be a reason to change or review her will.

Enough, Riley! He gave himself a mental slap. He had far too much work to do for useless speculation. But he was nosy by nature, and he'd keep his eyes open for confirmation of… something.

Once everything was tidy, he grabbed the delicate teacups and let himself out of Gabrielle's office.

"What are you doing sneaking around?"

The harsh accusation made Riley jump, nearly sending the fine china to the floor. He whirled around to face the speaker: Floriana, early for her meeting with Gabrielle.

Riley drew his shoulders back and announced in his haughtiest tones, "I was not *sneaking*. As you can see, I was retrieving dirty teacups." He brandished them at Floriana in case she'd missed them. "Otherwise known as doing my job."

Floriana gave him a little grimace but didn't apologize. She didn't like him, hadn't from the first. Riley didn't know why. Homophobic, perhaps, or resentful that Gabrielle relied on him. Or maybe she was just nuttier than peanut brittle.

"Where's my mother? I can't believe you moved my meeting and then didn't even bother responding to my email. I don't want it changed. I have too much to do without you messing with my day. Don't you know we're only days from the most important launch of my career?"

Riley took the teacups into the executive kitchenette around the corner, placed the cups in the sink, and returned. Floriana's tirade didn't let up for a moment.

He sat at his desk and blinked innocently up at her. Probably he should have stayed in the kitchenette and washed the damn cups, but that might have been like tossing grain alcohol on her crazy wildfire.

"Well? Where's my mother? And who is this Hanover you gave preference?"

"I rearranged her schedule at her request." He narrowed his eyes. "And I'm well aware she won't be pleased if you second-guess her decisions."

Floriana pressed her lips together, looking like she'd been force-fed a handful of sour Skittles.

"And as for Mr. Hanover, if Gabrielle wants you to know about her other meetings, she can discuss them with you. I am not at liberty to do so." Presumably he wasn't one of the company lawyers, or anyone on regular retainer for Gautier Cosmetics.

Floriana found her voice again, unfortunately. "Well, where is she now? I can't wait about all day."

"At lunch. And you're early."

"Lunch? Impossible. My mother would never slack off this close to a launch. Why are you lying?" If Floriana could spit venom, Riley would be dead right now.

Riley had dealt with a number of irritating and unusual people over the course of his varied career, but Floriana was a bitter woman who spent her life competing with her mother and failing. Perhaps she'd have become a nicer woman if she hadn't joined the family business.

"*Mon Dieu*, Floriana. I was not slacking, I had a business lunch."

Floriana grimaced and faced her mother, her tone smoothing into something a great deal more syrupy and a thousand times more fake. "More important than the launch?"

"Irrelevant. It needed to be taken care of, since I'll be making a special announcement at the launch party."

"What announcement?" Floriana's eyes widened. This was the first Riley had heard of an announcement, but he was surprised Floriana didn't know what was going on.

"You'll hear it with everyone else Friday night."

Riley nearly laughed. He could practically hear Floriana's teeth gnashing in frustration.

"You can wait in my office, *ma petite*." Gabrielle's patronizing tone made Floriana's nostrils flare.

Nevertheless, she stomped into her mother's office, effectively dismissed. Gabrielle patted Riley's shoulder in a manner that was supposed to be comforting, but it was obvious she wasn't particularly skilled at it.

"Can you review the file for the launch party? Make sure everything is in order? I think a few confirmations need to be made with caterers and such. Aaron left it pretty well finished, I believe. If you could take it on, I'd appreciate it."

"I'd be happy to."

"And please feel free to bring a date Friday night if you'd like."

"Oh. I didn't realize I was invited." Temps and contractors so often were left out of celebrations as part of controlling costs.

"Of course you are. You must show up. You've been absolutely indispensable these past two weeks." Gabrielle gave him a cheeky grin that stripped decades from her face. "If you enjoy yourself, you might consider my offer to stay on permanently."

Riley laughed. He wasn't surprised she had an ulterior motive, but it was the sort he didn't mind at all. "I'll be there."

"And a date?"

"We'll see."

Gabrielle winked and swanned into her office.

Maybe he didn't need a date, exactly. He slipped on his headset and called the front desk.

"Gautier Cosmetics, how can I direct your call?" Alisha was every bit as perky on the phone as she was in person.

"Hey, it's Riley. Are you bringing a date to the launch party on Friday?"

"Uh, no. I like my job and I want to keep it."

Riley snickered. "Wanna be my date?"

"You don't have some nice hunk of man you want to bring?"

"Where am I going to find one of those in the next five days? My friend Shaun would be happy to come for free booze and munchies, but I'd feel bad if I had to leave him to fend for himself."

"Then consider me your date."

After Floriana left, a steady stream of people came in and out. Riley directed the flow in between digging into the party file.

The file included a couple of minor errors, and an enormous one. Right before he cut out for the day, he took advantage of a fifteen-minute gap and stuck his head in Gabrielle's office.

"Oh, Riley. You should be on your way home."

He moved into her office, letting the door close behind him. "I'll head out in a few minutes. Did you need me to order in dinner?"

"*Mais non. Merci.* I'll be heading home after this conference call."

Riley waved the party file. "We're good on the party. I found a couple of typos, one of which was fairly significant, to the tune of twenty-five thousand dollars. The party isn't quite as expensive as it looked at first glance." Although he was pretty sure most people got married for less. Not that it was any of his business.

"Again?"

"Again?" Riley parroted.

Gabrielle huffed. "Aaron has been getting sloppy. That's the second typo of that nature recently."

Riley wasn't about to bash the man he was temporarily replacing, but he wondered if illness had affected Aaron's focus. "No harm done. We caught it in time." Before any money was moved around. It wasn't earmarked for any specific vendor, so it wasn't like checks would be issued with bonus money. Probably the money would have sat in the party account until the next launch, and they'd wonder why there was twenty-five large just sitting around doing nothing.

"It shouldn't have gotten past François's money monkeys either."

Riley had no response. Since this was a family-owned company, the Finance department might rubber-stamp certain expenses, no matter how ill-advised it might be. And he wasn't pleased about discovering one of Aaron's slipups. Ideally, he slid into a role, performed well, and slipped away again. He liked leaving a pleasant memory, not a gaping wound for a boss aggravated by the return of their regular assistant.

Chapter TWO

THE IMPENDING launch party had infused the office with a festive atmosphere. Most of the employees had been given the option to leave a couple of hours early to go home, freshen up, and snag their dates before returning to the party. Those with long commutes simply dispersed to nearby pubs and bars to get a head start on the drinking, letting their dates trickle into the city and meet them there.

Even with Gabrielle booked in back-to-back meetings, Riley'd had just enough time to get home, shower, and change. Alisha waited for him inside the building, but a reminder notification about his brother's birthday made him pause outside.

A few weeks ago, he'd suggested he and Jonathan go out for dinner or something to celebrate, but Jon's wife, Meredith, had planned a weekend away. Although Riley wasn't surprised Meredith would plan something special for Jon's fortieth, it did make him a little sad to know there was yet another milestone they'd spend doing their own thing. With nine years between them, they'd had little in common growing up, even less so after their parents died and Jon got stuck raising him. By the time Riley had grown up enough to meet his brother on equal adult footing, Jon had married and was working on opening his fledgling plastic surgery practice.

So often it felt like Jon didn't give a shit whether Riley was around. Maybe Riley had been more of a trial than he'd realized, but Jon never gave him a chance to apologize, or make it up to him, or anything. He just never seemed to have any time for Riley.

It wouldn't hurt to call Jon and at least wish him happy birthday, even if it was only on his voicemail.

"Hello?"

Stunned that Jon actually answered, Riley lost his words for a moment. Jon repeated his greeting, prompting Riley to speak past his surprise.

"Jon. Happy birthday."

"Thanks, Riley! I'm glad you called. I wish you'd been able to come over." Loud background noise almost obscured Jon's words.

Come over? What did Jon mean by that? Riley didn't get a chance to ask, because Meredith spoke loudly or close enough that Riley heard every word.

"Jon, dear, please put your phone away."

"Of course, Merry." The abbreviated form of her name brought a huff that even Riley could hear. Perhaps shortening her name was Jon's only form of rebellion. "I'll be right there."

"Hurry up. You're being rude to your guests."

Guests? Riley gritted his teeth. Surely that didn't mean what he thought it meant.

"Jon?"

"Yes, sorry, Riley. Wish you'd been able to make it to the party, but I know how busy you are. I appreciate the call."

Before Riley had a chance to say anything, Jon terminated the connection.

That fucking bitch. She'd told Riley they had plans for Jon's birthday. Plans that apparently included a birthday party Riley hadn't been invited to. He gripped his phone until his knuckles whitened, trying desperately to control his upset to avoid throwing his phone or bursting into tears.

As tempting as it would be to kick his professionalism to the curb and take full advantage of the open bar, he couldn't let his brother and his harpy of a wife continue to get under his skin. He was an independent adult, and maybe the time had come to stop trying to battle Meredith for tiny crumbs of Jon's attention.

Riley carefully tucked his phone into his pocket and scrubbed at his burning eyes with the backs of his hands. Jon hadn't disowned him when he'd come out in high school, so things could be worse. Other people had it worse than Riley. It hurt, but he was okay. He'd be okay.

He took a few calming breaths and strode into the building.

Alisha waved at him from behind the enormous rubber plant that served as decoration at the northeast corner. The sight of a friendly face did wonders to help him let go of his upset.

"Are you hiding?"

She shrugged. "No. Well, maybe. Gary the lab tech can be a little creepy, and it gets worse when he drinks. When the lab techs showed up a few minutes ago, I thought I'd just take a phone call over here instead of waiting around in plain view."

"Yeah, I guess I can understand that. You look great. I didn't think you were planning to go home."

Alisha gave him a very unladylike raspberry, completely at odds with her sleek red dress. "I keep a dress under the desk for emergencies such as this. Or last-minute dates."

Riley lifted an eyebrow. "Really?"

"Ha. As if. No, I changed my mind. Pregaming at a pub and then attending a work function doesn't actually sound smart. At least not for me. I just know I'd say something awful. I'm super sunny when sober, but my sarcasm gene is activated when I add alcohol."

"You are a very wise woman." Riley was rather looking forward to seeing other Gautier Cosmetics employees who weren't as savvy as Alisha.

"What about you, hot stuff? I thought you said you weren't going home between work and the party."

Riley fought off a blush but suspected he failed. Objectively he knew he looked decent, but a part of him never reconciled his exterior changes with the awkward, gangly teenager he'd been. "My friend Shaun convinced me I *had* to go out with him tonight. It's been a while, so I agreed. Which meant going home and changing."

"Friend?" Alisha wiggled her fingers in suggestive air quotes.

"No, we're not friends with benefits." Riley's laugh was only partially bitter. His life would be so much easier if he and Shaun could make a go of it, but it wasn't ever going to happen. "Shall we go up? I should probably be there in case there are issues."

Alisha rolled her eyes but nodded, and they headed to the elevator. "Since we both look hot as shit, can I invite myself along tonight? Or is it boys' night at the gay club?"

It only took Riley a split second to decide. "Sure, come along. It'll be fun." More fun than fending off Shaun's attempts to get him to fuck any halfway attractive man. In university, Shaun had helped him transform his look from nerdy and unremarkable to blond, twinkish, and slightly more remarkable. The dyed blond hair, blue contacts, and better sense of style contributed to Riley's self-confidence, but Shaun still seemed to think, years later, that he needed to direct Riley's social life.

"Awesome."

They entered the elevator. Alisha pressed their floor, then slid her arm through his. "Since you're the man of the hour, wanna tell me what this announcement is going to be?"

"Ugh. I have no idea." Riley had received no less than five invitations to join the preparty happy-hour festivities, all of which he'd declined. He'd like to think people were starting to warm up to him, but the more cynical side of him assumed everyone wanted the inside scoop. He didn't resent Alisha asking, though. She hadn't spent the past three weeks buttering him up.

"Really? I'm a little surprised."

"Not even Floriana knows what it is." He could impart that tidbit, at least.

"No shit?"

Riley snickered. Alisha truly was off the clock if she was swearing. "No shit."

"The rumors are rampant. Half the people think Gabrielle is closing the company down and letting us all go, a bunch think she's moving the operation to Quebec or China or Mexico or wherever and letting us all go, and the rest think she's expanding and there will be a slew of possible promotions."

Riley had wondered if it wasn't something more personal. "Wouldn't Floriana know about that?"

Alisha shrugged. "Eh. Maybe, maybe not."

"What do you think it is?" Riley wasn't really ready to share his own speculations, nor the fact that Gabrielle had been reviewing her will.

"Well, you aren't my only friend in this company. Heather—you know, the HR admin? We get pedicures together sometimes. She probably knows more than she's saying, but from the hints she's dropped, I think we're getting a new VP."

No fucking way. "I can't believe Gabrielle would let François or Floriana go easily."

"No, no. I mean an additional one. For a new department."

"Huh. Maybe that's why she's keeping it secret. Might put some noses out of joint bringing in a non–family member."

"You are as smart as you are hot, my friend."

Riley rolled his eyes but was saved from making a self-deprecating comment by the elevator doors opening.

The first thing Riley did was check in with the catering staff. Then he returned to Alisha's side and they inspected the canapé stations. A commotion at the other side of the room caught their attention.

Gabrielle strode in, looking as glamorous as a Hollywood heyday actress. On her arm was a tanned, extremely good-looking blond man who had to be younger than Riley, if not by much.

"Holy shit," Riley whispered and yanked on Alisha's arm. "Who the hell is with Gabrielle?"

"You don't know?" Alisha whispered back and led him off to the side for as much privacy as possible. "That's Gabrielle's latest flavor of the month. Cody Rosenberg."

He grimaced. "Crude. But I didn't know she had a… boyfriend."

Alisha's laugh was evil and gleeful at the same time. "He's younger than either of her kids, he's stuck around longer than most of Gabrielle's 'man friends,' and Flo and Frank just *despise* him."

Riley stared thoughtfully at the couple. Yet another dimension to the puzzle of Gabrielle asking him about love at first sight. They certainly seemed happy together, even if Gabrielle could be Cody's mother.

François and his wife, Bethany, strolled in a few minutes later, closely followed by Floriana, apparently solo. When François and Floriana looked at Cody, they grimaced like they'd swallowed rotten oysters. Bethany's face had the dead plastic look of a recent Botox treatment, so Riley couldn't be sure if she cared about Cody's presence.

As soon as Gabrielle noticed and waved them over, her children pasted on smiles. They weren't particularly successful. Considering how they treated Riley and other admins, he couldn't help but feel a bit of uncharitable delight at their discomfiture.

While Gabrielle and her entourage made their way through the throng, greeting everyone and stopping to chat here and there, Alisha dragged Riley to meet a few people, and Riley quickly lost interest in watching the royal family of Gautier Cosmetics.

ABOUT HALF an hour into the party, Riley excused himself from Alisha's side to take a quick tour. Being nominally in charge of ensuring there were no snags made it difficult to enjoy himself. Each food station he visited, he checked to make sure they were filled rather than eating anything himself. He had a personal rule about limiting the amount of alcohol he drank at work functions—like Alisha, he didn't want to say or do anything stupid—so he'd probably be nursing one glass of champagne for the rest of the night.

Going out with Shaun after this would actually be quite welcome. After the painful conversation with his brother, he could use a drink. And with Alisha along, Shaun might dial down his attempts to get Riley to pick up random men. Tonight might end up being one of the best nights he'd had in a long time. Anything was possible.

"Bonsoir, Riley."

He knew who was speaking without taking his eyes off the canapés. Turning, he smiled at his boss. "Good evening, Gabrielle. It's a lovely party, thank you."

Gabrielle gave him a tiny nod, still managing to look like a queen while carrying a plate of munchies, and Riley tried desperately not to stare at Cody. Cody wasn't Riley's type, but since he was straight, that hardly mattered. Nevertheless, Cody had the kind of good looks that belonged on a magazine. Gabrielle was a beautiful woman too, but Riley was surprised he hadn't heard much about Cody.

"Cody, let me introduce you to my new assistant. This is Riley. He's been taking over since Aaron left."

She'd made it sound as though Aaron was no longer with the company and Riley was filling the role permanently. However, it wasn't like she'd said anything *wrong*. "Nice to meet you, Cody."

Cody's handshake was firm, without any macho posturing. "Same, Riley."

"Cody is a marketing director at Treyhorn Associates."

Riley blinked. Treyhorn Associates was the company Gabrielle had contracted to take care of marketing and promotions for Gautier Cosmetics, since Gautier didn't have its own marketing department. "I didn't realize you were associated with Gautier. Do you work on their account?"

"He does. That's how we met, in fact." Gabrielle smiled at Cody like she was sharing a secret, and he returned that smile. "I'm going to be giving him plenty more work soon."

Riley made a noise in his throat, not sure he was supposed to understand the undercurrent in their words, and he hoped desperately they were actually talking about work and not fucking. He applauded Gabrielle for landing a sexy man like Cody Rosenberg, but he did not want to think about his boss fucking. That was out of the scope of his job requirements.

The pair stood close, almost giggling. He certainly understood why François and Floriana wouldn't approve, but Gabrielle had a glow about her. Whether or not she'd been referring to herself when she'd asked Riley about love at first sight, she cared deeply for Cody, and her feelings were returned.

"Riley, *mon petit*, please let the caterer know that I'm not happy. Others might like a lot of garlic, but it is just excessive."

"Of course, Gabrielle." He'd not heard any other complaints along those lines, but it was Gabrielle's party—she could be finicky if she wanted.

"If you will both excuse me, I just need to powder my nose. I'll return shortly."

"Hurry back, Gabby."

Gabrielle kissed Cody's cheek and glided away.

Gabby? Riley had never heard anyone call her Gabby, and he'd gotten the distinct impression when he'd first met her that any nicknames would mean death.

"It was nice to meet you, Riley. I have some more mingling to do."

Cody was more polite than either of Gabrielle's kids, so Riley didn't begrudge him his escape. Riley had more canapés to inspect and a complaint to lodge with the caterers.

OVER AN hour into the party, a pointy finger tapped Riley on the shoulder, and he bit his lip against an annoyed "What?" that wanted to escape.

He turned as slowly as he could. Floriana stood behind him, a scowl marring her features. "Have you seen my mother?"

"Not lately."

"If you see her, tell her she should get started with her announcements." The bitter twist to Floriana's lips could indicate she didn't approve of her mother's intentions, but more likely she was still pissed that she didn't know what Gabrielle had planned.

"Of course." Riley wasn't all that concerned, though. Gabrielle had mentioned announcements and speeches and such shouldn't take more than fifteen or twenty minutes, and she wasn't going to start them until the very end of the party. Wherever she was, he was sure she'd be ready when the time came.

About twenty minutes later, François approached and interjected himself into the conversation between Riley, Alisha, and a few of the junior lab techs—fortunately Gary was nowhere to be seen.

"Riley, find my mother. It's time we wrapped things up."

François's brusque, dismissive manner—and Riley wasn't the only recipient of his disdain—got his back up. Nevertheless, François was right—it was getting late.

From somewhere, perhaps the bottom of the champagne flute he'd almost drained, Riley dredged up a smile and a moderate tone of voice. "Certainly."

François returned to the small knot of upper-level employees pretending to be accessible to the lower echelons.

He didn't see Gabrielle's sleek updo anywhere. Probably she'd snuck back up to her office to do more work. He admired her work ethic, but she could use a lesson or two in taking a break.

"Alisha, can you take point with the caterers if something comes up?"

"Sure, sure. You gotta work, I know."

Riley smiled at her, a real one this time. For the most part, the party had gone smoothly, only requiring his intervention a couple of times. This close to the end, he didn't anticipate any issues.

There were two ways to get to the executive offices on the opposite side of the floor from the reception area, both of which were accessed by nondescript doors in the lobby. He eased his way through clumps of employees, most of whom had had far too much to drink for a work event, and their spouses or dates, aiming for the door farthest from the crowd and coincidentally closest to Gabrielle's office.

Only the much dimmer overnight lights were on in this part of the offices. The long shadows and near dark made the normally welcoming office space slightly eerie, and a tiny shiver raced down Riley's spine. Behind him, the lobby door shut with a bang, making Riley jump. His embarrassed laugh sounded loud and brash in the atypical silence.

Straightening his back, he strode down the hall, fruitlessly straining to hear the sounds of the party. But this building was too well made, and the door might as well have been soundproof.

Gabrielle's office was as far from the lobby and reception area as possible. A yellow glow spilled out from the space between her office door and the industrial carpet that muffled Riley's footfalls. Riley smiled. Just as he suspected.

Riley opened the door. "Gabrielle, you're missing your party."

His first indication that something was wrong was the folder on the floor by his feet, the yellow manila garish against the serviceable charcoal carpet. His smile fell away. "Gabrielle?"

Gabrielle sat at her desk, sprawled inelegantly in her chair, head back as though sleeping. But the pose was all wrong, as was the disorder on her desk, like someone had shoved at the paperwork, sending half of it to the floor. Her phone was off the receiver. Her laptop wasn't visible, but Gabrielle put it away when she didn't need it.

Heart pounding, prickling with sweat, Riley crept toward the desk.

"Gabrielle?" He raised his voice a little louder this time, hoping she'd fallen asleep. Passed out. A faint scent of garlic hung in the air.

Gabrielle didn't respond. Riley bit his lip and stretched out a trembling hand to shake her shoulder. "Are you okay?"

Gabrielle slipped sideways.

Stomach roiling, Riley felt for a pulse on her neck. Nothing. He'd taken CPR courses, but the cool clamminess of her skin told him there wasn't any point in trying. She was dead.

He backed away, afraid he was going to hurl. He closed her office door quietly and slumped, shaking, at his desk. This was the first dead body he'd come across, and he couldn't help but superimpose the fuzzy memory of his mother's face over Gabrielle's. His parents' funeral had been closed casket because his brother wanted him to remember them as they were when they were alive.

For a hot minute Riley considered calling his brother, but what was Jon going to do? Stupid impulse. His hands trembled, the sound of his rapid breathing harsh in his ears.

He hugged himself, tucking his suddenly chilled fingers under his arms as he forced himself to suck in deep, even breaths.

The cops. 911. That's what he needed to do.

Extricating one of his hands, Riley grabbed his handset and dialed, then waited interminable moments until the 911 operator answered.

By the time he'd given her all the information, he'd started to regain his composure. Emergency services were on the way and... oh shit. Would they go tearing through the party? However much he disliked Gabrielle's children, he didn't want them to find out about their mother like that. Nor did he want them to start looking for their mother and, well, find her.

Another moment went by while he considered options; then he ran back to the lobby. He let himself through the door, moving swiftly but not fast enough to draw attention. Fortunately Alisha's sexy red dress was easy to spot in the crowd, and he homed in on her.

"Excuse me," he apologized to the people she was talking to. "I need to borrow Alisha for a moment."

He dragged her almost out to the reception desk.

"What the fuck is going on, Riley?" She wasn't angry, just concerned. Obviously he wasn't pretending to be composed nearly as well as he'd thought.

"Gabrielle's dead."

"What?"

"Shush!" Riley had spoken in a whisper, but Alisha's response had been loud and shocked.

Alisha gripped his arms so tight he might end up bruised, but she spoke quietly enough. "What happened?"

"I don't know. I went to her office and found her dead."

"Oh my God. That's awful. You have to tell François. Floriana. The police?"

Riley tried to be patient, because he'd done the same panicked freak-out. "Would you want to break that news to them?"

Alisha's eyes widened. "No. Hell no."

Her children would fall more to the "shoot the messenger" side of the spectrum.

"I called 911. I don't know who'll show up, though. EMTs or fire department, maybe? Anyway, I want to go back to the office, prevent anyone from going in before emergency services show up."

Alisha sucked in a breath. "Oh my God. She was murdered?"

The words hit like a slap in the face. "What? No. I don't think so. Why would you say that?"

"Because you want to keep anyone from going inside. Protecting the crime scene."

The skeletal fingers of another chill played with Riley's spine. He'd not once considered Gabrielle had been murdered. "That's far too melodramatic. Seriously, I just want to keep her kids from barging in and having to see her like that."

Alisha's eyes teared up. "You are a good man, Riley Parker. After this all blows over, you're going to have to help me find your straight doppelganger."

The ridiculous statement was unexpected enough to return Riley's equilibrium. He'd dealt with all sorts of emergencies and last-minute issues as part of his job. Just because this situation was atypical didn't mean he couldn't deal with it.

"Later. First thing, though, will you wait by the elevators? Maybe we can get them in through the back way at the emergency exit, before anyone sees. I don't want to create a panic." If he could get officials inside using the back stairway, he could keep this quiet for now.

"Yeah, yeah. Go."

Riley took a deep breath and went back into the party. Floriana caught his eye, and he tried to mime that it would be a few minutes. She glared but turned toward the wine station.

That slight deception felt terrible. Riley didn't have any idea how to break such bad news without causing a scene, and he was pretty sure none of the Gautiers would be happy about that, once they'd had time to think about it.

He let himself back into the office area and made his way to Gabrielle's office with all the enthusiasm of a man going to the gallows.

Slumping into his chair, he tried desperately to think of anything but the scene beyond Gabrielle's door. A sniffle and a tear caught him by surprise. Gabrielle wasn't always the warmest woman, and she'd stepped on a lot of necks to get where she was, but he'd liked her. He was going to miss her.

RILEY DIDN'T know how long he waited, but the troop of emergency personnel burst into the office area with an explosion of sound. Stamping feet, the jingle of keys, the rattle of a gurney, and the low murmur of somber voices.

The woman in the lead, an EMT, made eye contact with him. "You're the one who called in the report?"

Riley nodded. "She's... in the office."

For the next few minutes there was a whirlwind of activity and chatter inside Gabrielle's office. A uniformed police officer stood next to Riley's desk, but he didn't know if that was because too many people were in Gabrielle's office or if the cop was performing guard duty.

"What the fuck is going on?" Floriana's shriek cut through the cacophony, sharp and pointed. She was running as fast as she could in her stilettos, and hard on her heels were François, Bethany, and Cody. Riley knew it had been too much to hope for that the Gautiers would wait much longer before they came looking for Gabrielle. Riley stood and moved toward Floriana, trying desperately to think of the best way to explain.

Like a tornado, Floriana whirled up into Riley's face and grabbed his lapel. "What did you do?"

"Excuse me, ma'am. I'm going to need you to step back." The officer spoke with a tone of command at odds with his youthful appearance.

Floriana didn't even glance at him. "This doesn't concern you. Riley, I want to know what the fuck you did, and then you're fired. Or did my mother already do that?"

The venom in her voice surprised Riley almost as much as the words, and he didn't know how to respond, not even when she shook him hard enough that he heard fabric rip.

This time the officer acted while he spoke, and separated them. "Ma'am, one more outburst like that and I'll have to take you into the station."

Although François was also glaring daggers at Riley, he at least had the sense to pull his sister back. "Calm down, Floriana. We're not going to find out anything by losing our cool." François looked at the officer, while Bethany clung to his arm. "What's going on?"

"Please just remain calm and let them do their work." The officer's implacability helped to mute Floriana, but Riley couldn't figure out why she'd attacked him. But the time he'd been dreading had come, and he had to step up.

"I'm so sorry. François, Floriana… when I came to remind Gabrielle of the time, she was…." His throat constricted as though trying to prevent the words from escaping. "She had passed away. I'm so sorry." His eyes filled again.

"No. That's not possible. She was just at the party." Floriana wobbled, and the officer snagged a couple of nearby chairs, directing Floriana and Bethany to sit. The women took seats while François glared at Riley.

However cold Riley found the siblings, witnessing their shock and grief was heartbreaking. He grabbed the box of tissues from his desk and offered it to them.

"When can we see her?" François demanded in a haughty tone that didn't faze the officer one bit.

"As soon as possible, sir. For now, though, you can wait here, or if there's another room where you'd like to wait...?"

"François, what about the party? Should we tell the guests? Or send them home?" Bethany spoke up for the first time.

Riley stood. "I can go tell them. I mean, not tell them. But maybe say there's been a medical emergency and they should head home?"

No expression crossed the cop's face. "It would be better if you stayed here. Is there someone else who could take care of that?"

That didn't make sense either—sounded terribly official too. A cold sensation formed in the pit of his stomach. Was it a bad thing the cop didn't want him to leave? Had he been wrong about Gabrielle being dead? Should he have tried to give her CPR? But he didn't think that was enough to get him in trouble with the police.

"Um. I could call Alisha, the receptionist," he said for the cop's benefit. "Everyone knows her."

The officer nodded. "My partner will take contact information for everyone before they leave."

After Riley finished his phone call, he hung up and turned back to the cop. "What now?"

"Is there a conference room where you all can wait?"

"Wait?" Floriana shrieked. "Wait for what? You to do your job?"

The officer turned to look at her. Whatever she saw made her shut up.

"Yes. Sure. Just down the hall." Riley couldn't be happier that they had conference rooms back here in addition to the fishbowl conference rooms that flanked the lobby. "The blue conference room." There was an executive conference room closer, but it might be too small.

François turned to his sister. "I'm sure we'll be more comfortable waiting there." His words were a command, if nothing else, and Floriana seemed willing to acquiesce. "Riley, bring some coffee in."

Riley nodded again, feeling like a damn bobblehead, but making coffee would give him something to do.

François then gave Cody a very pointed look. Riley had almost forgotten he was there. He'd lost his cocky, arrogant air and had faded back beside a potted plant. Riley didn't know how long he'd been dating Gabrielle, but he looked like he was about to throw up or burst into tears—but Gabrielle's relationships were so volatile he wondered if he'd mistaken how genuine Floriana and Bethany's tears were.

"Cody, this is a family affair. We can handle it from here." Riley didn't know if he'd have the balls to contradict anything François said in that tone—he'd half expected to see a swirl of snow in the room.

Cody stiffened his spine and he snarled. "I'm not going anywhere, you sanctimonious pile of shit."

"This is a family affair," François repeated more forcefully. "You don't belong here."

"I have every right to be here."

"You do not."

Floriana glared at Cody. "There's nothing left for you, you gold-digging bottom-feeder."

"Everyone calm down." The cop appeared between Cody and François, blocking Riley's view of Floriana, his presence convincing Cody to swallow whatever poisonous retort he'd been ready to launch. "We're all going to head to the blue conference room and wait." He gestured for François to lead, and Riley took that as permission to move into the kitchenette to make coffee.

Unsure if the medical people would want some as well, Riley pulled out the largest carafe. The methodical routine of preparing coffee helped calm him, although he wondered if he should make decaf or regular. Probably everyone could use a jolt of caffeine. Tea might be better—but he didn't want to get anywhere near Gabrielle's body to get some.

All too soon, the aroma of coffee filled the kitchenette. There would be cups in the conference room, so Riley poured coffee into a smaller insulated serving carafe. He gathered creamers, sweeteners, and the carafe onto a tray and left the kitchenette, only to be stopped by a tiny, wizened woman wearing a coroner's windbreaker. She was accompanied by another uniformed cop. He didn't think she'd arrived with the rest of emergency services, but she was short enough he might have missed her.

"Who are you?" Considering they were all strangers, her brusque and impatient air seemed odd.

"Riley. Riley Parker."

"Mm-hmm. I'm Dr. Nehru. Coroner. What are you doing here?"

"I'm… I mean, I was Gabrielle's assistant. I just made coffee for the family. There's more ready in the kitchenette if any of you want some." He carefully set the tray down on his desk.

The cop thawed a bit, but the older woman flapped her hand in exasperation. "Were you the one who called 911?"

"Oh. Yes. That was me." And just like that, his temporary calm hung in tatters.

"And did your boss have any allergies?"

Riley shook his head. "Nothing she told me about. If she'd been allergic to any type of food, she would have said, because of the party we had catered." And the few restaurant reservations he'd made for her.

Dr. Nehru pursed her lips. "And that party was tonight? Here?"

"Yes." Riley checked his watch. "The caterers might even still be here. It hasn't been that long since we told everyone to pack up and go home."

She tapped her cheek thoughtfully before turning to the cop towering over her. "Make the call. If the caterers are still here, we'll want to talk to them."

The cop strode off, muttering into his radio.

God. Riley had never been so happy he hadn't eaten anything. Had Gabrielle died of food poisoning? No, that was stupid. Food poisoning would have included some sort of gastrointestinal issues, wouldn't it? And if Gabrielle had been hit that quickly, surely other people at the party would have been affected. It must have just been a heart attack or stroke or something.

Unsettled, he picked up his tray and made his way to the conference room.

TWO HOURS ago Riley hadn't realized the import of Dr. Nehru's words *Make the call*. But as soon as he'd shown up in the conference room, the uniformed officer told him he wasn't allowed to leave, which was apparently the first anyone else in the room had heard of that.

Riley was pretty sure both of the Gautier kids had come within a hair of being zip-tied and arrested, but time had deadened their responses. François had called their lawyer, hoping that would get them out of the room, but the lawyer, currently out of town, had told them to sit tight and he'd find someone to fill in. So far that mythical beast hadn't arrived.

Floriana had not been pleased about missing the official launch party. The executives had planned to go straight from the office to an upscale club, complete with press and celebrities. Even the stoic cop had winced at her shrill tone when she'd informed the event planners that their account manager was going to have to host the event.

Everyone was tired, sullen. The tears had dried up a while ago and the coffee was long gone. Riley hadn't been allowed to make any more. Of them all, Cody was the one who still looked the most ravaged by grief, but that might have had more to do with his fairer complexion.

It looked more and more like Alisha might have been onto something, because the police seemed to be treating Gabrielle's death as suspicious.

Fuck. Alisha. He'd completely forgotten about her. He pulled out his phone and realized, from the excessive number of notifications, that he'd also forgotten about his plans with Shaun. He must have been in shock or something, because he hadn't felt one vibration.

The cop gave him a look but didn't say anything as Riley shot off a couple of quick texts. At least Alisha had given up on him and gone home after dismissing the partygoers. Shaun's messages were angry, but he wouldn't hold a grudge. Especially not when he finally left his one-night stand's bed and found out why Riley had blown him off. Alisha made him promise to text when he got home, no matter what time.

"What is taking so long?" Floriana couldn't let the silence go unbroken for too long. She glared at Riley. "We wouldn't be in this mess if it weren't for you."

"Me?" He'd called 911. That was normal procedure after finding a dead person.

"Oh for fuck's sake, lay off, Floriana," Cody spit out.

Riley wanted to groan. If they just let Floriana rant for a bit, she'd eventually wind down, but not with Cody throwing fuel on the flames.

Floriana narrowed her eyes and turned her Medusa's gaze on Cody. "Why are you even here? You're nothing. No one. You don't belong here. This is for people who loved her."

She glanced Riley's way. "And for assholes who call in the police."

On top of it all, Riley was pretty sure Gautier Cosmetics wouldn't be keeping him for his whole contract.

"Fuck you, Floriana." Cody pushed his chair back from the table and rose to his feet. Out of the corner of his eye, Riley saw the cop straighten, ready to take action if required. "I belong here. I loved Gabby."

"Gabby?" Floriana's voice rose, incredulous. "No one calls my mother Gabby. She'd eviscerate you."

Cody leaned over the table and wagged his finger in her face. "I call her Gabby. I loved her. She was my *wife*."

"You filthy fucking liar!" Floriana shrieked as she practically climbed over the table in an attempt to lay hands on Cody.

Riley stumbled to his feet and pressed back against the wall while the room erupted.

At that moment the door banged open, although Riley, on the other side of the room, couldn't see who'd arrived around the chaos.

"Sit down and shut up." The androgynous, gravelly voice stunned the near combatants into silence. They obeyed her like she was the voice of God, rather than a tall, hawkish woman in her late forties wearing a tailored plum suit. "I have no time for nonsense."

A glare from icy blue eyes leveled them all. She pointed at Floriana and Riley. "You two, come along."

It had been a long time since Riley had been actively scared, but he was edging into fear. He followed the nameless woman into the hall, Floriana trailing behind.

"You, that office." She directed Riley to one of the manager's offices, then gestured for Floriana to enter the adjacent office. At least they weren't on the south side of the conference room, or this woman might have appropriated Floriana's or François's office, and wouldn't that be weird for everyone?

Riley took a deep breath and knocked gently before opening the door. A man sat at Sandra Cheng's desk, dark head bent as he jotted in a notebook.

"Have a seat."

That voice, like aged whiskey, flowed over him. It sounded vaguely familiar, but Riley didn't know any cops, and despite the dark blue sports coat, there was no mistaking him for anything but police.

Riley sat and waited.

After several moments the cop lifted his head as he spoke. "I'm Detective Tad Martin. And you are?"

The room swam as Riley struggled to breathe. Or not throw up. This couldn't be happening to him.

Tadeo Martin had been a fucking god in high school. Watching him on the lacrosse field had pretty much catapulted Riley into fierce, aching puberty. Two years ahead of Riley, he had no reason to know who Riley was. After all, the jocks had only mingled with the A/V and drama geeks that one year because the head cheerleader broke her leg and decided to star in the school play.

No need to humiliate himself by trying to get Tad to recall someone even Riley barely wanted to remember. It wasn't like they'd been friends.

He stared at Tad, cataloging all the ways Tad's face had changed and all the ways it hadn't. His skin was still kissed with gold, as though the sun never quite stopped shining on his face, even in deepest winter. But there were fine lines at the corners of his eyes that probably crinkled when he laughed. A few silver threads sparkled in the smooth sheen of his dark hair. It was hard to tell, but Riley suspected they'd be about the same height, unless Tad had also experienced a late growth spurt after he'd left high school. Perhaps the absolute worst for Riley's equilibrium, though, was the stubble. He didn't know if it was a personal fashion choice or the result of overwork. Either way, Riley had spent so much time imagining Tad's lips gliding along his jaw and down his neck. Now he could add the rasp of dark stubble marking his skin with beard burn to the sounds in his mind, and goose bumps rose along his collarbone.

Fucking hell. Why had the universe seen fit to drop this on him today? The only thing good about Tad sitting in front of him was that there was no way Tad would know who he was.

Tad's jaw firmed and his nostrils flared ever so slightly. "Your name?" The words were almost glacial.

Riley made a sound that could generously be called a squeak as he sucked in a breath. He'd completely forgotten Tad had asked him a question.

"Riley Parker. Gabrielle's temp admin assistant." Heat flooded Riley's face as his voice broke like he was back in high school, rather than a twink facing the wrong side of thirty.

Tad tilted his head to the side and narrowed his eyes. Riley didn't quite like the speculation in his gaze and needed to divert it.

"T—" Riley swallowed the rest of Tad's name and coughed. If he started calling Tad by his first name, he'd either piss him off or amp up the speculation. "Er… Detective Martin. Can you tell me what's going on? Why have we been held all this time?"

Tad's official mien dissolved into incredulity. "Didn't my partner say anything?"

"Would that be the terrifying woman in the next office?"

A tiny laugh escaped from Tad, but he controlled his mirth too quickly for Riley to note if the corners of his eyes did indeed crinkle.

At least Riley wasn't going to get in shit for his imprudent, thoughtless description.

"Sorry about that. She quit smoking a couple of weeks ago."

Riley nodded because it did explain some things, but he didn't imagine Tad's partner exuded rainbows and buttercups even after smoking all the tobacco in the world.

Tad's amusement quickly faded. "You're the one who discovered Gabrielle Gautier?"

"Yes."

Tad made a couple of quick notes. "At the moment, we're treating her death as suspicious."

Suspicious? Riley's stomach flipped, and he got light-headed so fast he was insanely glad he was already sitting down. But he was truly afraid he might throw up, and he couldn't do that in front of Tadeo Martin. His mortification would be infinite.

"Hey. Are you okay?"

Riley waved him off, afraid to open his mouth. He took a couple of deep breaths and his stomach settled a bit. "Sorry. Low blood sugar or something."

"Are you diabetic?" Tad braced himself as though ready to launch out of his chair.

"No. Not that serious. I've only had half a glass of champagne since breakfast." Because he'd intended to take Alisha somewhere with giant burgers after the party, before they met up with Shaun. When he finally got home, he'd have something to eat, but it would be more along the lines of crackers or rice.

Tad sat back down. "So you didn't eat anything at the party?" This time the question had a hint of menace in it, unless Riley was imagining it.

"No. I was the liaison for the caterers. I was too busy making sure things went smoothly, and, well, there wasn't time for lunch today. Gabrielle's schedule was booked solid."

"I'm going to need a copy of her calendar."

"Just for today?"

"If you can get it for the last three months, that would be better."

Riley paused for a few moments, because he suspected the rest of the Gautiers wouldn't be happy with him handing over any information, but morally he was obliged to cooperate, wasn't he? Legally, though, he was a bit murky. But there wasn't anything confidential or proprietary in her calendar. Surely his nondisclosure agreement didn't apply.

"If you're worried about anything, like your job or other retaliation, I can promise you we'll protect your identity. No one will know who provided this information. It's simply more expedient to get it sooner rather than wait for a warrant."

Riley wasn't particularly worried about his job—if this one dried up, there'd be another around the corner—but retaliation? That seemed ridiculous—no one would do that. Ultimately, though, his loyalty was to his boss, however temporary the post had been, and that loyalty included making sure the police were able to figure out what happened to her.

"I can do that. Is that all you need from me?"

Tad's dark eyebrows rose. "No. Not at all. You said you were the temp? How long have you been working here?"

"Nearly three weeks."

"And were you aware of any allergies Mrs. Gautier had?"

"Madame."

Tad narrowed his eyes. "What?"

Another tide of blood surged into Riley's cheeks. "Sorry. She was French… Québécois. She was Madame Gautier, not Mrs." If there was a French equivalent for Ms., Riley didn't know it, and Gabrielle might have been too old-fashioned to use that term anyway.

"Right. Madame Gautier. Allergies?" Tad clearly thought Riley's clarification a waste of time. He'd have to be careful not to provide irrelevant details.

"No. None that she mentioned to me."

"Do you know of anyone who would want to harm her? Anyone who disliked her?"

"Enough to kill her? Not at all. At least, not that I've seen. But I've only been here a short time."

"So everyone liked her?"

"Well, no. From what I saw, lots of business rivals found her ruthless. Many found her cold. She was a bit of a perfectionist. But... I can't see anyone hurting her for that."

Although after the fiasco in the conference room, if Floriana had her way, Cody wouldn't be long for this world. Maybe the provocation didn't have to be as great as Riley assumed.

"And what about you?"

"Me?" Riley squeaked again. He was going to have to do something about that. He cleared his throat. "Sorry. Tickle in my throat."

Tad's complete lack of expression said that maybe he didn't believe Riley, but he wasn't going to challenge him on it. "Did you like her?"

"Of course." Did he reply too fast? Suspiciously fast? He rubbed sweaty, clammy palms on his no longer perfectly creased pants. "I mean, I admired her. She was refined, and she had this Old World glamor, but she still grabbed the cosmetics world by the throat and insisted on taking her piece of it."

The only reply was more of Tad scratching a pen across paper. A few moments later, Tad lifted his head, and Riley was struck anew by his magnetism, all the more intense for Riley having been indoctrinated as a teenager.

"What about the party today? Would anyone gain anything if Madame Gautier were no longer in the picture?"

"Just call her Gabrielle. It's faster." Riley sucked in another breath and clamped his lips shut. Hadn't he *just* promised himself he wasn't going to offer up any more irrelevant information?

Tad somehow managed to nod in a patronizing manner. God, Riley had to remember that Tad wasn't one of his buddies. He represented authority with a capital *A*, and he was investigating Gabrielle's death as a possible murder. He might even consider Riley a suspect.

"Gabrielle, then. Is there a reason someone might have chosen to act now?"

Riley raked a hand through his hair and tucked it back in his lap before Tad noticed the tremors. Tad probably didn't give a shit if Riley looked weak, but Riley would rather not add to his already bad impression.

Besides, he was having a hard time concentrating, and he didn't think it was entirely due to Tad. He'd been holding off an incipient freak-out for a while, but it was coming, and it was coming soon. He desperately wanted to be at home when it happened.

"I don't think so. The product launch for Invigorate, their new caffeine-infused skin-care line, is a done deal, as far as I know. The launch party for the public went ahead as scheduled—Floriana called from the conference room to let them know. There are probably reports and reviews online already."

"Anything else? Business deals not related to *caffeinated* beauty products coming up?" Tad didn't sound particularly impressed. "Mergers, buyouts?"

"I don't believe so, but honestly, depending on what it was, there might be no reason for me to know. I am only a temporary employee." He clamped down on the temptation to tell Tad that Gabrielle had asked him more than once to stay on permanently. More irrelevant information.

"Yes, you mentioned that. Tell me how that all came about."

Shit. He really was under suspicion. "Gabrielle's previous assistant, Aaron, had to go on long-term medical leave. She called my agency, and they sent me over."

"Right. And her last name is?"

Riley waved a finger at Tad's notes. "Aaron Brown, not Erin."

He spelled it out, and Tad frowned at him. "Both male secretaries. Was that something Gabrielle insisted on?"

"We aren't *secretaries*. We're *administrative assistants*. And aren't you a little too young to be that bound up in traditional gender roles?"

Tad blinked at him, and Riley thought he was trying not to laugh. Great. He'd *sooooo* been hoping to come off as laughable and pathetic. Tad, in one of the most alpha roles a man could have, also probably thought Riley was somehow less masculine.

"Sorry. Administrative assistants. But many jobs still tend to skew toward one gender, and I'd imagine that there are fewer men in your profession. Correct?"

Riley shrugged. "Yes, I suppose." This was the first time he'd temped in replacement for a man, and most of the admin assistants in the other places he'd worked were women. Tad had a point, however distasteful.

"Then the fact that Gabrielle had two male assistants is something of an anomaly. Did she ever make any sort of overtures? Sexual advances?"

"What?" Riley rocked in his chair, wanting to stand up and pace but not wanting to antagonize the man with a gun. "What a terrible thing to suggest. I'm sure she didn't request a man from my agency. I'm actually very good at my job, you know. I'm not just some eye candy for degenerate CEOs and company presidents."

Tad held up his hands, palms out. "Calm down. I didn't mean to suggest anything."

Riley had to get the fuck out of here before he combusted. Or said something irretrievably stupid. "Are we almost done?"

Without answering his question, Tad asked another one. "Do you know why Aaron was out on medical leave?"

"No, of course not. Human Resources might know, but they certainly don't share that information." He knew it wasn't parental leave, but that was about it. He'd heard a number of theories, though, and he'd gotten the impression that people weren't terribly fond of Aaron Brown, which might explain Gabrielle's repeated job offers. It could have had nothing to do with Aaron's performance and everything to do with his personality.

Tad shrugged. "You might have heard something. He might have friends around the office who know."

"If anyone knows for sure, they haven't told me."

"Do you have a list of everyone who was at the party?"

The odd jump in topic jarred Riley's brain. It was difficult to prepare answers when he didn't know where Tad was heading. "Maybe? It wasn't exactly mandatory, but it would have been frowned upon if any of the employees didn't attend. Most of them wanted to, simply for the free food and drinks. Everyone was allowed to bring a date if they wanted, but there was no list for plus ones. There were caterers. I think someone already went to talk to them before they left."

Tad didn't appear too happy with Riley's answer, but it wasn't like Riley had been tasked with taking attendance. "Who was your date?"

Be nice if Tad was asking for personal reasons. Riley grimaced. What was he thinking? He didn't really want to get picked up while answering police questions about discovering the dead body of his employer. No, no, and no. Definitely not a story to tell the grandkids. And he shouldn't have to keep reminding himself of this, but Tad wasn't gay, no matter how delightfully filthy and naughty he'd been in Riley's wet dreams.

"I didn't bring a date." Again, he was tempted to explain that both he and Alisha were between relationships and had decided to be each other's date, but that was probably more frivolous information Tad didn't have the time or patience for. Alisha wasn't a stranger who'd need to be tracked down.

"Okay, then. Can you get me a list of employees?"

"Yes." Again, not private information. Floriana and François wouldn't be pleased, but Tad's requests didn't seem unreasonable.

Tad asked for his contact information and made note of it, then stood. "Where's your desk?"

"Uh, you want me to print stuff out now?"

"Might as well, since you're here."

Riley didn't want to read the subtext, which was basically that he might not have access by Monday morning, although he agreed. Tad had undoubtedly pegged him as the one most likely to cooperate.

"Then can I leave?"

"Yes."

Riley stood and faced Tad, perhaps a bit longer than necessary. After all was said and done, Riley had ended up a couple of inches taller than Tad, rather than the half a foot or so shorter he'd been the last time he'd laid eyes on Tadeo Martin.

Tad stared up at him, expression morphing from politely expectant to quizzical, especially as he inspected Riley's hair. This time Riley could definitely put a label on Tad's expression: *This guy seems familiar—have I met him before?*

Last thing he needed was Tad figuring out just where they knew each other from.

"My desk is right outside Gabrielle's office." He could hold it together long enough to get Tad the required printouts. There simply wasn't any other option. Not if he wanted to keep his self-respect.

Having Tad follow him halfway across the floor was nearly as nerve-racking as having him hover while Riley pulled up the required information as efficiently as possible.

Gabrielle's office was still a hive of activity, and lights brighter than anything she would have authorized cast unfamiliar shadows along the walls.

The moment Riley pulled up the calendar, two coroner's employees wearing dark jumpsuits guided a covered gurney out of Gabrielle's office. His hands started shaking again, and he stared fixedly at the screen, trying not to watch as Gabrielle's body was transported out of the office. None of the letters on his screen coalesced into words, and he couldn't remember how to export a schedule.

Then Tad's hand, warm and comforting, landed on his shoulder. "It's okay. Just breathe."

A couple of tears slid down his face, which Riley ignored as he tried to do as Tad suggested. After the gurney had finally rattled away, Riley composed himself enough to get the information Tad wanted.

Handing it over, hot off the printer, Riley spoke again. "So I can leave now?"

"Certainly. I'll walk you out."

What, did he think Riley was going to collapse or something? Surely he'd held up better than that. "Thanks, but that's not necessary."

"It's no trouble at all." Tad stood, waiting.

Then it struck Riley. It had nothing to do with being overly solicitous. Tad was making sure Riley actually left the building and didn't come back to muck about in the crime scene. The distrust was like a slap in the face, and yet he should have expected it.

They started walking down the hall, and Riley tried to pretend he wasn't being "escorted" out of the building. He cleared his throat. "You didn't actually say why you think Gabrielle's death wasn't natural causes."

She wasn't that old, true, but Riley had just assumed it was a heart attack since she was a bit of a workaholic. When they'd started asking about allergies... well, anaphylaxis shouldn't be suspicious, either. She might have recently developed an allergy to nuts or shellfish.

"No, I didn't say."

Riley bit back the sarcastic response that danced on the end of his tongue. "It seems like you think it was a severe allergic reaction. I don't understand what's suspicious about that."

They walked a few more steps in silence. "We can't say for sure until the autopsy, but the coroner is leaning toward anaphylactic shock. The EMTs found a medical alert necklace that said she was allergic to penicillin, but she died alone in her office, and there was no trace of a penicillin prescription, pills, or bottle."

It was late and he was tired, but it only took a couple of seconds for the significance of that to register. "So how could she have come in contact with penicillin?"

"Yes, that's exactly it. Questionable enough to call us in."

As though the night didn't have enough surprises, Riley suddenly realized Tad had become a real-life homicide detective. He wasn't entirely sure this day hadn't been a weird sort of fever dream.

He couldn't think of one single thing to say after that, and they continued in silence to the elevator. Tad hit the Down button before reaching into his jacket and pulling out a business card.

"If you remember anything else, anything odd or that you think might be significant, give me a call. If I'm not at this number, just dial zero. The switchboard should be able to connect you to my mobile, or to Emma."

"Who is Emma?"

Tad laughed self-deprecatingly. "That's right, she probably didn't introduce herself either. Detective Emma Wilson. My partner."

Oh hell no. If he decided he needed to contact the police about this case, he'd be talking to Tad or no one. But Riley had sense enough not to say that aloud. "Thanks." He pocketed the card.

"And we'll be in touch if we have further questions."

Riley didn't know if he was a person of interest, but he was, unfortunately, still interested in Tad's person. Who probably wasn't any more gay than he'd been in high school, more's the pity.

"Are you going to be okay?" Tad asked as the elevator doors opened.

Sending his shoulders back and stiffening his spine, Riley got onto the elevator. "I'll be fine, thanks."

Chapter THREE

RILEY STUMBLED into his condo and shut the door behind him with a bang. He rested against it for a couple of seconds before securing the dead bolt and chain. He'd never been so fucking happy to be holed up all by himself in his apartment. By the time he'd been allowed to escape, the Friday drinkers were reveling all over the public transit.

His short commute on the King streetcar saved him, though. Just when he'd thought he might lose his mind, he arrived at his stop. Liberty Village had its share of bar-hoppers wandering the sidewalks, but they didn't make him feel almost claustrophobic like those on the streetcar had.

Being able to shut it all out in the haven of his condo was a blessing he'd never appreciated until today. He threw himself onto the couch and stared at the picture on the end table. The last family photo with him, his parents, and Jonathan. He'd managed to avoid dealing with deaths other than his parents' over the past years, mostly by luck.

Thinking about his parents lying around lifeless like Gabrielle had been, vibrant personalities just snuffed out, made his teeth chatter. His eyes burned, but he didn't want to cry. A breath hitched in his throat. He desperately wanted someone to talk to, to come over and drink with him or just hold him while they watched something mindless. He had friends he could call, but as they'd all be well into Friday-night libations, they probably wouldn't be all that comforting. He should be able to call his fucking brother right now since Jonathan knew what it was like to lose someone, but odds were Meredith would scold Riley for calling so late and make Jonathan hang up.

He was so fucking cold, he started shaking. With a growl, he launched off the couch and slammed the photo facedown on the table. Right there in his living room, he stripped off his clothes, which suddenly seemed unbearably grimy.

In the bathroom, naked and shivering, Riley started the shower, thankful for excellent pressure and a responsive hot-water heater. Steam curled around the curtain, fogging up the edges of the mirror. Riley stepped into the shower and let the near-scalding water camouflage the tears he could no longer hold in. He slid to the tiled floor and let the water beat down on him. By the time he'd cried himself out, he was no longer sure if he was mourning his parents, Gabrielle, the loss of a brother's love, or all of them, but he knew he was tired of being alone.

He clambered to his feet and got out, quickly dried himself, and put on his coziest pajamas before the warming effect of the shower wore off. He usually only wore pajamas during the winter, but his need for comfort hadn't diminished when the tears and shaking stopped.

The emotional firestorm dulled his agitation, and he picked up his phone to make sure there wasn't anything he'd missed.

He answered Shaun's inebriated yet concerned texts—better late than never, he supposed—and sent Alisha a message confirming he was finally home before turning his phone off and putting it on the charger. He didn't want to answer any questions about what had happened. Not tonight.

Then he got into bed and tried to sleep. But no matter which position he chose, every time he closed his eyes, all he could see was Gabrielle slumped in her chair, surrounded by the scattered array of files. Underlying all that was the worry that he was somehow a person of interest in her death, and he wondered if he should have had a lawyer with him. But seeing Tad again after so many years had flustered him, and he hadn't done anything wrong, dammit.

There was no hope for it. He got out of bed, took a sleeping pill, and choked down a handful of crackers so he wasn't going to sleep with an empty stomach.

EARLY SUNDAY morning Riley rolled out of bed, refreshed and mostly feeling good. He had vague memories of getting up late Saturday afternoon and spending several hours dozing in front of the television before returning to bed. The sleeping pill might have hit him harder than normal, but Riley suspected it was the stress of finding Gabrielle on top of the highly soporific effects of his sleeping pill that had kept him zonked for over twenty-four hours. Giving up a precious weekend day was well worth it, though, because it no longer felt like ants were running through his brain and over his skin.

After plucking his phone off the dresser, he turned it on, pleasantly surprised by the lack of "WTF?" texts from his friends. Riley quickly shot off an email about bailing on gaming later that afternoon. For many things in his life, gaming was and had been a welcome distraction, but he'd never be able to concentrate.

Most importantly, he had no messages from his agency. Which meant that until further notice, he would be returning to Gautier Cosmetics. If nothing else, they might need some assistance redistributing Gabrielle's files and fielding phone calls, keeping the lights on while the family mourned.

Thinking about redistributing files twigged a memory that had completely escaped him when faced with Tad while trying to recover from the shock of finding Gabrielle dead. Before he could enumerate all the reasons he shouldn't or couldn't talk to Tad, he retrieved the business card from the pants he'd stuffed into the laundry hamper—and dialed the number.

"Detective Tad Martin." Tad's words were alert and brusque, despite the delivery in a voice thick and rough like he'd just woken up.

A delicious shudder shook Riley as he imagined Tad naked in bed, hair mussed, a sheet barely covering sleek hips, and he manfully resisted the urge to palm his cock.

"Hi, it's Riley Parker?" Riley grimaced. Between the breaking voice—again—and Riley saying his name as though he wasn't sure who he was, Tad was probably silently laughing on the other end of the line. Embarrassment killed Riley's burgeoning arousal. "Uh. From Friday. Gabrielle Gautier's death? I'm sorry I woke you up."

Tad cleared his throat. "Riley. Yes. It's fine, you didn't wake me up."

Sure he didn't. But there were more important things at stake.

"I remembered something else. Something unusual—or at least I think it was unusual—happened about a week before Gabrielle died."

"Okay. Think you can meet me at the Golden Griddle on Carlton in an hour for breakfast?"

Stunned, Riley couldn't reply. He'd remembered such a tiny tidbit of information, hardly worthy of an in-person meeting, and yet the temptation, however foolish, to see Tad again was irresistible. "Yes, I can do that."

"See you in an hour." Tad disconnected the call before Riley could second-guess himself. It wasn't a date, but his fascination with Tad had already come roaring back when he'd thought he'd successfully buried it and salted the earth over those fruitless feelings.

OUTSIDE THE Golden Griddle, nerves almost got the better of him, and for the millionth time he thought about calling Tad back and just giving him the information over the phone. Hell, he hadn't fretted over his wardrobe this much for his last actual date.

This was work—at least it was for Tad. Who wasn't gay, which Riley needed to keep reminding himself. The world wouldn't stop turning if Tad never saw Riley in a favorable light, but he still wanted at least one interaction with Tad where he wasn't at his worst.

"Not a date, not a date, not a date," Riley muttered under his breath like a mantra. He took a deep breath and walked in.

Tad, ensconced in a booth not far from the door, waved him over. Whatever sleepy rumplement Riley had imagined earlier was not evident. Tad appeared freshly showered, and his clean-shaven jaw was every bit as sexy as the stubble. As Riley took his seat across from Tad, he got a whiff of a spicy scent, warm and woodsy. As much as he wanted to think Tad had put on cologne for him—Riley had barely refrained from slapping on some of his most seductive scent—it was probably something simple like a soap that maybe his girlfriend or wife had purchased for him.

"Good morning." Tad had been waiting long enough to order coffee.

"Sorry to have kept you waiting."

"No, no. I got here a little early. I live fairly close."

Riley could barely take his eyes off Tad's lips as he took a sip from his mug. Then he shook himself. "Oh good." He wasn't even going to touch on the fact that Tad living close to Golden Griddle meant he also lived not far from Riley.

Riley savagely bit the inside of his cheek. *Tad isn't gay*. Riley had to get out of this mental fun house where he viewed everything as though they were on their first date.

"Do you have time for breakfast?"

The loud grumble from the vicinity of his stomach answered before Riley could compose any sort of reply. A tiny grin lifted Tad's lips as he handed over a menu.

Face flaming—it was becoming endemic to his encounters with Tad—Riley stared hard at the menu, trying to take it all in when his senses were swimming.

The waitress returned, and Tad ordered an egg-white omelet with a side of fruit. Riley thought for a brief second of ordering something light, but he didn't think he'd eaten anything since the crackers late Friday night. He ordered stuffed french toast with sausage and a side of scrambled eggs.

"Did you want coffee or juice with that?" The waitress was almost as perky as Alisha.

Riley hadn't worked for Gabrielle long enough to break his coffee habit, but she'd definitely been responsible for a burgeoning enjoyment of tea in the more basic varieties, and he thought it would make a tiny tribute to a complicated woman he'd liked, despite her faults.

"I'd like a cup of tea, please."

"We have several varieties. Do you have a favorite?"

He certainly wasn't going to order lapsang souchong or oolong, even as a tribute to Gabrielle. He doubted they'd be readily available at a low-key restaurant like Golden Griddle.

"Do you have Earl Grey?" Gabrielle hadn't liked the bergamot that gave Earl Grey its distinctive scent, but Riley had taken to it right away, and Gabrielle was more than happy to let him make inroads on her supply.

"Sure do. I'll get that order in immediately." The waitress glided away with a shimmy of her hips that Tad did not even notice, amazingly enough.

They sat in silence for a few minutes. Riley didn't want to blurt out his wee piece of information before their breakfast arrived, because he was afraid doing so would make the rest of the meal incredibly awkward. He didn't know why Tad wasn't saying anything.

"I didn't take you for a tea drinker. I thought just about everyone was addicted to coffee." The comment might have been meant as a dig, but Tad's inflection held no trace of scorn.

Riley tried to relax and be himself, or he was going to make a complete ass of himself. "Oh, I drink coffee too, but Gabrielle introduced me to the joys of tea, and well…." He didn't know exactly how to articulate his sentiment. Also stupid to bring up Gabrielle right away, because he wanted to put off the official reason for their meeting as long as possible.

"Sure. Yeah, I get it." Tad flashed him a sad smile, one he probably kept on tap for all the grieving people he came across in the course of his work.

Riley wanted to volley the conversational ball back, but he had to do it in a way that didn't lead the conversation to Gabrielle's suspicious death or make Tad wonder why Riley was acting overfamiliar. It was hard, though, to pretend Tad was a complete stranger.

"How long have you been a homicide detective?"

A faint ruddy hue highlighted Tad's cheeks. "Not long, actually. Just over a year."

"You've been a detective for a year?" Riley couldn't keep his tone from expressing his shock. Even with a more experienced partner—and he suspected Detective Wilson had been ripping murderers a new one since the womb—how wise could it possibly be having a newbie on Gabrielle's case?

The reddish tone intensified, making Riley feel a little bad about embarrassing him. "Sorry, I shouldn't have said that."

Tad gave him a tight smile. "I've been in homicide for a year, but I've been a detective for four years."

"Again, sorry. I just… I don't know. It's not like I know what's normal. How do you become a detective?" Riley only knew what he'd seen on television, which wasn't going to tell the whole story.

"I got my criminology degree at the University of Toronto, then went to the police academy. Spent six years in uniform before I got a chance to get bumped to detective."

"Wow."

Riley was saved from further inanities by the arrival of their breakfast, and Tad's eyebrows lifted.

"That's a lot of food. Busy night last night?"

If there had been anything other than curiosity in Tad's tone, Riley would have thrown a few biting verbal barbs his way, but as it was, he just laughed ruefully.

"I wish. Nah, I took a sleeping pill with some crackers when I got home Friday." He bit his lip at the uncomfortable reminder that this wasn't a social occasion. "They have a tendency to knock me out pretty good. I spent most of yesterday sleeping. Those crackers haven't exactly filled in the hollow belly."

Tad frowned. "I wish you'd told me you were going home alone on Friday."

Riley laughed uncomfortably. "Why? What difference would that have made?" Not like Tad would have escorted him home and cuddled him in bed.

Silence returned to the table. Riley was too hungry to be put off by awkwardness, especially with the gorgeous spread of food laid out before him, the aroma tantalizing his nostrils.

Tad applied himself to his own breakfast. At one point he shifted and his knee brushed Riley's under the narrow table. Riley froze midchew as he tried to figure out how best to respond, electricity zinging through his body at the contact. For a split second Riley wondered if Tad was going to leave his leg there. He stared at Riley, almost as though daring him to say something, but then the moment passed, the contact ceased, and Tad chased his mouthful of omelet with a sip of coffee, leaving Riley flustered and unnerved.

Once the worst of their hunger had been sated, Tad spoke. "So how did you become an admin assistant? And why temping?"

After a quick dissection of the words, Riley decided Tad wasn't being disparaging. He spent more time in his life defending his choice of profession, and after nearly ten years, he was hypersensitive to criticisms, overt or implied.

"I went to York University for performing arts, and although I loved what I learned, I also discovered I didn't like being in the spotlight. I much preferred being in the background, working the lighting board or behind the scenes."

As a scrawny, runty, super gay nerd in high school, he wasn't given many opportunities to act in real roles in the drama club. If he had, he might have figured out that important aspect of his personality sooner. But he'd been obsessed with acting and the stage, and he was proficient at playing roles—he just didn't enjoy being the center of attention.

"Acting, huh? Seems a far cry from being an assistant in a cosmetics company."

"Yeah, well, after I graduated, I needed a job and couldn't get one in the theater. Not one that paid, although there were plenty of volunteer positions. My, uh, brother… he's the only family I have left. He raised me, and I couldn't go back to needing his financial support after I graduated." Especially since Riley would have been subjected to continual criticism for his lack of ambition and direction. He still had some money socked away from his share of his inheritance, even after buying a decent condo, but it wasn't enough to live off for the rest of his life.

"Your brother raised you?" Tad waved off the interruption. "No, no. Continue with what you were saying. We can circle back to that later." He gave Riley a feral grin. Riley wasn't sure if it was supposed to be sexy or terrifying. It would depend on if these questions were simply Tad making small talk to get to know Riley or whether he was being subtly interrogated as a suspect.

Riley took a bite of french toast, getting a mouthful of cream cheese, raspberries, and maple syrup all at once, and nearly moaned it was so fucking good. He licked his lips, took a sip of his tea to cut the sweetness, and returned his attention to Tad, whose expression had shuttered into blankness.

He cleared his throat. "Okay, well, I needed a job, but my degree didn't offer much in the way of marketable skills. I applied to an agency that provided temporary admin assistants, because just about the only thing I knew besides acting was computer programs—self-taught, though, nothing like having a computer-programming degree. Anyway, I was able to ace the office support programs and could type really fast thanks to MMORPGs. They hired me and sent me out to my first job. I realized that a good assistant can be vital to the way a department is run, and I quickly racked up enough experience and accolades that my agency started offering me contracts for senior executives when their assistants went out on medical or maternity leave. Then I realized how even more critical those assistants were in the running of entire companies, and now I work exclusively with senior executives."

"But why not take on a permanent position? Obviously you could if you wanted to."

Riley smiled before taking another mouthful of his sinfully delicious french toast.

"I like the challenge of new environments, new people. I think I'd get bored doing the same thing every day. Lots of people bounce around to different roles in different companies—I do the same, but at the end of the day, I'm still technically employed by my agency. I have benefits through them that remain consistent. I do miss out on bonuses or profit sharing that some permanent roles at my level include, but I command top dollar for what I do, and I think I do okay." He'd do better with a boyfriend or husband, but he had a great condo downtown and had enough money left over each month to max out his retirement savings as well as contribute to his rainy day fund. All without "sponging" off his brother, as Meredith had frequently accused him of doing.

Tad nodded thoughtfully. "What's an MMORPG?"

"Massive multiplayer online role-playing game. Everyone joins a story in session online, and you interact with each other to accomplish missions. You can pick and choose people to play with or join new groups depending on what scenarios you want to engage with. Like *World of Warcraft*."

"Huh. Yeah, I've heard of that one. That actually sounds fun, although I work long hours, and they can be somewhat erratic."

Riley huffed out a laugh. "I guess, since you were called out to a party on Friday night and probably got to bed later than I did." Oh shit, he hadn't meant to mention Tad going to bed. The idea of it just made him squirm.

"I might have. Makes it hard on relationships."

For the first time, the conversation veered into truly personal territory. Riley couldn't help but liken it to the many first dates he'd been on, but he also had to wonder if Tad had some ulterior motive.

"Uh, yeah, I guess, but your job is… admirable." And sexy, but Riley wasn't going to say that. "An incredibly valuable civic service."

A defeated look crossed Tad's face. "Maybe so, but the hours are long, as I said, and we see the worst humanity has to offer every day. It's hard not to bring some of that bleakness home, and even if other people think they can handle the canceled plans or sudden callouts in the middle of movies or dinner or romantic weekends, the dark underbelly is often the last straw."

"Huh. I guess I never thought of it like that, but surely most people would realize how hard the job is on you. Because shit, I had a minor freak-out when I got home, but you must have to deal with death, grieving people, and angry people on a daily basis. I should think anyone who cared would want to help… I don't know… give you a way to protect yourself."

Tad's whole demeanor softened ever so slightly. "I think if more people thought the way you did, there would be fewer divorces on the force. But unfortunately, too many think being a cop is glamorous or something, without realizing the gritty reality of the everyday grind."

Riley desperately wanted to give Tad a hug or pat his hand or something. It made his heart clench to see that Tad had obviously been hurt just for doing his job. But they weren't friends, and it wasn't his place.

He was biting holes in his tongue trying not to ask if Tad's current girlfriend or wife—although he wore no ring—was understanding about his job, but that was none of his business.

"You mentioned that your brother raised you?" Tad forked the last of his omelet into his mouth, a bit of grease giving his lips a shine that Riley would love to lick away. He sighed. There wasn't much point in not answering—Tad could probably just look through police records or whatever to find out what had happened, and then he'd figure out they'd attended the same high school.

Unlike some of the men he'd dated, though, Tad paid attention to everything Riley said and appeared to file it all away. Riley wondered if that was a side effect of being a police detective, or because Riley was at best a witness and at worst a suspect. If that attention to detail carried over in Tad's romantic life, Riley couldn't believe Tad didn't have potential girlfriends swarming over him.

"Our parents were killed in a car crash when I was twelve, and Jonathan was given custody."

Tad's eyes widened in shock. "Shit, I had no idea.... I mean, I'm so sorry. That must have been hard. Both my parents are still alive, and I can't imagine losing one of them even now. Weren't there any aunts or uncles or grandparents? Your brother must have been very young as well. I'm surprised he got custody."

"He's nine years older than me, and we didn't have any other family." Riley did his best to keep his voice even, but many, many times he'd wished his situation had been different. He hadn't liked feeling like a burden, alone in his grief.

Holding his half-full coffee cup, Tad tilted his head as he inspected Riley. "You weren't happy about being placed with your brother? I mean, you're lucky. If he'd been younger, you could have easily been placed in foster care. Most times family is better."

Riley shrugged. "Oh, I get that. I mean, either way, kids and teachers at school treated me different because I was that kid whose parents had died. But Jonathan, as I said, was nine years older. We didn't have a lot in common and hadn't even seen much of each other for a couple years before that because he was in premed at McMaster. He could have easily moved me to Hamilton, because there was no way he could be my guardian from an hour away, but he transferred to the University of Toronto so we didn't have to sell the house. Sometimes I think a brand-new start might have been better, instead of limping along in a life and home that had two great gaping holes. Three, really. Jonathan didn't have a lot of time for me, with his schooling and all."

"I am really sorry. I have two older brothers and a younger sister, and there's only six years between youngest and oldest. We're quite close, and, well… that sounds like I'm rubbing it in, but I just wish you'd had that."

"Thanks." Riley didn't know how to feel. This sincere, invested sympathy seemed out of character for a detective. Tad's partner, Detective Wilson, wouldn't have sat and made small talk over breakfast, of that Riley was 1000 percent certain.

Riley stared down at his plate. One enormous piece of french toast loomed; breakfast had been delicious, but he really couldn't pack away any more. He shouldn't have eaten all the sausage and eggs; they'd been good but didn't compare to the stuffed french toast. Tad had already cleaned his own plate, but then, Riley wasn't sure a simple omelet and fruit would have satisfied him today.

"It's sad, but I can't eat any more."

"That looked really good. You sure you don't want any more?"

"Ugh. No. I might just burst."

"Not even a wafer-thin piece?"

Riley let out a smothered gasp of laughter. Love of Monty Python had run rampant through their school during Tad's last year, since one of the dramatic productions had been a collection of their *Flying Circus* skits. But he couldn't assume Tad was making a joke based on shared experience. He didn't dare. That would just be too fucking embarrassing.

"Not even that," Riley replied, resolutely not commenting on the Monty Python reference.

Tad grinned at him. "Mind if I finish it off?"

Riley couldn't have been more surprised. "Go ahead. No sense in it going to waste."

Like they'd been friends—or boyfriends—forever, Tad swapped plates with him and made short work of the last of Riley's breakfast. He didn't actually moan, but Riley got treated to a pale imitation of what Tad might look like in bed. And it just wasn't fucking fair. Did Tad make a habit of finishing people's breakfasts?

"Can I get you anything else?" The waitress appeared like magic the moment Tad finished chewing, and gathered up the dirty dishes.

And just like that, they were done with breakfast, without ever once having discussed Riley's information.

"I'll have some more coffee. Riley, did you want more hot water for your tea?"

Huh. Maybe breakfast wasn't over. "Sure, yes, please."

As soon as their drinks were topped up, Tad leaned back, relaxed, like they were two friends who'd met for brunch.

No, scratch that. Any friend of Riley's who brunched always drank something alcoholic—Caesars, Bloody Marys, or mimosas. Tad maybe didn't drink, but if *Flashpoint* was any sort of guide, Tad might be working on the weekend, trying to solve Gabrielle's death or any number of other cases. Toronto was a big city, and he suspected homicide kept Tad quite busy.

Riley still found himself reluctant to break their surprisingly easy camaraderie by bringing up the reason he'd called Tad in the first place.

When Tad grimaced slightly and pulled out a notebook, Riley knew his reprieve was over.

"You said you had some more information about Gabrielle's death?" Tad wasn't nearly as brusque as his partner, but there was a definite difference between Tad wearing his metaphorical cop hat and Tad shooting the shit—or more like fishing for information.

Riley blew out a breath, then sipped at his tea, stalling. He didn't want Tad to get upset that Riley had wasted his time. "It's not much. I'm sorry if I made it seem more important than it was."

A smile cracked Tad's cop mien. "Why don't you tell me *what* it is before we figure out how important it is."

"Oh, right." Flustered again. "I don't know if you've had a chance to go through Gabrielle's calendar yet."

Tad made a noncommittal noise that Riley couldn't interpret, and gestured for Riley to continue.

"Anyway, Gabrielle had a meeting the Monday before she died. With Mr. Hanover. It was sort of last-minute, and she had me rearrange several important prelaunch meetings to accommodate it. Mr. Hanover is a lawyer, but as far as I know, he's not associated with any of the legal counsel for Gautier Cosmetics. Certainly Floriana said she didn't know who he was. After the meeting, they went out to lunch. I had initially suspected they might be seeing each other."

Tad held up a hand. "Wait a sec. So you didn't know she was involved with Cody Rosenberg? At all? I mean, I know the marriage came as a shock to her family, but they all knew about him."

"No. I'd heard occasional snatches of gossip about boy toys but assumed it was idle speculation. I didn't know Cody existed until Friday night. So they are—I mean, were—actually married? He wasn't lying about that?"

"Nope. It's why they flew to Vegas, apparently."

"Shut up. *That's* why she went to Vegas?"

"You weren't aware that the trip was personal?"

"I assumed part personal—does anyone go to Vegas for work and do nothing but work? But I was sure she was meeting with a vendor or two while there. Maybe that was simply to keep her kids from finding out before it was too late."

Tad tapped his pen against his notepad. "You could be right. I'll follow up with those vendors, just in case it's relevant. Was there anything else?"

Riley blushed. This was maybe the worst part. "So, uh, while she was out, I went into her office. Nothing unusual. She drinks a lot of tea during the day and offers it to anyone in meetings with her. I go in several times a day to collect teacups and wash them."

"Washing dishes is part of your job description?"

There it was: just a hint of judgment, and Riley narrowed his eyes. "My job description is to make my boss more efficient. Tea is one of those things that made Gabrielle efficient. So yes, at this post, I wash dishes. I still get paid top dollar, even if my only task is to sit at my desk and look pretty."

Tad's eyebrows rose. "I'm sure you'd do well at that."

Wait, was that a backhanded compliment?

"But I didn't mean anything. Obviously I don't have an assistant, so I don't really know what an executive would require."

Riley opened his mouth to give him a rundown, but Tad tapped his notepad again, speaking before Riley could. "You picked up dirty dishes. What then?"

Right. Back to business. Riley's varied job duties didn't really matter. "I noticed some files on her desk were messy. Gabrielle practically uses a ruler to align things on her desk."

He sucked in a breath as the memory of the disarray in Gabrielle's office returned, unexpected and vivid.

"Hey. It's okay." Tad's voice was low and soothing. "Drink some tea, take your time. I know finding Gabrielle like that was a shock."

Riley obeyed, thankful Tad didn't appear impatient with him. "Sorry. It was the mess on her desk that was my first clue that something was really wrong."

Tad nodded. "Sure, sure. I can see that." He made a notation in his book.

"Anyway, the files were messy, but not like… Friday night. So I straightened them up, but, well, I could tell the files were old. I know I shouldn't have, but I flipped through them." The heat returned to his cheeks.

Instead of reprimanding him, Tad gave him another noncop grin. "Snooping, eh? Why am I not surprised?"

Riley gasped. Why would Tad assume such a thing, even if it was true, and one of Riley's vices?

"Kidding, kidding. I swear. Files on your boss's desk, not locked away, when you, as her assistant, are accustomed to entering her office while she's not there? No expectation of privacy. Confidentiality, yes, but you didn't mention this to anyone else, did you?"

Riley let out a relieved breath. "No. Of course not." The realization that a cop had more or less given him tacit permission to snoop was slightly heady.

"I assume there was something in those files that you think is relevant."

"It was her will. Signed around ten years ago. After I saw it, I assumed that maybe Mr. Hanover was her personal lawyer and she'd been reviewing it with him. I don't know if she was planning to change it, though."

"I'll follow up with Mr. Hanover, thank you. Her previous will would have been invalidated by her marriage. If she did manage to get a new will drafted, any changes might give us a direction to follow."

"So this wasn't a waste of time? Don't most murders need to be solved within like forty-eight hours or something?" Riley didn't think his tiny bit of information would help put Gabrielle's murderer behind bars.

Tad laughed, but the sound was devoid of true mirth. "Sure, that's the theory. But it's not a hard and fast rule, as much as we'd like it if every investigation could be tied up in two days. Unfortunately, there's a backlog at the coroner's and a backlog at the lab." He wagged a finger at Riley, voice filled with mock recrimination. "Don't believe what you see on television. It's not all instantaneous results with trace evidence that can narrow down a suspect to a left-handed assailant with a preference for Italian food and a hothouse full of rare orchids."

Riley rolled his eyes. "I know, I know. I mean… I don't know, but I assumed that to be the case. It might surprise you to know I've never met a homicide detective before."

"Anyway, we're still waiting on the autopsy report. I'm working off the prelim data we got Friday night at the scene."

Okay, now they seemed to be truly venturing into collaboration territory—unless providing all this information was some elaborate trap to get Riley to act or admit to his guilt. Good thing he wasn't guilty of anything but overdeveloped curiosity.

"And if anything else strikes you as odd—are you going to be working there, or will you be sent on a new assignment?"

"Honestly, I don't know. I haven't heard from my agency, so if nothing else, I'll go in Monday. Since I'm still under contract, I intend to go in, help things continue as best they can until François and Floriana—or whoever would end up in charge—takes over."

"Good, good. Keep your eyes open, and if you remember anything odd or if anyone does anything unusual, give me a call. Please."

A buzzing sound emanated from the vicinity of Tad's inner pocket. He pulled out his phone and frowned at it. "Sorry, I gotta get going. Work."

Riley dug in his pocket for his wallet, but Tad had already dropped a couple of twenties on the table.

"That's too much for your breakfast."

Tad stood up and winked. "I got this. You can get it next time. By the way, you can get into Gabrielle's office now, if you need to."

And then he was gone, leaving behind a trace of spicy cologne and a flabbergasted Riley, who had absolutely no idea how to fit that wink and the assumption they'd be eating together again with the straight cop who'd questioned him so impersonally Friday night.

He really, really hoped Tad wasn't trying a version of a honey trap on him. Nevertheless, he'd definitely be keeping his eyes peeled.

It was almost like Tad had told him he *had* to snoop. Or at least implied he'd appreciate Riley's help. And if his curiosity could help Tad arrest the person responsible for Gabrielle's death, his curiosity would have a purpose besides his own satisfaction.

Most times, people found him charming and harmless. It was time to take advantage of that. The opportunity to keep in contact with Tad, at least for the duration of the investigation, had nothing to do with his newfound eagerness to get back to Gautier Cosmetics.

Chapter FOUR

MONDAY MORNING hadn't come soon enough. Riley had been so anxious—good and bad—about his first day back after Gabrielle's death, he ended up waking before his alarm. He was undecided whether he should just go in early, even if that meant getting in before anyone else, or if he should linger at home until the last minute. He certainly wasn't going to waste time eating breakfast—his uncertainty about the day and the possibility he'd been mistaken about his contract continuing had his stomach in a snarl. Once he knew better what was going on, he'd dash out for a snack.

In the end, he decided to split the difference and show up about thirty minutes early. He did take the time to stop at a Second Cup for a tea. He didn't think coffee would sit well on his anxious belly, and he didn't think he could bring himself to use any of Gabrielle's teas. Not today, at least, although he suspected they'd all end up in the garbage. Most people, including her children, drank tea with Gabrielle because she insisted rather than as a result of any true preference.

Despite his early arrival, Alisha was already at the reception desk.

"You asshole! How could you not text me this weekend, let me know how you're doing?" Despite her harsh words—Riley had never heard her swear at her desk—Alisha bounded toward him and enveloped him in a hug.

Riley sighed and let himself be hugged. It had been a fucking long time since someone had hugged him like this. Shaun was more of a cheek kisser than a hugger, and his brother certainly had never engaged in any sort of hugging behavior. Most of Riley's human contact had been in the form of well-meaning but ultimately incompatible boyfriends.

Eventually Alisha let him go. "Seriously, though, how are you doing?"

"I'm holding up okay."

"I cannot believe how long you were stuck here on Friday night. And it's all over the office that they suspect Gabrielle was *murdered*. Do they know who did it?"

Riley blinked. "What do you mean it's all over the office? Hardly anybody's here this early on a Monday."

A derisive snort escaped Alisha's glossy plum lips. "Puh-lease. They might be upset she's dead and concerned about what this means for the company and their jobs, but nobody wanted to miss out on a scrap of gossip or any developments. You're practically the last one here."

That did not bode well. He hadn't really wanted to be alone next to Gabrielle's empty office, but he should have listened to his first instinct and come in early.

"Well, I'd better get in there. I imagine there will be a lot of messages and emails to deal with." Gabrielle's death had made the evening news on Sunday—including the information that it was being investigated as suspicious—and he expected a deluge of emailed requests for information. Thanks to Tad, Riley knew more than the news reporters.

He assumed at least one of those emails would be from Gautier's legal team, complete with a scripted response that he should use when responding to messages or rescheduling or canceling Gabrielle's meetings. Alisha would be fending off the majority, but plenty of people had Gabrielle's direct phone line or email address. They were both going to have a busy day.

Without an actual board of directors, Riley didn't know if there was a clear line of succession. With or without it, the entire company was going to be in disarray, possibly for months.

Before he could head in, Alisha grabbed his hand and looked into his eyes. "Listen, if you need anything, even just a break or a shoulder or anything, you call me. Understand? I will put those phones to voicemail and we will find a bottle of Scotch or something."

That surprised a laugh out of Riley. "I got it. Thanks for having my back."

"Hey, us cool kids have to stick together."

Riley walked past the reception desk, slightly more buoyant than he'd been a few minutes prior.

The buoyancy didn't last when he made it to the other end of the floor. A small knot of people were crowded around his desk, but they weren't waiting for him. They were discussing whether they could open the door, since the crime scene tape hung limply from the doorframe.

Riley clapped his hands sharply, making them jump and spin like a pack of startled meerkats. "If you all don't go back to work, I'll call both HR and the police and you can discuss this with them."

That sent them scurrying on their way. Vultures, the lot of them. Glancing around to be sure he was alone—only his desk and the kitchenette had a direct sight line—he opened Gabrielle's door.

What a fucking mess. Gabrielle would have been horrified at the state the police and crime scene technicians had left her office. Hell, Riley was horrified, and he wasn't nearly as tidy and precise as Gabrielle had been.

It would be hours of work before the office was even ready for her successors to sift through documentation, never mind how long it would be before someone else could work in it. Another thing that Riley would have to take care of, assuming his contract continued.

He quickly backed out and shut the door before he fired up his computer. As expected, his inbox—and Gabrielle's—were inundated.

It didn't take long to find the expected official email from Legal with a carefully crafted response employees could use to answer questions about Gabrielle and the fate of Gautier Cosmetics. First thing he did was clear all Gabrielle's meetings for the week, canceling until further notice. Once that was done, he prepared to tackle the mountains of messages. Then someone moved into his peripheral vision and stood there expectantly.

Riley looked up and found the attractive yet haggard visage of Cody Rosenberg. There may have been more than twenty years between him and Gabrielle—he still looked younger than Riley, although maybe not by as much as Riley had thought Friday night—but he looked like a man in the throes of grief. Behind him stood the head of HR, Mattie Tran. It wasn't clear if Cody and Mattie were together or if Mattie was merely waiting her turn. If the latter, odds were good Riley would be clearing out before the end of the day.

"Mr. Rosenberg." Riley stood and held out his hand. "I should have said something Friday. I'm so sorry for your loss."

Cody shook his hand. "Thank you. I appreciate that."

"Is there something I can do for you?" Riley glanced over Cody's shoulder at Mattie, still trying to determine if they were a united front.

Mattie stepped closer. "Riley, if you don't mind, we'd like to have a chat with you. Is the executive conference room available?"

Riley nodded. "Sure." He grabbed the key from inside his desk. Gabrielle never wanted anyone else to use the small conference room without her express permission because she never wanted to search for a meeting room if she needed it, and therefore it was locked when not in use. He had no fucking clue what was going on, but Cody's presence with Mattie meant he wasn't getting fired today.

At least not yet.

"Can I make some coffee for us?"

Cody nodded. "Yes, thank you. I could use a cup. Decaf, please." Riley handed Mattie the key to the conference room, earning a tiny but genuine smile.

"Thank you, Riley. I'd love some too."

"I'll be in there in a few minutes."

TEN MINUTES later the three of them sat around the conference table, steaming mugs in front of them. Riley still wasn't sure he could handle the acidity of coffee, but he'd found a package of hot chocolate. Riley hadn't felt warm through since Friday, so maybe the hot chocolate would help.

Cody and Mattie looked at each other before Cody turned his gaze on Riley. The man still looked more like a model than any man in real life had a right to, but Riley's assessment of Cody's looks was impartial and objective, not like the warm, squirmy feeling he got when confronted with the sexy Tadeo Martin.

"Gabrielle was going to make two announcements on Friday. The first one was about our marriage, which took place in Vegas last week."

There was an uncomfortable pause while Cody visibly pulled himself together. If Riley's spouse had died, he'd still be at home hiding under the covers with a bottle of booze and box of tissues. The fact that Cody was suited and more or less functioning despite his grief was awe-inspiring. Riley was certain other people would take it as evidence Cody didn't love Gabrielle, but Riley didn't think he was misreading Cody's grief.

Under normal circumstances, he'd have been offering congratulations, but now Riley didn't know what to say, so he kept silent.

"Sorry." Cody took a deep breath. "The second announcement was going to be the creation of an in-house marketing department, headed up by myself as vice president. Technically, I'm supposed to be starting today."

"You're kidding." Riley clapped a hand to his mouth. "I'm sorry, that was terribly rude, but you took me by surprise."

Cody chuckled weakly. "It was supposed to be a surprise, so I guess that worked. Treyhorn Associates didn't want to publicize that I was leaving, and Gabby didn't want to fight with her kids about it."

"But don't they have some say? How could she possibly start a new department without involving François? Because that all takes money."

Mattie spoke this time. "I counseled her against doing it this way, but you've been here long enough to know Gabrielle had her own way of doing things. She and François worked together to ensure funds were available for the new department, but she kept Cody's employment a secret. She doesn't actually need consensus for hiring whoever she wants for positions that report to her."

Huh. That was fucked-up. Floriana and François would be furious. "Wait, does her death mean that these plans won't go forward?"

"No. The contract, although initiated by Gabrielle, is a company contract. It's still valid, even without her. Cody might be in for a bit of a fight once everything shakes out, but François and Floriana will have a hard time ousting him without just cause."

Cody cleared his throat. "I was hoping you'd work with me while I transition."

"Um. I'm sorry, what does that mean?"

"You're contracted with the company to cover another admin's long-term medical leave. While we could absolutely use some help tidying up Gabrielle's office, Cody and I think you might be able to take on the role of his assistant, at least until we've figured out where we're going from here. We're happy having you work for us," Mattie said.

"Gabby said a number of times she'd like to hire you on permanently. As far as I'm concerned, there's no better recommendation than that." Cody's expression was pleading, and that alone would probably have convinced Riley if he hadn't had other reasons for wanting to stay.

Nevertheless, it could become uncomfortable. Floriana hated him, and François might start if he reported to Cody.

"I'd half thought you'd tell me my contract was up now."

Mattie shook her head. "As Cody said, Gabrielle wanted you on board. I have a contract template set up on her order, in case you ever took her up on her offer."

He knew he'd get bored if he stuck around one place too long, but Gabrielle's near-instant belief that she wanted Riley to stay gave him the warm fuzzies.

Thinking of Tad and his tacit permission to snoop gave Riley the best reason to accept Cody's offer. Riley wasn't an idiot. Cody needed someone in his corner who wouldn't be caught in the upcoming civil war between him and his stepchildren, both of whom were older than he was. Cody needed someone who could put his interests first without worrying Floriana would retaliate by getting him fired. If things didn't end well at Gautier, it would be upsetting, as Riley had never left any position with less than glowing references, but either way, his agency would have a new posting for him within a week.

"Thank you. I'd be happy to accept."

Cody's shoulders dropped in relief. "Thank you, Riley. I appreciate it."

"You're not seriously thinking about working today, are you?" It wasn't hard to make the mental switch to being Cody's assistant, and that included looking out for his interests in all areas.

Cody's jaw firmed up. "I must. If I'm to protect Gabby's legacy, I need to make myself every bit as visible as she would have wished."

"Where are you planning to work?" Riley shook his head. "Never mind. I think I know. The empty office on the other side of the conference room?"

Mattie nodded, a pleased smile hovering on her lips. "You guessed right. It was originally supposed to have been François's office, but he wanted one closer to the rest of his department, and Floriana spends so much of her time in the lab she never needed a big office on this floor. When Gabrielle suggested adding another vice president, the empty office sitting there waiting was almost serendipity."

Serendipity. Doubtful. He hadn't known Gabrielle long, but he didn't think many of her moves relied on anything so specious as serendipity.

He wasn't sure how he was going to wind up Gabrielle's outstanding work affairs and provide a buffer between Cody and the Gautiers, but he'd do his best. Somewhere in there, he'd poke around, see if he could figure out who might have had it in for Gabrielle.

"When are you going to make an official announcement?" Mattie and Cody made the same sour face. But if this truly was a done deal, someone was going to have to break the bad news to François and Floriana, and it sure as shit wasn't going to be Riley.

"I've put a meeting on their calendars for after lunch. Once we've told them, we'll send out an email to the entire company," Mattie said.

"Wait, François and Floriana are both working today?"

Mattie nodded, but her expression mirrored what Riley was thinking. Bereavement leave wasn't just some nice, fluffy, feel-good perk. There were damn good reasons people should have some time to get their heads back on straight after the loss of a loved one.

"Right. Well, I'd better get back to my desk and finish dealing with the messages."

"I've talked to IT. Cody's inbox is set up already, and now they're going to close down Gabrielle's email account and route any messages to your inbox. They'll let you know when they're going to do that," Mattie said.

"Thanks. Cody, where will you be in the meantime, in case something comes up?"

Cody smiled, but it didn't quite reach his eyes. "Hiding out in my office, setting up the accounts I'm going to need."

"Got it. As soon as you get the chance, give me access to your calendar and email."

Cody nodded, and they all stood. Riley shook their hands before gathering the coffee cups, his mind awhirl as he returned to his desk.

"Back to work," he barked at the fresh knot of people craning their heads around the corner by his desk, probably hoping Gabrielle's office door was open.

They scurried away like frightened mice, and Riley grimaced as he realized the office door was open a couple of inches. He specifically remembered closing it, which meant one of those vultures had opened the damn door.

Indecision hit him hard. All those messages needed replies, but if he was going to be working for Cody, it might be better to get Gabrielle's office cleaned up so there wouldn't be anything for the damned gawkers to see when there was no gatekeeper at his desk.

He had express permission to clean—Tad had said the police were done with the office. Riley sighed. It wasn't a task he looked forward to, but it would be better for everyone to have the office put back to rights. He sent quick messages to Alisha and Cody to let them know where he'd be if anyone came looking for him.

SEVERAL HOURS later, a soft knock startled him out of his concentration. He strode to the door, prepared to deliver a blistering dressing-down, but it was only Alisha.

"I'm ordering lunch. What do you want?"

Riley frowned. "Ugh. Nothing for me, thanks."

Alisha narrowed her eyes. "No, I don't think so. You need to eat. You've had a rough couple of days, and you already told me you didn't have any breakfast. So you'd better think quick about what you want."

There were so many different types of food in the vicinity: Greek, Asian of just about any variety, Indian, Lebanese, Ethiopian. But what he really wanted was some comfort food. Macaroni and cheese or something that involved mashed potatoes or maybe spaghetti. Riley glanced down at his pale blue button-down shirt. Penne instead of spaghetti if he wanted to save his shirt.

"Italian maybe, or someplace that's got mac and cheese."

"If I go Italian, what do you want?"

"Red sauce and penne."

"I've got you covered. I know just where to go."

Suddenly Riley remembered his new responsibilities, and that responsibility was currently hiding out in his new office, hoping François and Floriana didn't notice he was there until their afternoon meeting with HR.

"Uh, could you also pick me up a meatball sub? With a side salad?"

Alisha's eyes widened. "I thought I was going to have to hold your nose and stuff food in to make you eat."

He did his best to look unconcerned and innocent. "Just… I can't quite decide what I want. This way I'll have a choice." He could offer Cody his choice of both, and Riley could pick over what Cody didn't want.

"Then two lunches you'll get. By the way, you did a great job in here."

Riley wrinkled his nose. He had done a lot of work—the office was almost back to normal. "How do you know?"

Alisha rolled her eyes. "I took a peek when I got here this morning."

"I've been chasing vultures away all morning, and you were one of the first!"

"I don't count. Remember, I was there Friday night. And honestly, I mostly wanted to check to make sure we didn't need to call in special cleaners."

The thought of needing cleaners specializing in crime scenes made him shudder. "Go, get out. Any more of this talk and I won't be able to eat anything, no matter where you get it from."

As it was, he'd shoved Gabrielle's office chair into the corner and given it a wide berth as he worked. He was pretty certain the chair would have to be disposed of—he didn't know anyone who'd want to sit in the death chair. One place he'd worked at had a pregnancy chair. Everyone who'd used it got pregnant within six months, whether they'd been intending to or not. Riley'd had a bit of fun with that one, pretending he'd also managed to get pregnant.

The death chair was no laughing matter.

Alisha slipped out of the office and closed the door behind her. Riley checked his watch. Not too much longer before the fireworks would start, and they would probably be easier to deal with if he was fortified. A quick glance around the room confirmed he was mostly done.

After ensuring all the file cabinets and Gabrielle's desk were locked, he approached the massive tea caddy and opened it. All the teacups and teapots were covered in fingerprint powder, and Riley sighed. Presumably the police hadn't found anything useful, or the china would have been absent entirely. After washing all those dishes again, he'd be done.

Then he frowned. One of Gabrielle's favorite teas—the lapsang souchong that tasted and smelled like campfire leavings—was missing. He traced a finger over the gap where it was supposed to be. The rest of the squat airtight containers on that shelf had been shuffled, just a bit, to make it look less like there was a specific gap, but Riley remembered everything on that shelf.

It was possible the police had removed it—and it gave Riley chills to think that he might have held the murder weapon in his hand just last week. But it was an unusual detail, one he'd tell Tad about when he let him know about the new marketing department.

After he made quick work of washing the china, he put everything back and inspected the caddy once more. Surely no one would mind if he took a little keepsake. No one was going to keep this around. Riley selected the best Earl Grey and a masala chai, as well as three of the honeys—plain, blueberry, and cinnamon flavored—and tucked them all in his top desk drawer.

But it wasn't really his desk, was it? It was Aaron's. Aaron Brown, who thought he'd be coming back to work for Gabrielle after he recovered from whatever he had. It hadn't even occurred to Riley to ask Mattie or Tad—had anyone let Aaron know about Gabrielle's death? Riley had seen it briefly on the news, but she wasn't a beloved celebrity. It wasn't trending on social media. If Aaron didn't watch the news, he might not know.

And really, how awful would that be, to turn on the television and find out that way? Riley did a quick search of his email—Gabrielle had directed him to send Aaron a fruit basket on his first day of work. There it was: Aaron Brown's address, and it wasn't out in the fucking suburbs or anything.

Riley went back into Gabrielle's office. She'd received a gift set, three types of teas with rose honey that she'd only opened enough to place on the shelves. The individual containers were still sealed. He took those back to his desk. He'd go visit Aaron Brown, make sure he knew about Gabrielle, and find out if Aaron wanted a little memento from Gabrielle's tea caddy. The china itself might be valuable enough for Bethany or Floriana or even Cody to want it, but he knew none of Gabrielle's family cared about tea with the same passion.

ALISHA DROPPED off an aluminum container filled with penne, marinara, and giant aromatic sausage meatballs, and another bag with a sub and salad. She also offered to eat with Riley, but he needed to deal with the ever-increasing messages, and he also wanted a bit of privacy to call Tad.

As soon as Alisha was out of sight, he grabbed the bag of food and a couple of soft drink cans from the kitchenette and made his way to Cody's office. He didn't see anyone else, which wasn't exactly a surprise, but it was also lunchtime. On most days, the second the clock struck noon, Gautier Cosmetics bore an unfortunate resemblance to the stark, desolately empty lab in *Resident Evil* before they figured out the zombies were hiding around the corner, waiting to pounce. Riley just hoped the zombies were out getting their own lunch, instead of milling around his desk hoping to catch a glimpse of a potential crime scene.

He tapped on Cody's closed door and placed a hand on the handle. His heart skipped a beat, because the last time he'd done this, he found Gabrielle dead. The odds of that happening again were astronomical, but that didn't stop an irrational niggle of fear from spawning in his gut.

Fuck it. Riley swept the door open, and Cody looked up from his computer with a strained smile. "Riley. What did you need?"

He held the bag aloft. "Penne marinara or meatball sub with salad?"

Reddened, puffy eyes blinked at him. "It's lunchtime already?"

"Yes." In other circumstances, like once everyone knew Cody was here and working for Gautier Cosmetics and Riley hadn't spent the last hours clearing away the evidence of crime scene technicians, he'd be sure to ask Cody what he wanted for lunch and figure out his preferences. But today wasn't a normal day.

"I'm not really hungry."

Riley had a moment of sympathy for Alisha. "Maybe not, but you need to eat." They both did. "So pick one."

A half smile brightened Cody's face for a split second. "You're going to be a pushy assistant, aren't you?"

"Yes. Stubborn too, so you might as well just give in and eat something."

"The sub and salad. Thanks, Riley."

Riley nodded and pulled out the meal, leaving it on Cody's desk with napkins, utensils, and a drink.

"I, uh, have a favor to ask."

"What is it?" Riley asked.

"Can you sit in on the HR meeting with François and Floriana? I know I have to face them down, but it might help if it looks like it's not just me taking on Gautier Cosmetics on my own."

The reasoning was almost sound, but Riley also didn't begrudge Cody simply not wanting to be alone. He felt bad for the whole family. A death was stressful enough without having to add all this other drama. "I can do that."

"Thank you." Cody's eyes brightened, but he ducked his head, attention back on his computer, before Riley could do anything to try to comfort his new boss.

Taking his cue, Riley grabbed the rest of the food and left, making sure to close Cody's door behind him.

AT QUARTER after twelve, his own desk was almost as silent as it had been when he'd come looking for Gabrielle on Friday night, although all the lights were on, making it less creepy. He ate a few bites of pasta before getting his phone out.

Riley pulled up Tad's name and called him.

"Detective Tad Martin. Leave a message."

So that was how he always answered the phone, even voicemail. Riley had been expecting to leave a message, but hearing Tad's voice still rattled him a bit. "Uh. It's Riley. Parker?"

Again he'd introduced himself as though he couldn't remember his own fucking name. Tad was going to think he was completely clueless.

"I found out something. A couple of things actually. Call me back when you can."

Riley disconnected the call and stared at his phone, tapping his desk impatiently as the seconds crawled by. Tad wasn't at his beck and call, but dammit. Why wasn't he calling back?

An email notification dinged, and Riley leaped for it, anxious for the distraction. Unfortunately, it postponed the meeting with HR, and that meant even fewer distractions for him.

If he stayed here waiting for the phone to ring, he would simply go mad. With a huff, he dumped the remainder of his lunch in the trash, then got up and shut himself in Gabrielle's office. Plenty still to do to prepare for her successor, and he might as well do something useful with his time. He was too antsy to simply answer emails.

A FEW hours later he emerged, only slightly dusty and disheveled, to find he'd missed a couple of phone calls from Tad.

Slightly mollified, although he should have taken his phone with him, he quickly called back.

This time, thankfully, he didn't have to introduce himself.

"Well, hello, Riley Parker. What can I do for you?"

Oh, so many things. But there was a divide the size of the Grand Canyon between what Tad *could* do and what he'd be *willing* to do. And none of that pertained to the investigation.

"As I said in my message, I found out a few things."

"I'm not close to your office, but perhaps we could meet for an early dinner."

It might have been Riley's imagination—or more like his wishful thinking—but Tad's voice sounded warmer than Riley would expect. He also hadn't been angling for a dinner invitation, but he'd take it.

"Sure. I'm off work at five thirty, so any time after that." Since it was quarter to five now, he didn't have too terribly long to fret.

"What about Alberto's? At six?"

"That's fine. I'll see you then." Riley disconnected the call quickly before he said something stupid, like he was looking forward to it.

He didn't care that he'd be having Italian two meals in a row—he loved the stuff, although with just about anyone else, he'd have suggested another option. There wouldn't be enough time for him to go home and take another shower before meeting up with Tad, but since it wasn't a date, that shouldn't matter. Riley assumed the only reason Tad had chosen a restaurant with cozy little alcoves tailor-made for romantic dates was so they could talk undisturbed without worry of being overheard.

None of the logic calmed the tiny flutter of excitement in his belly, but he had no right to feel excited about meeting with Tad. Not when the whole point was to catch whoever had killed Gabrielle.

What was with him getting all hung up on unavailable or uninterested men? It was like his subconscious had decided he needed to be alone forever.

Chapter FIVE

AT FIVE thirty on the dot, Riley stood by the reception desk, wondering what to do with himself. If the HR meeting had happened as scheduled, instead of getting postponed to the next morning, he might have worked late, because he was certain as soon as Cody was officially confirmed, there'd be plenty of additional work on his plate. But as it was, he had little to do, and he had zero desire to hang about in the rapidly emptying office, trying not to jump at every sound.

The problem was that it wasn't going to take him long to get to Alberto's. He didn't have time to go home first, and he didn't want to be early. Most times he didn't mind showing up early—it was being late that he despised. But waiting for Tad at a restaurant? Unbearably nerve-racking.

Alisha was just closing down her station.

"Doing anything exciting tonight?"

Alisha snorted. "Not hardly. I have a date to catch up on my recorded episodes of *Arrow*, and I have a brand-new bottle of malbec desperate to be opened."

Riley smiled. More proof that they were destined to be friends. Underneath Alisha's glamorous exterior beat the heart of a fellow nerd. He might try inviting her to game night sometime, although some of the guys might faint at the presence of an actual female.

"What about you?"

Well, he hadn't thought that out, had he? For all that his heart and libido had been treating his interactions with Tad like they'd met on a dating site, his brain was adamant that letting it be known he was meeting with one of the detectives in charge of Gabrielle's case would not be smart, even if it was only Alisha.

"Uh. Just meeting up with a friend for dinner."

"Shaun? I still have to meet that guy. I can always postpone my solitary drinking night until tomorrow and come with."

Heat flashed into Riley's cheeks. Bringing Alisha along was pretty much the last thing he wanted to do. "It's not Shaun, no."

"Oh." Alisha looked a bit embarrassed too, before she laughed wickedly and got her air quotes out again. "A 'friend.' I see. I wouldn't want to be a third wheel, but I'll be expecting details."

Details? Riley's face got hotter.

"Oh my God, I'm not trying to give you a stroke. I only want details if it's a date and if you like him. If you're just fucking, well, my imagination will suffice."

"Alisha!" Riley glanced around, making sure no one had overheard her.

She just rolled her eyes. "I'll see you tomorrow, Riley, and hopefully you'll be less uptight." Her expression became solemn. "All joking aside, you could use some relaxation. I know how difficult the past few days have been, and it's probably not going to ease up for a while. So go have fun with your friend and know you can always call me if you need."

"Thanks, Alisha. I appreciate that. And I promise I'll get you out to meet Shaun soon." Riley took a look at his watch. "I'd better get going." Not that he was going to be late, but because he was too damned nervous to wait. If necessary, he'd walk around the block a few times or twelve.

Before he left, Alisha gave him another hug. If they'd moved their relationship into hugging territory, he was okay with that.

RILEY STOOD on the sidewalk outside Alberto's. His conversation with Alisha had killed some time, but he was still fifteen minutes early. Maybe they had a bar he could wait at. One drink shouldn't impair his ability to control himself.

He sucked in a deep breath and peered at the shiny glass front, confirming his reflection was tall, blond, and well-dressed, instead of the short, nerdy, braces-on-teeth and bespectacled face that he'd been around Tad in high school.

His new image gave him a tiny boost of confidence, and he walked into the restaurant.

The bar was more crowded than the restaurant, which wasn't a surprise. Most places offered happy-hour specials every weekday. Riley was still able to get a stool at the bar. The bartender winked at him and came over immediately to serve him, reinforcing his confidence.

When his wine came—also in flatteringly record time—Riley took a large mouthful and swallowed, letting some of the tension of the day drain away. Arriving early wasn't so bad, even though he was alone.

Shit. He'd completely forgotten about his plans to visit Aaron after work. Not that there would have been enough time to head over to Aaron's place even if he hadn't stopped to chat with Alisha, but he couldn't believe one conversation with Tad pushed all other thoughts out of his head.

Tomorrow. He'd go visit Aaron tomorrow, for sure.

With the glass of Chianti at his side, Riley pulled out his phone and started playing a game to help pass the time.

"Hey."

Riley looked up, startled, to find Tad well inside his personal space. "Oh, hi." Breathlessness was not an improvement over asking his name like a question. The bar was simply crowded. That had to be the explanation for Tad's pulse-raising proximity.

"Sorry I'm late."

Riley tucked his phone away. "I, uh, hadn't realized." Although he should have. He'd passed a level in his game and almost finished his Chianti.

"I'm not sure if that's good or not," Tad teased.

God. For Riley's self-preservation, Tad needed to knock off the good-natured likable shit and start acting like a hard-hearted detective, or Riley really was going to do something stupid, like become infatuated all over again.

"Well, you complained last time that your job had challenges. You should be happy I can entertain myself if you get delayed." *Riley, what the fuck?* He'd have to settle for a metaphorical smack on the forehead. He wasn't out to prove he'd make good relationship material. And for the six millionth time, they weren't dating.

"That is a good thing." Tad's voice lowered to a deep rumble that Riley felt in his balls. Which really wasn't fair. Maybe Tad was just fucking with his head, messing with the gay guy for a laugh, but if Tad had been capable of that sort of maliciousness, Riley would have experienced it in high school.

He shouldn't have had the glass of wine. The alcohol was starting to dissolve his hastily built defenses against a grown-up and blindingly attractive Tadeo Martin.

"There's no wait for tables. Did you want to go eat or have another drink?"

"Let's eat." No more booze for him tonight.

Tad led the way to their table, and as Riley had feared, it was every bit as cozy and romantic as he'd remembered.

The round table in a half-circle booth hadn't felt this small when he'd been here last. But then, he hadn't been worried about the consequences of touching the man he'd been with.

Riley slid into the booth, doing his best to stay close to the edge without falling off. Tad, on the other hand, sat on his side of the booth and sprawled. Riley might have an inch or two on Tad in height, but Tad was wider and seemed to take up all the air in the vicinity.

The waiter came to take their drink order, and Tad ordered a cranberry and soda.

"I'll have the same," Riley said. Slightly more interesting than water, and absolutely no alcohol.

The waiter left, and Tad shifted so he could look at Riley better. "You can have another glass of wine if you'd like. Just because I'm not drinking doesn't mean you can't."

So tempting to ask coyly if Tad was trying to get him drunk. Riley was a damned job for Tad. He wished it was easier to remember that.

Instead, he laughed nervously. "That's okay. One drink on a work night is pretty much my maximum." Not that Shaun hadn't convinced him otherwise on occasion, but going into work hungover was never fun, and much less so after he'd hit thirty.

Riley hid himself in his menu, but it didn't take long to decide what he wanted. Fortunately, the waiter returned with drinks before things got too weird, and took their order.

"How was your day?" Tad asked.

"I found out—"

Tad waved his hand. "No, no. I mean how was your day? I know it had to be difficult going back to work. Or… they didn't give you the boot because your boss died, did they?"

Riley heaved a sigh. Tad seemed determined Riley wouldn't escape with his sanity intact.

"No, I'm still there for the foreseeable future." He'd get into specifics once Tad had his notebook out. "And you're right. It was… tough. Gabrielle had a lot of energy. She was a force to be reckoned with, and there was a distinct emptiness in the office today."

"I understand. And I'm sorry you've had to go through this." Tad moved as though he were going to pat Riley's hand, but then he didn't and Riley wondered if he'd imagined it.

"Thanks. And your guys left quite a mess in the office." Riley smiled, hoping to lighten things up a bit.

Tad rolled his eyes. "Oh I know. You didn't have to clean that all up, did you?"

"I suppose I could have called in a cleaning service, but I had to refile all of the files that were out anyway. Get things prepared for whoever takes over. It just made sense that I do the cleaning as well."

"Oh. That's rough."

Riley didn't mention the death chair. He wasn't sure he was up to joking about that yet.

"What about your day? Everything go okay?" So much for Riley's hope it wasn't going to get weird. Brunch yesterday, dinner today, and asking about each other's day. This felt like the beginning of a promising relationship rather than cooperating in a homicide investigation.

Did all of Tad's witnesses and possible suspects get this sort of treatment?

Tad smiled at him. "Could have been better. Emma's still being a bear, but she hasn't caved yet. But a couple of our cases are dragging on, leads fizzling out."

There was a short pause before Tad continued. "So, what sort of things do you do for fun?"

Riley blinked. This was seriously fucking with his head. "Uh. Gaming mostly."

"Like, video games?"

He shrugged. "Sometimes, sure. But I meet up with a bunch of guys and we play board games, like strategy ones. Sundays mostly, but sometimes other days too."

"You mean like Monopoly?" Tad grimaced. "I hated playing that. My oldest brother, Lucas, always insisted we play to the bitter end, even though the last half of the game everyone knew who was going to win. I usually preferred playing street hockey or football or something."

Or lacrosse, but Riley bit back yet another comment that might let Tad realize they sort of knew each other. "No, no. Not like that. They're more strategic, less dice oriented. Often called European style." Riley clamped his lips shut. He could talk about games for hours. Then again… this wasn't actually a date. "There's a café called Coffee and Conquer not far from here where you can eat, get coffee, or have a beer while you play."

"Really? I've seen that place. And the café has these games there?"

Riley nodded. "They have a bunch, sure. Sometimes we bring our own, though. Sometimes we play role-playing games."

Tad's eyebrow lifted. "You don't say. And they allow that in this café? I might have to drop a tip about this place to the Vice squad."

"Not that kind of role play," Riley sputtered. Although he'd been to a couple of those clubs over the years too. "Like Dungeons & Dragons. We run a campaign once a month."

"Nah, I know about that, I was just pulling your chain. I didn't realize people still played that, though. There was a group of guys in high school who played all the time."

Blood heated his face so much his ears started sweating. There had only been one group who'd played D&D in their high school, and Riley had been in that group. One more thing Tad's friends had bullied them about. And the last thing he wanted to do was hear how Tad really felt about Riley's band of geeks.

Seeing Tad again stirred up so much emotional muck from high school, garbage he thought he'd long since buried. He was thirty-one, for fuck's sake. He shouldn't care, and yet, he hadn't changed much. Inside, at least.

"Anyway, yeah. If I ever wanted a permanent job, I'd want to open one of those board game cafés. I'd get to order all the new games as they came out, be one of the first to see how they worked." There was something almost magical about opening a new game, punching out the cardboard game pieces. Riley liked the ones with lots of fiddly pieces, although most of his gaming group didn't enjoy them as much because setting up the game and putting it away took such a long time.

Tad laughed. "Owning board game café as a life goal? That's the first time I've heard that. Awesome."

The heat in Riley's face receded somewhat. At least Tad wasn't making fun of him for such a weird dream. And that's all it was, really.

He wasn't sure if the downtown area needed another board game café, and honestly his job, even as a temp, was far more stable than running a retail food-and-beverage establishment, however much fun it would be. He'd never mentioned that particular idea to anyone before, but desperation to redirect the path of the conversation made other things leap out of his mouth.

"So what about the gym? Ever go there?" Tad asked.

Like Riley had forgotten for half a second that he was talking to a jock turned cop. "Sure I go, but not for fun." Exercising was a necessary chore.

"Huh. It can be fun. We should go together sometime."

What? Law & Order, *Criminal Minds*, *Castle*, and *Flashpoint* had completely failed to prepare him for this situation.

Their food came, saving Riley from having to reply, and Tad shifted in his seat again. This time his leg, muscular and warm, pressed heavily against Riley's thigh. The unexpected contact sent a zing through his veins. Tad's entire body radiated heat that warmed Riley's skin all along his right side. If he relaxed at all, more of their bodies would end up touching, but if he moved away, he'd fall right off his seat. Did Tad not realize how close they were sitting? Completely against Riley's better judgment, he was getting hard. Probably because that useless piece of flesh didn't have anything resembling good judgment.

Riley had no idea what he'd ordered. Holding himself motionless to avoid drawing attention to their touching thighs took a ton of concentration. On top of that, he needed to respond intelligently to Tad's questions and occasionally volley a question back without sounding as though lust had swamped him. There was no brainpower left over for anything else. He simply ate by rote, and at some point both of their plates were empty.

Tad shifted again, rubbing their legs together, and Riley almost moaned.

"Can I get you anything else? A dessert menu?" The waiter gathered up their empty dishes as he spoke.

Tad turned to Riley. "Do you like tiramisu?"

"Uh, yes, but I don't really need any dessert." What he needed was to go home and jerk off and then maybe check the news, make sure he hadn't dropped into some sort of alternate reality.

"Good. Don't bother with the menus, just bring an order of tiramisu with two spoons."

Stunned into silence, Riley stared at Tad. Who *did* that? People on *dates* did that. People in *relationships* did that. Why was Tad fucking with him?

The waiter nodded and left; then Tad slid out of the booth and got to his feet. "Gotta hit the bathroom. Back in a few."

Great. Now Riley was wondering if his "date" was going to ditch and leave him crying in the tiramisu he hadn't ordered, stuck paying the bill.

Riley sat up straighter. That might have happened once or twice before he had Shaun help him reinvent his look, but he could probably go home with the bartender at this very restaurant if he wanted. Which he didn't, but Tad wasn't running out—hell, they hadn't even gotten to the notebook portion of the "date."

Before the turmoil in his brain settled, Tad returned, followed shortly by the waiter, who set the dessert down with a flourish.

Tad dove in first. "That is so good. Maybe it's a bit of a stereotype for a cop, but I could drink coffee all day, and I love tiramisu and coffee ice cream. Coffee chocolates."

"Uh-huh. I think what I'm hearing is someone using a stereotype as an excuse for a sweet tooth." If Tad was going to act like they weren't here for business, then Riley was too.

"Maybe." Tad laughed. "Are you going to try it?"

Riley could smell the creamy goodness. Screw it. He picked up his spoon and swiped a mouthful. "Oh. That is good."

"And sharing sweets is how I keep the spare tire at bay." Tad patted his extremely flat stomach.

"Uh-huh. I'm sure finding the gym fun has nothing to do with it."

Tad gave him a bashful grin.

Alternate reality. It was the only logical explanation.

Bite by bite, the tiramisu disappeared, and they laughingly fought over the very last bit.

Tad patted his stomach again. "Wow, that was great."

Riley agreed, even though he still couldn't recall what he'd eaten before the tiramisu. He was seconds from asking if Tad wanted to go get coffee or come back to his place when Tad pulled out the infamous notebook and pen.

Oh, right. Not a social occasion.

"Why do you use a notebook? I mean, wouldn't a tablet or something work better?" At least in this day and age.

"Tablets have some advantages, sure. But I never have to worry about my notebook's battery running low or the screen breaking. I do take photos of my notes and type up more detailed information later on."

Huh. All those shows sort of skimmed over that aspect of it. Detectives could probably use admin assistants every bit as much as CEOs. Maybe more.

"Right. Well, you asked about my day earlier. I was expecting to either be cut loose today or maybe given a week or two to help wind up Gabrielle's work. But that's not what happened. I mean, you might know all this, but… actually, I guess it's still confidential until tomorrow." Shit. If that meeting with HR hadn't been postponed, this would be company-wide knowledge.

"I told you before I'd keep your identity confidential. And I'm not planning to call a press conference about whatever this is."

Riley was going to drown in these murky ethical waters. "There's a meeting tomorrow. After that, it'll be common knowledge."

Tad nodded. "Okay, then. Tell me now, then text me tomorrow as soon as they've pulled the trigger on this. I won't act before that."

"Thank you." That eased his conscience. "Gabrielle's husband had been offered a contract to come on board as a VP, equivalent level to François and Floriana. He started today, and HR says the contract's binding even though Gabrielle's dead."

"That is very interesting. And let me guess, they want you to finish your contract out as Cody's assistant."

Riley blinked. "Yes. That's exactly it. I said you might know this all."

"Nope. Educated guess."

Huh. Not that he'd had a reason to think otherwise, but this was pretty clear evidence Tad was good at his job.

"If François or Floriana didn't know the details of his contract, this might make motive."

"They didn't know about Cody being hired at all. Mattie told me Gabrielle insisted it be kept secret. Floriana apparently didn't even know about the creation of the new department."

"But François did?"

"As VP of Finance, he had to make sure the money was available."

Tad scratched on his notebook, angling it so Riley couldn't casually peek at what he was writing. "Mattie who?"

"Mattie Tran, head of Human Resources."

More scratching. "Well, all we know for sure is that Mattie and Cody believe François and Floriana are in the dark. But it's possible either or both found out this secret. Thank you. Was that everything?"

"No. Not exactly. While I was cleaning Gabrielle's office, I noticed one of her containers of tea was missing. I don't know if maybe the crime scene guys took it with them for some reason."

"Hmmm. I think they took samples of everything, but I don't believe they'd have reason to take a whole container. Are you sure it's missing? Maybe Gabrielle used it up and threw it out."

Riley considered that for a moment. "No, I don't think so. It's one of her favorite flavors—lapsang souchong—and I know it was in the caddy just after lunch on Friday because I made some for her."

Tad pulled out his phone and scrolled around a bit. "Here. This is her schedule for Friday. Can you pinpoint when?"

Wow. Tad really hadn't been kidding about taking pictures of everything. A tablet would be easier to view some of this stuff on, but then again, a tablet wouldn't fit as well in his pocket.

Riley skimmed through the calendar. "Here. She had a meeting with one of the wholesale distributers at one. I made tea for them; Gabrielle had a cup then. The two representatives from the distributers had assam. Then she had a meeting with all of the senior executives and staff throughout the afternoon. She had more tea, but either she or the staff made it. I just know there were additional cups to be cleaned, so I don't know if anyone used the lapsang after that or if it was still in the caddy."

"This is good stuff. I'll follow up with the CSIs."

The bill came and Riley wasn't quick enough to grab it. Tad merely smirked at him and dropped some cash. "Want to go grab a coffee?"

Riley hesitated for a moment. "Sure." Why the hell not? He was already lost and confused; it could hardly get worse.

THE SECOND Cup within walking distance of Alberto's had been crowded and noisy; they finished their drinks quickly and with a minimum of conversation. At least there hadn't been any additional touching.

Riley wouldn't have been able to hide just how much he enjoyed Tad's proximity while slouched in the coffee shop's armchairs.

In short order, they were back out on the street.

"Let me walk you home," Tad offered.

Already drowning in mixed messages, Riley agreed. Tad had already proven to be a better date than the last half dozen Riley had endured. It didn't even matter that his teenage infatuation predisposed him to like Tad. After tonight, he'd have been suckered in regardless.

He was a fucking idiot, but since he'd already leaped without a safety net, he might as well enjoy getting escorted home. Not everyone could have a big, strong policeman take them right to their door.

"You're in Liberty Village, right?"

Riley blinked at him a moment before he remembered giving his address as part of his interview after Gabrielle's death. "Yes."

They weren't far from his condo, and they walked in silence. Riley couldn't quite figure out what was going on. Tad seemed to be thinking hard, and Riley didn't want to do anything to destroy the illusion that he and his date—or even better, his boyfriend—were heading home for some rather more carnal entertainment.

Normally the sight of his gray-bricked building filled him with contentment. Not so tonight.

With a sigh, Riley opened the security door and turned to say good night to Tad, who merely gestured for Riley to go ahead and followed him to the elevator.

He fidgeted a bit as the elevator plodded up to his floor. Had any date walked him right to his door? But this wasn't a date, and he needed to remember that. Maybe Tad needed privacy to talk about Riley's information? He should probably invite Tad in.

Shit. He'd had another allergy attack that morning and had been moving sluggishly until the antihistamines had kicked in. What if he'd left dirty laundry or other embarrassing items out in the open? Although he usually kept his condo neat and tidy, he hadn't been expecting company.

Tad followed him in silence. At his door, Riley paused before putting the key in the lock and turned to offer an invitation inside.

Only to find Tad right up in his space, close enough that Tad's body heat sent his own temperature soaring. Shock kept him paralyzed while swarms of butterflies erupted in his belly. He was nervous and excited in a way he'd never been. Tad's warm brown eyes were dark with hunger, and Riley barely refrained from whimpering aloud when Tad cupped his face in his strong hands.

Blood surged into his groin as Tad's lips covered his, the kiss swallowing the sounds Riley could no longer hold back.

Oh God. Tad was definitely not straight.

The touch of those lips broke his paralysis, and almost involuntarily, he wound his arms around Tad's waist.

Tad pushed him up against the door and devoured his mouth. Riley licked and nipped and sucked in response, the kiss hotter than molten lava.

Time came to a standstill as their mouths merged and dueled. The thick ridge of Tad's erection bumped against Riley's, the sensation weakening his knees. He wanted to get them inside to a bed, but he didn't want to stop long enough to make the offer.

Instead he moved his hips in a restless rhythm, more and more frantic the deeper and longer they kissed. Riley clutched at Tad's back while Tad gripped the sides of his head as though Riley might escape. No fucking chance of that. Orgasm was too close.

Before either of them tipped over the edge, Tad pulled out of the kiss, his brown eyes glittering and his heaving breath skating warm across Riley's cheek. He took a deliberate step back and shoved his trembling hands through his tousled hair.

Riley blinked and licked his kiss-swollen lips, trying to restore cognitive function and figure out why they'd stopped. Coming in his pants like a teenager wasn't maybe the most dignified, but he hardly cared.

"Inside?" His voice had deepened well into phone sex operator territory.

Tad groaned. "I can't. Jesus H. Christ, but I can't."

His suit pants did nothing to conceal just how much Tad would like to accompany Riley into his bed, and he curled his hands into fists to keep from stroking that hefty erection.

The short respite allowed some blood back into Riley's brain. This was a phenomenally bad idea. Tad was investigating the murder of Riley's boss, and until just minutes ago, Riley had thought Tad was straight.

"I...." Riley had no idea what to say here.

Tad bit his lip, then looked away. "Shit. Riley." The husky rasp of a still-aroused Tad did nothing to put a damper on the desire still raging through Riley's veins.

"I'm sorry, Riley. This shouldn't have happened. If… if you could maybe not mention this to anyone…."

The sour twist of Tad's lips indicated dislike of what he'd just said, and Riley decided to gamble.

"If I'm not going to say anything, can't we go inside? Finish what we started?"

The silence lengthened while Tad stared at the door over Riley's shoulder. Had he overstepped? Had he somehow misread things? Although it was hard to misread a tongue down the throat and a hard cock seeking a playmate.

"I can't tell you how much I want to follow you to your bed and fuck your brains out."

A shiver ghosted down his spine. Did Tad have any idea how good that sounded? But he waited as Tad chased after the right words.

"We shouldn't. I'm investigating a suspicious death."

Fuck it. "I didn't have anything to do with that, but we probably shouldn't have been kissing either. What's that expression? Something about being hung for a lamb or a sheep?"

A laugh burst out of Tad, surprising them both. "That's not even close."

Riley shrugged. "Yeah, well. You know what I mean. We've already crossed a line, right?"

"It… asking you to keep it a secret isn't right. It makes it seem like I'm ashamed, and I'm not. Even if we were to do this, it couldn't be anything but sex. Just sex."

Had he lost his fucking mind? Probably. And he was probably going to lose his heart in the process too, but he couldn't stop himself. "No strings. We don't tell anyone. And you're not asking, I'm offering." Like a desperate, lovesick fool, but he didn't have the willpower to say no to this chance to have Tadeo Martin in his bed.

"I need you to think about this. Think if this is something you can live with."

Riley thought it might be more whether it was something Tad could live with, because Tad actually had more at stake, strings or not. But he understood it would be wiser to make a decision like this without the influence of mind-melting lust.

He nodded, because he couldn't quite trust himself not to beg.

Tad brushed a thumb over Riley's bottom lip, the conflict obvious.

"Good night, Riley." Without waiting for a response, Tad strode down the hall and banged through the door leading to the stairwell.

For all that Riley was the drama major, that had been a rather dramatic exit. Riley smiled as he let himself into his condo.

Offering Tad a secret friends-with-benefits might backfire in a major way, but it wouldn't be the first time he'd decided on a course of action that didn't seem altogether wise.

Chapter SIX

THANKS TO another sleepless night, for which he blamed Tad, Riley arrived at work before Alisha and was able to get to his desk without any interrogation. He had no idea what to tell her about his "date," mostly because he had no idea what had happened. They'd decided to "think about things" and Riley had spent the night—after jerking off—weighing the pros and cons and waffling about his decision.

The only thing he knew for sure was that he wanted to keep seeing Tad. Since Tad was so adamant about no strings, obviously no romantic relationship would come out of this. No boyfriend, no husband, no forever, but Tad was good company. Being friends Riley could handle. Being friends with benefits, at least temporarily, was better than nothing.

Eventually Riley would meet a man he could share his life with, and his misplaced affection for unavailable men would vanish. He hoped.

If it weren't for his promise of discretion, he'd like to get Shaun's or even Alisha's perspective on the situation. Maybe if he swore them to secrecy.... Although he could guess what Shaun would say. Most of it would be variations on the theme of "dumbass."

Hell, he'd even like to talk to them about the investigation. Riley wondered if maybe Tad had told him more than he should have. Nothing in the news had mentioned penicillin, and to be fair, Tad hadn't referred to it since the night of Gabrielle's death. Riley didn't know if they'd confirmed penicillin or if Tad had merely been testing various stories to check for media leaks.

Riley chuckled. That sounded far-fetched even to him. If Tad stayed in Riley's life after this investigation was over, then Riley could figure out why Tad did what he did. And if Tad was only around for the investigation? Then Riley would have his answer—he was being used.

He spent the next couple of hours whittling down the messages he'd ignored in favor of cleaning out Gabrielle's office, and then it was time to get ready for the fireworks, otherwise known as the Cody bombshell.

Riley made coffee and took it to the executive conference room, making sure he had everything set up a good fifteen minutes before the scheduled start time.

Ten minutes to detonation, Cody showed up. François and Floriana were both legendary for showing up late to meetings, but if Riley had been in Cody's place, he'd want to make sure he was in the conference room before the others. Less likely to be ambushed that way.

"Good morning, Riley."

"Morning."

Cody didn't look substantially better than he had the previous day, but Riley supposed that was normal for a man preparing to face down angry stepchildren mere days after his wife died. Riley was expecting François and Floriana to look haggard when they showed up too.

"Would you like some coffee, Cody?"

"Yes, thanks. You don't have decaf, by chance, do you?"

Riley was fucking good at his job. Most times decaf went to waste, but he'd thought there were about equal odds that people would either want a pick-me-up or had been drinking so much coffee since Gabrielle's death that they'd need a break.

"I do." Riley poured Cody a cup from the black carafe. "Do you normally drink decaf?" He'd need to know for future reference.

"Yes, I do. A few years ago I practically bathed in the caffeinated stuff, but then it started to give me heart palpitations."

Riley raised an eyebrow. Cody seemed too young to have those sorts of problems, but he supposed there could be underlying issues, or he could have been drinking coffee by the gallon.

Cody sat back at the head of the conference table. Riley had to admire the psychology of the move. He was here waiting for everyone to come to him, in the seat reserved for the most important person in the meeting. Riley hoped he was going to try for true collaboration and compromise with the Gautiers, or the battles and manipulation might never end.

There was no time for any more chitchat—Floriana flung open the door and strode in, François and Mattie on her heels. Where Riley stood, he'd only be visible if anyone turned around to sit at the table, which he was sure they'd do momentarily.

"What could possibly be so important you had me clear my schedule, Mattie? Our mother is barely.... Our mother just died." Floriana sniffled and brought a tissue to her eyes.

Riley would have bet his week's pay that Floriana had been about to say her mother was barely cold in her grave, but remembered at the last moment that her mother hadn't been buried yet. The funeral was scheduled for Saturday, assuming the coroner released her body in time.

Cody chose that moment to stand, the movement drawing everyone's attention.

"You," Floriana snarled like a second-rate actress in a bad B movie. "What are you doing here? Isn't it enough that you got your gold-digging hands on part of my mother's money, but you have to show up at the company she worked for years to build? You're an infection in the very air."

"Can we please calm down?" Mattie tried her best, but after having seen Floriana's vitriol on Friday, Riley had sort of expected this to devolve into a shit-slinging melee. He'd even brought in paper cups for the coffee, just in case.

"I'd choose my words more carefully if I were you." Cody's measured tone made his implacability undeniable. Here was a man who'd easily be as successful as Gabrielle, once he had a couple more decades under his belt. "I have every right to be here, as we'll soon explain."

François and Floriana sat in stunned silence as Mattie and Cody outlined the basics of Cody's contract and the fact that the three of them were now more or less equal.

However volatile Floriana had been, Cody's contract had incredibly, amazingly, and perhaps alarmingly stunned her into silence.

"I can't accept this." François shook his head. "I just can't believe my mother would do this to us. First her ill-advised and secret marriage— which I hardly believe can be legal. She must have been coerced. But then, to plan this… this… alteration. Gautier Cosmetics has always been a family company." The tone was calm but the words inflammatory.

Despite the provocation, Cody kept his cool, although his jaw tightened, emphasizing its model-like squareness. "Gabby was not coerced. And since I'm her husband, the company would still be a family company. Didn't you question this when you signed off on the new department?"

"You knew about this?" Floriana turned on her brother.

"No." François held his hands up defensively. "I mean, I knew we were adding the new marketing department, but that's all I knew. I didn't even know she had anyone in mind, and certainly not him."

The sneer said it all. François might not be as hotheaded as his sister, but he wasn't any more thrilled with Cody's presence.

"Now that I'm here, I guess we'll all just have to get along."

"Get along?" Floriana had recovered both her equilibrium and volume. "Like hell. As soon as we take you to court, you'll be out of here, without one fucking penny of my mother's money."

"Wrong." Cody wasn't just being contrary, he was confident Floriana wasn't going to be able to get rid of him that easily. "I have lawyers too, you know. And the law on my side."

Floriana's face screwed up in a vicious scowl. "You're probably the reason the cops are crawling all over our lives, asking questions. You probably married her while she was drunk or something, then killed her before she could get it annulled, you useless *branleur*."

Riley blinked. Not only was that quite the accusation, but the slip of a French term into her speech—even if it was more or less to call Cody a wanker—made it sound almost like Gabrielle had possessed her.

"Really? Are you sure you didn't kill her to keep her from marrying me, only you acted too late?" Cody's sneering response sent François to his feet, face flushed in outrage, and Floriana shrieked wordlessly.

"Right, that's enough of that." Mattie finally spoke, trying to calm the waters. "Accusations like that have no place here."

It was brave of Mattie, because Riley was pretty sure François and Floriana could fire her, even if they couldn't legally do anything about Cody. Yet. Riley was sort of surprised Cody was pushing to work here. No matter what happened, Floriana wasn't likely to bend, and it would remain a never-ending hostile work environment.

But if Cody had legitimately married Gabrielle and he was legally entitled to part of her legacy, then Riley supported his right to fight for it. There wasn't any arguing against the employment contract Mattie had produced.

Then François seemed to notice Riley's presence. "And what are you doing here?"

Riley opened his mouth, but Cody beat him to it. "I have need of an assistant, and Riley was available."

François snarled, every bit as viciously as his sister. "I guess you have no loyalty at all."

"You do know I've only worked here three and a half weeks, right? And I'm contracted with Gautier by my agency. The one I've worked at for ten years?"

Oh shit. Riley had not meant to get involved. He was supposed to be providing silent support, not mouthing off to vice presidents. Mattie shot him an exasperated look, but Cody looked pleased.

"I'll thank you not to speak that way to my assistant. Or should I file an official complaint with HR?" Cody tilted his head toward Mattie, who blanched but did her best to appear unruffled.

If Riley were Mattie, he'd be stopping by the LCBO for some vodka or something on the way home from work. She was definitely going to have to balance on a fine line to keep the peace among the three VPs and make sure the company kept on ticking.

However, François did take his attention off Riley. "Enjoy your undeserved 'promotion' while you can. You may have lawyers, but so do we, and I'll bet ours are better." François got to his feet. "I see no further need to continue this meeting, Ms. Tran. Unless you've got more unsavory information you need to impart."

Mattie shook her head. "No, nothing."

"I will want the company lawyers to review those employment contracts, though. I'll be in touch about that."

Riley wasn't sure if his contract was included in François's pluralization or if it was merely a slip of the tongue, but he wasn't worried about himself. He suspected Cody was in for a long haul, but if rumors were to be believed, getting a slice of the Gautier empire might well be a worthwhile endeavor.

"I'll have my assistant put something on both your calendars so we can discuss a transition plan to in-house marketing."

Riley nearly scoffed aloud. There would be no plan agreed upon until everyone's lawyers were satisfied, and maybe not even then.

"Oh, you do that," Floriana sneered. "But my schedule is pretty full, Cody. I might not be available for the foreseeable future. Since François and I will have to do mother's work as well."

"Ah, no. We'll all three be sharing that burden. Remember? I'm your equal. And until we unanimously agree on a new CEO, we'll be working together."

Unanimous agreement between these three? Not in a million years. Riley sighed. If this kept up, Gautier Cosmetics would be nothing more than a memory in a year, no matter how well received their new product was. The product reviews had been inextricably linked to Gabrielle's death, but on the whole, Invigorate appeared to be successful, although Riley was hardly the best judge of such things. He had seen an article or two speculating on the possibility Gabrielle had been poisoned by her own product, but it had smacked of sensationalism.

"In your fucking dreams, usurper."

Floriana rose and turned with a flourish, ready to storm out.

"If it's easier, you can just call me Dad."

Riley glanced at Mattie in horror. They were both expecting immediate bloodshed, but aside from another angry shriek from Floriana, the Gautier siblings left without another word. François did slam the conference-room door shut behind him forcefully enough to rattle the picture frames on the walls.

All of Cody's bravado seemed to disappear, leaving him shrunken and not nearly so commanding. "Thank you both. I appreciate your support. However, I guess I should get back to work."

"I'll leave you to it." Mattie swept out, probably thankful this skirmish was over.

"Is there anything I can do for you now?"

Gone was confident Cody. In his place sat a beaten-down man. "I said a lot of shit I shouldn't have said. But I was serious about getting time on Frank and Flo's calendars."

Riley refrained from rolling his eyes. François and Floriana weren't averse to going by Frank and Flo, but their mother hated it, and they were fussy about who was allowed the privilege. Undoubtedly Cody didn't make the cut.

"Are you sure?"

Wearily, Cody waved a hand. "Yes, unfortunately. If I'm going to do what Gabby wanted, I need them to work with me, even though it's going to be an uphill battle. Do your best. I'm sure they'll decline, but we'll just have to keep at it. At some point there's going to be something they need my consensus on, and then we'll see. I'll have some other work soon, including scheduling interviews." Cody smiled, but it was weak and watery, like viewing him through the surface of a pond. "Got a department to build."

Riley gathered up the cups and returned to the desk outside Gabrielle's office. Soon he'd have to move to the desk outside Cody's office. The first thing he did was put in a requisition for IT to move his phone and computer. It was getting a trifle morbid sitting where he was when Gabrielle was gone, and Riley would have long since moved on by the time the remaining Gautiers squabbled their way into appointing a successor.

Riley sat at his desk and did his best to look busy. He'd heard a number of suggestive things, like the fact Floriana suspected Cody and Cody suspected either of the siblings, or possibly both, of bumping Gabrielle off.

Interesting, to be sure, and filed away for later perusal, but nothing of enough significance to justify calling Tad.

Riley was already at the point where he wanted to see Tad every day. He was especially ready to pick up where they'd left off at the door of his condo. He'd enjoyed getting to know Tad as a person and interacting with him one-on-one, which he'd never done before. Didn't hurt that the kissing was hot enough to scorch the sun. If only they'd met in a different way, Tad might just be perfect for Riley.

As it was, the need for secrecy made him a ridiculous target for Riley to fixate on.

He whipped out his phone and texted Shaun.

Dancing this weekend?

Seconds later, his phone buzzed with a response.

YEEESSS! 'Bout fuking time! Saturday night, Anaconda. 10pm

Ten? He was thirty-one now. Couldn't they start earlier? Riley didn't bother asking, because he knew Shaun would tell him only the old farts showed up early and the sexy guys wanted to party all night. At some point Riley was going to have to ditch the twink act, because he wanted a real relationship that factored things like working and errands and brunch into the equation. And he didn't mean "so hungover I have to wear sunglasses inside" brunch. He meant a relationship where talking was at least as important as fucking.

'K—can I bring Alisha?

Yup. Since u never bring nice men home to meet me, I cn meet ur work wife ;)

Riley snorted out a laugh. He'd be more than happy to introduce Tad to his friends, but that wasn't quite in the cards.

Step one: go out and meet eligible men instead of isolating himself. Check. Fucking was out of the question, at least until whatever it was with Tad had run its course, but it wouldn't do any harm to look. Maybe meet someone to date. Nice boyfriend-material men must exist out there somewhere, and if Riley wanted to find one, he should get started, no matter how abysmally it had ended in the past.

Besides returning messages and attempting to set up meetings for the three VPs, Riley didn't have much to do, so he busied himself indulging more insatiable curiosity. He wanted to compare some of the files for previous launch parties and similar events. Something was nagging him about the particular typos in the estimated costs.

A COUPLE of hours later, Riley messaged Cody.

Heading out for lunch—can I pick you up anything?

No thanks. I've got an appointment. Back in the office around 2.

An appointment? Riley pulled up Cody's calendar. Sure enough, the time had been blocked out without any details. Had to be recent, because he hadn't seen it when he was setting up meetings earlier. Maybe he was meeting with a funeral home.

Given the tug of war between the Gautiers and Cody, Riley wasn't sure which one would have responsibility for setting up services or final disposition of her remains. Then again, he also hadn't heard if the coroner had released her body.

He'd really like it if someone could make a decision soon, since most of the messages now pouring in were requests for information about services or flowers or donations and he didn't have any choice but to let them know that all information pertaining to that topic was still pending.

A grumble from his belly reminded him he was supposed to be getting some lunch. Riley took a look at the files on his desk. Nothing terribly confidential, but nevertheless he gathered them up and tucked them into his desk drawer, which should be good enough to deter prying eyes.

Most prying eyes were more interested in Gabrielle's office these days, not completed files for past launch parties.

A few people stopped him along the way, inviting him to lunch. He smiled gently and turned them down with the excuse of having other plans—and he did. If Alisha wasn't free, he'd be eating on his own, with a book on his phone to keep him company. Making friends—or just being social with coworkers even if they'd never become friends—wasn't a terrible thing, but the timing was incredibly suspicious. They probably wanted to "subtly" dig for more information about Gabrielle and possibly where the police were in their investigation. Which Riley should know absolutely none of, if Tad hadn't been so bizarrely forthcoming over their two… meals.

Even in his head, he'd started to think of them as dates, and that was mighty dangerous. At least the email about Cody's new marketing department and Riley's shift to Cody's department hadn't shown up yet. The employees who didn't beat down Mattie's door would likely mob him in an effort to get inside information.

If he were Mattie, he'd hit Send about thirty seconds before walking out the door at five, and hopefully any panic would recede overnight.

He waited by the desk for a moment while Alisha finished up her spiel and redirected the incoming call.

"Lunch?"

"Yes. And you're buying."

"I am? Why is that?"

Alisha rolled her eyes. "As if you don't know. But come along. I'll explain when we get there."

Riley wasn't opposed to buying Alisha lunch, but he did wonder why she thought he was supposed to.

The sidewalks were busy enough with people taking advantage of the long-missed sunlight that they couldn't really speak. Alisha led them to the food court, where they quickly ordered and found a free table way at the back.

Alisha stabbed a french fry in his direction. "One. Seriously? Gabrielle was murdered? Why the fuck didn't you tell me I was right?"

"I don't think anyone has actually said 'murder.'" Not even Tad, but Riley wasn't about to use that as proof. The last thing he needed was to try to explain exactly what Tad was doing when he didn't understand it himself. And unless he discovered something else funky and unusual, he wasn't sure he'd have the nerve to call Tad again.

"Oh really? Then how come there hasn't been any notice of a funeral? How come the police keep showing up?"

"The police keep showing up?" Why hadn't Tad.... Riley gave himself a vicious mental slap. Tad had no damn reason to come seek him out, whether he'd been spending time at Gautier Cosmetics or not.

"Yeah. They keep asking for access to records, access to the lab, access to personnel information. As far as I know, though, the lawyers have kept them stymied. But it all points to murder, and even on the news, they've been calling it 'death under suspicious circumstances.'"

Riley shrugged. He didn't think she was wrong, but he wasn't sure Tad would be happy about him discussing this. "I guess it could be, but I'm hardly in a position to know. I'm just the temp. You do realize that almost no one tells me anything." The other admins were social but reticent. Riley was slowly winning them over.

"Puh-lease. Besides the caterers, you were one of like half-a-dozen people detained by the police Friday night. You still haven't given me any details about that, and I was nice enough not to pester you about it."

Riley laughed ruefully. "Thanks for the less-than-a-week reprieve."

She smiled wickedly. "I wouldn't want to give you time to forget."

"Fine, fine." Riley gave a quick rundown of the tense few hours Friday night after he'd found Gabrielle's body, and his medication-induced sleep, but avoided mentioning the penicillin thing—he was sure Tad hadn't meant to tell him that—and the fact that he'd had two meals with Detective Tadeo Martin since. Two very enjoyable meals where he'd learned a number of new things about his longtime crush, including how well he kissed, but that were completely irrelevant to this discussion.

When he was done, Alisha slumped in her chair. "This is so fucked-up. I mean, we know someone who was probably murdered. And if she was, we probably know the murderer."

"I think we're getting ahead of ourselves. It could still be just an accident. Or a bad reaction to food poisoning or something." He didn't think that, though. That one tiny piece of information about penicillin had influenced his thinking, just as it had Tad and his partner's.

"Sure. Sure. Whatever you say. But I'm pretty sure the police don't push so hard for information when they're expecting a verdict of accidental death."

Riley couldn't answer that. After all, the sum total of his exposure to police methods came from television and the couple of nerve-racking hours Friday night.

"I'm not sure this qualifies you to a free lunch, though." Riley had already paid for it—and many other lunches; he didn't begrudge the expense. Receptionists didn't make a lot of money, especially when they were also trying to put themselves through school and keep themselves in a decent apartment.

Alisha laughed. "Oh, you're not off the hook yet, monsieur. Want to tell me about Cody Rosenberg and how he works for the company now?"

"Jeez, Alisha. How do you know that? I only found out, like, just over twenty-four hours ago."

That earned him a mock glare. "Exactly. And I still had to find out about it from Heather in HR. What is he going to be doing? Why are you going to be his official assistant?"

This was something he could probably share, or at least partially share. Mattie had confirmed the welcome email would be out at some point today, and if Alisha already knew a portion of the story, others might as well. Maybe even some of those others who'd asked if he wanted to get lunch with them.

It took the rest of their lunch to go over the development of a new department and the extremely tense meeting with the Gautiers, although he carefully excluded the mutual accusations of murder. They also discussed what sort of situation had to occur to allow Cody any sort of power, especially with the company, but together what they knew about Gabrielle's plans for the company wouldn't even fill up a mosquito.

"Seems weird, though, doesn't it? I mean, Gabrielle was all over her shit. She didn't miss a trick; she knew everything. I can't believe she would have ignored such a vital thing like a current succession plan." Alisha sucked back the last of her lemonade.

"I know. But thinking about death has a funny effect on some people. I've met a lot of people who seem to think that death is something for other people." Riley, for example, had no will. He wasn't ready to put that admission down on paper, even though he knew all too well how unexpectedly death could occur. But Gabrielle had had a will, one that had been updated when Floriana joined the company. She wasn't entirely against them, and Riley assumed she'd been planning to update it again. But that was also information he hadn't shared with Alisha and wasn't going to.

"François and Floriana must be losing their minds. This has to be a bit of a slap in the face."

Riley nodded. "Uh, yeah. And I was afraid Floriana was going to slap Cody's face right there in the conference room."

Alisha laughed. "Oh my God. That would have been something to see. She can be such a snobbish bitch, you know?"

He wasn't going to say anything about one of the VPs, but he agreed. He didn't find François any more sympathetic, from that perspective. "I do feel bad for them, though. I mean, they all lost someone close to them not even a week ago, and they're all back at work and trying to deal with an extremely difficult situation."

Alisha responded with a loud, wet raspberry. "I don't know if any of them cared as much about Gabrielle as they pretended." A sad, pensive look crossed her face. "I'm pretty good at picking out when someone's pretending to care about you."

"I'm sorry." Riley patted her hand. He could sympathize.

She shook herself. "Men. They can be assholes."

Riley didn't take offense; he was well aware she meant men she'd dated, and he had to agree. A lot of the men he'd dated, or been interested in, were assholes.

"On that cheery note, I've decided I need to get out there and meet some eligible men." If he considered Tad one of those eligible men, well, he'd cut himself some slack. His brain told him it was a bad idea, but his heart and his cock couldn't help but hope.

"Oh yeah? So I get to hear details about your date yesterday? Or are you 'getting out there' because he was a total dick?"

What Riley wouldn't give for a chance at Tad's total dick. Tad might refuse his offer and Riley would never see the man naked. He sighed. "It was a very nice dinner, but it's not going to go anywhere." No matter how many times Riley had hoped and prayed to whatever deity looked out for horny gay boys. "No, Shaun and I are going to a club Saturday night. Did you want to come?"

"Yes, I do. Gay bar? Eh, doesn't matter. I'm okay if there aren't any eligible men for me, because as we've agreed, most of them are giant dicks."

"Shaun is looking forward to meeting you." However happy Riley was to introduce Alisha to his best friend, he sort of wished—okay, he wished a lot—that he could also introduce Tad. At least he could use Alisha as an excuse not to get picked up. By Saturday night, he hoped to have Tad in his bed, but a night out with his two friends might distract him from his dismal love life.

"Ha. Me too."

They gathered up their garbage, threw it out, then headed back to the office.

RILEY STOOD on the sidewalk outside a dilapidated little semidetached house on Ossington. Judging from the mailboxes on the front, the right half had been converted into three apartments, one on each floor. A couple of doors down, a silver Mercedes sat by the curb, looking a little out of place. The location wasn't bad—close to restaurants and public transit. But the faded, chipping paint and scraggly lawn told of a landlord's neglect. This was hardly the only place on the street that could benefit from some TLC.

God. Was he doing the right thing? Was he overstepping? He'd been totally convinced this was the right thing to do, but now that he was here at Aaron Brown's address, his certainty had fled along with his courage.

Then he remembered what had brought him here in the first place. He'd have hated to find out about his boss's demise through an impartial news report.

And if Riley was practically invisible at Gautier Cosmetics, Aaron had almost been erased. No one mentioned Aaron; no one asked when he'd return. It was weird. Most of the contracts Riley worked had people asking him about the welfare of the person he was replacing, and usually the baby pictures for maternity leaves were shared with him. Sometimes he was responsible for distributing them throughout the office. Once, he'd even attended a baby shower when the assistant's leave started early for her to go on bed rest. Her wife attended the shower in her place, and Riley had set up a Skype session so Amy could see the cake and the presents as Sarah opened them. Granted, Aaron wasn't on maternity leave, but it was weird how just about the only things Riley heard about Aaron had been Gabrielle denigrating him.

Yet aside from a few glaring errors in the event folders—the one from Friday night and a few more he'd unearthed that hadn't been caught—he hadn't seen anything to indicate that Aaron was a bad assistant. Not as good as Riley, of course, but not horrible. Even if he had been horrible at his job, Riley would have expected to hear that too.

He'd come all this way, and he definitely needed something to distract himself from the fact that he had no reason to call Tad, so he might as well finish his self-assigned mission.

He rang the doorbell and waited. Hell, Aaron might not be home, or he might not open the door if he wasn't expecting anyone. But Riley had to try. Once more, he rang the bell. Maybe Aaron was recovering from surgery or a broken leg. If so, he might need more time to get to the door.

Finally a faint creak that might be a footstep sounded from the other side of the door.

When the door swung open, Riley nearly took a step back but recovered in time. "Aaron Brown?"

"Yes?"

Aaron Brown bore a startling resemblance to Cody Rosenberg. Not like twins or anything. More like the before-and-after-the-makeup-chair pictures for celebrities. They were both blond-haired, golden-skinned, and brown-eyed. Aaron was the adorable boy next door—grown up into an adorable man—whereas Cody's genetics had taken a similar baseline and fabricated looks that were runway ready. Which would totally suck when Aaron's medical leave was up and he possibly had to go back to work for Cody.

"Uh. Hello. I'm sorry to stop by unannounced. I'm Riley Parker. I'm actually temping for you at Gautier Cosmetics."

Aaron frowned, clearly confused. As well he should be. This was highly unprecedented. "What brings you by?"

"Have you… been watching the news at all? Since Friday?"

"What, the launch for Invigorate? I'm sure the launch went fine, but no, I haven't been paying attention. I've found watching movies or streaming television shows better for my recovery."

"Yeah. I'm not a big fan of the news either." Riley sighed. "But there's been some bad news, and I wasn't sure if anyone had been by to break it to you."

Aaron paled. "I'm not getting fired, am I?"

"Oh, no. I'm so sorry. Can I come in?" Riley had always thought it odd when people invited complete strangers into their homes and offered them tea or coffee, and here he was, a complete stranger *asking* to be invited in.

With some reluctance, Aaron opened the door wider. "I just put on a pot of tea. Would you like some?"

Riley smiled sadly. "Did Gabrielle get you hooked?"

Aaron let out a chuckle. "Yes. But I can't stand that lapsang tea she likes." He led the way through a neat and orderly apartment.

Riley caught a whiff of what he thought was a woman's perfume, but then it was gone and he couldn't be sure. "I know. Awful." And just like that, the supreme awkwardness of his clumsy arrival disappeared. "I never drank tea very often, but it's definitely growing on me. I do like the Earl Grey."

"That's decent. I prefer some of the green teas, but I have a pot of english breakfast on."

English breakfast was good in his book.

Near the back of the house a faint chuff like a wooden door closing caught Riley's attention, but perhaps it was a neighbor.

In the kitchen, Aaron took another mug out of a cupboard and poured a second cup from a squat brown teapot that looked quite similar to Gabrielle's.

Riley took a seat at the table across from Aaron.

"So what's this bad news?"

"I'm really sorry to tell you this, but Gabrielle died Friday night. I was… I was the one to find her. In her office."

Aaron put a trembling hand in front of his mouth. "I… she's dead? I can't… I can't believe it."

"I know, I know." Riley had recently learned the power hugs could have, but he wasn't ready to start doling them out to strangers. "It was such a shock."

Aaron got up out of his chair and paced a bit. Riley took a moment to assess. No broken leg, and probably not surgery, given how easily Aaron appeared to be moving, but there was still a laundry list of ailments that wouldn't have any obvious physical symptoms.

"She was… still so young."

Aaron was probably Riley's age, and therefore twenty or twenty-five years younger than Gabrielle, but Riley understood. She was still too young to have gone so quickly, and there was something about her vivacity that had made her seem much younger.

Riley took a sip of tea, not sure how to go about comforting Aaron. "I am very sorry for your loss."

Aaron turned back, almost surprised by Riley's presence. He sat back down and picked up his mug. "How... how did she die?"

Aaron sounded so lost. Riley knew from personal experience that being an admin for the big boss was kind of a weird position. People were sometimes afraid because of the close relationship with the person who ostensibly signed their paychecks, and yet many considered admin assistants glorified secretaries hardly worthy of their time. Certainly no one but Alisha had reached out to him, and she'd have said if she was friends with Aaron.

Then again, Aaron appeared to be single and straight. Alisha had already told him a number of horror stories about her attempts to be friends with men who were attracted to her. He didn't blame her one bit for not making or accepting any overtures from Aaron.

"I... honestly, I don't know. The police were there, they said they were treating it as a suspicious death. Mostly it looked like she fell asleep at her desk."

Aaron waved a hand. "I think they have to call it suspicious even if it's natural causes but unexpected."

Riley shrugged. "Maybe." He didn't think it necessary to mention the police trying to gain access to company records and returning multiple times. If it turned out Gabrielle was murdered, Aaron would find out eventually.

"What about the funeral? When is that?"

"Not sure. It depends on when the police release her body. If you give me your email address, I'll send you the information when I get it."

"Thanks." Aaron grabbed a nearby pen and wrote his email address on a receipt lying on the table. Riley tucked it into his pocket.

"I don't know how close you were. I don't even know how long you have worked at Gautier."

"Just a couple of years, but I loved working with her." A couple of years, and he didn't know one coworker well enough for them to at least text Aaron the news? Horrifying, but Riley didn't know if that spoke ill of the corporate culture at Gautier or of Aaron's social skills.

"She's very exacting, but that's a lot better than someone who doesn't know what they want."

Aaron huffed out a laugh intermixed with a sob. "Oh, I've been there."

Riley nodded in commiseration. Yes, any admin who'd been assisting for any length of time had worked for that one hurricane, that Tasmanian devil who tore around so fast you could never anticipate, never keep up, never relax.

Aaron told a few more stories about Gabrielle while they drank their tea. Riley's was almost gone, and he realized he should have remembered his mother's adage and gone to the bathroom before he left.

"Sorry to be a bother, but can I use your bathroom?"

"Oh, sure." Aaron pointed. "Down the hall, first door on the right."

Once Riley had done his business, he turned on the faucet and opened the medicine cabinet. It contained zero clues as to why Aaron had taken medical leave. Not that Riley knew much about medication, but he had the internet and a smartphone and Google-fu that was pretty decent, if he did say so himself.

He recalled reading somewhere that it wasn't good to store medications in the bathroom because the heat from the shower could… affect them somehow. But it wasn't like he could go poking about Aaron's bedroom or kitchen cupboards, which were the only other places Riley thought someone might leave medications.

There weren't any obvious feminine products, although there was a Gautier face wash and moisturizer. But that skin-care line was designed to be unisex, so Aaron could merely be supporting the company. One green toothbrush sat in the toothbrush holder. The remainder of the items in the cabinet were standard and gave him no information.

A quick wash of his hands and Riley was out of there, sadly none the wiser.

"Thanks for the tea, Aaron. I should probably be on my way."

"Thank you, Riley. I appreciate you coming over here and letting me know. Please don't forget to email me the funeral information, and if something else comes up, you're welcome to contact me."

Riley patted him on the shoulder, then took his leave.

Throughout the entire commute home, Riley couldn't stop thinking about Aaron and how isolated he'd seemed at Gautier.

Shit. He'd completely forgotten to mention Cody coming on board and the chaos. Too bad he hadn't remembered until he was getting off the streetcar at his stop.

Riley considered his options. It probably wasn't his place to tell Aaron anything. If HR wanted him to make a permanent shift to be Cody's assistant, they'd be the one to tell Aaron, not Riley. The rest of it would just be gossip, and for all Riley knew, everything could change by the time Aaron returned to work.

Chapter SEVEN

AFTER WORK Thursday evening, Riley paused a block away from the restaurant and pulled out his phone. Nothing from Tad since his text earlier, which had been terse in the extreme.

Dinner tonight? Bier Markt at 6?

The request had unnerved him all over again, and it had taken him almost an hour to send an affirmative response. After, he'd spent most of the morning wondering if he should change his mind, or if Tad was going to take him up on his offer or not, and what Riley would do in the many scenarios he dreamed up.

Without much to do in the way of actual work, he'd had far too much time to brood about dinner.

He liked the Bier Markt, but it wasn't nearly as close to Riley's condo as Alberto's. Did that mean something? If so, what? He hadn't heard from Tad since they'd kissed on Monday. Did it mean something that he'd waited until Thursday to contact him? If Tad wanted to date while having no-strings sex, wouldn't Friday be a more appropriate date night?

Riley growled under his breath. Bad enough that a high school infatuation held such sway, but he was now resorting to teenaged angst and spending far more brainpower than he should teasing out possible hidden meanings and motivations.

He ran his hands through his hair and strode the last block with false bravado. Might as well face Tad head-on and find out his fate.

Tad waved him over as soon as he walked in. The place was full of people who'd obviously just left work. This didn't feel at all like a date atmosphere, more like colleagues meeting up for happy hour.

Disappointment swamped him. Tad most likely wanted to discuss the investigation or find out if Riley had any more information. Nevertheless, he smiled and wove through the crowded tables.

"What can I get you to drink?" The server appeared magically as Riley shuffled into a chair.

As tempting as it would be to get sloppy drunk and throw his dignity away while throwing himself at Tad, he did have to work in the morning. He was a long way from the days when he could party all night and roll into work without any sleep.

"Stiegl Grapefruit, please."

The server dropped a menu and disappeared. Tad raised a brow at him. "Grapefruit beer?"

Riley shrugged. "It's light and summery. Suits the warmer weather." It might still be spring, but his sinuses were convinced it was later in the year.

Tad's beer was dark but almost full, so he likely hadn't gotten here much before Riley.

By the time the server returned with his beer, they'd both decided on what to order for dinner, but Riley was still no wiser about the purpose of this evening.

"How are you doing?"

Riley smothered a sigh. He was going to tie himself into a pretzel if he didn't stop wondering if Tad's words had underlying meanings. Fuck it. He was treating this like a date with no prospect of sex until Tad gave him a reason to think otherwise.

"Fine. Things at the office are obviously strained. I'd heard the expression about walking on eggshells, but in this case, I think it's more that we're all tiptoeing over unexploded ordnance."

Tad let out a chuckle at Riley's wry tone. "I have no doubt. Gabrielle's kids are under a lot of pressure, and I get the impression they aren't exactly sunshine and rainbows at the best of times."

"That's my impression as well, although I've only had a few weeks with them."

"I guess that's a good thing about temping. If the people suck, you know it's only temporary."

"That can be a benefit, to be sure. On the other hand, it sucks leaving a good situation."

They talked a bit more about Riley's career path and some of Tad's work stories. By the time their dinner arrived, Riley was on his second grapefruit beer. Tad's knees had come to rest against his own almost immediately, and he relaxed a bit.

"You like where you're living now?" Tad asked.

"Yeah, it's a great location, and I like my condo." It could be a little lonely at times, but it was his sanctuary.

"You own or rent?"

"Own. I got an inheritance from my parents' estate when I turned twenty-one. It was an easy decision to use it to buy a place to live, although it took me a while to find a location I liked."

"Smart." Tad took another bite of his burger.

"Are you renting? Thinking about buying?"

"Dunno." Inexplicably, Tad blushed.

This could be good. "What? Where are you living now?"

"I'm renting my parents' basement."

"Oh?" That could be sweet, pathetic, or weird. Riley held his tongue, waiting to find out which.

Tad lifted his shoulders in a shrug. "My two older brothers got married and moved out a long time ago. Remember those storms a couple years ago with all the flooding?"

Riley nodded. "Sure, I know a lot of people with basements had issues."

"Yeah, so they needed some work done. My lease was up around the same time, so I moved back home and helped fix up the basement. Then my sister got engaged, and I moved into the newly renovated basement to give my parents a bit of financial assistance for the wedding."

How the fuck was Riley going to protect himself from heartbreak when the overwhelming sweetness melted any protective barriers he'd cobbled together?

"That was a great thing for you to do." Riley had only a sliver of envy that Tad still had his parents. "Is your sister married now?"

"No, not until the fall. But my mom's making noises about the stairs getting to be too much for her. I'm thinking after the wedding, they're going to put the house up for sale, so I'll have to make a decision then."

Riley ruthlessly quashed the sudden vision of living with Tad in his cozy little condo. This might not even get to the point of sex with no strings. Dreaming of commitments and relationships was going to have to wait until he met another man.

The conversation moved on to the price of real estate and desirable neighborhoods. Much less fraught with emotion.

After Tad paid for dinner—again—they walked out of the restaurant together. Riley hadn't had the balls to ask Tad about whether or not he was going to take Riley up on his offer, and Tad hadn't mentioned it.

"Look, Riley, I—"

An obnoxious chirping emanated from Tad's pocket. He frowned and pulled out his phone. "Fuck. I'm sorry, Riley. I have to go. Work."

"Sure. I'll talk to you later."

What the fuck had Tad been going to say? Didn't he know how agonizing this was? Every moment Riley spent with Tad left him wanting more.

But the anguished, almost yearning look Tad gave him before he turned and walked away kept Riley's foolish hopes alive. He'd just have to be patient.

He watched until Tad disappeared down a side street, and then headed for the nearest streetcar stop.

SATURDAY MORNING dawned bright, and Riley woke feeling far more congested than he had the previous week. He hadn't heard from Tad since their "date" and hadn't been able to come up with a reason to call him. Annoying, because he wanted more. He threw a bunch of clothes in the washing machine before running out to drop stuff at the dry cleaner's. He was almost out of clean everything, because his last weekend had been a total write-off. It was a long time until he'd be meeting up with Shaun and Alisha at ten, and he was supposed to meet the guys at Coffee and Conquer for gaming on Sunday.

Might be nice to get laid. Unfortunately, he didn't think just anyone would do now that Tad had dangled temptation in front of him. Hell, he'd be happier if he'd just seen Tad since their dinner on Thursday.

The lack of contact made it seem likelier that Tad had been using him. Trying to get some information that Riley gave up without knowing it. A sudden, unwelcome thought struck him, and he frowned. What if Tad was simply busy dotting his i's in order to come and arrest Riley? He'd let himself forget that he might just be a suspect in the eyes of the police.

He didn't think Tad was the sort to manufacture evidence, but if Gabrielle *had* been poisoned, Riley was in an excellent position to have administered it. The fact that she'd died at work would also indicate it was someone she worked with, rather than someone she shared a home or private time with.

But his capacity for dwelling was only so big, and if he didn't think of something else, he'd be miserable all weekend, dammit. He'd already had to add a decongestant to his antihistamines in the hopes of heading off an allergy-induced migraine.

In between recorded episodes of *Criminal Minds*, Riley got his laundry washed and dried, did the dishes, and vacuumed. If he cleaned out the toilet in the bathroom, he could spend all day tomorrow nursing a hangover and whatever regrets he was going to find tonight.

A little grumble in his tummy reminded him he'd slept through breakfast and skipped lunch.

"Don't worry." Riley patted his stomach. "After the next episode, I'll figure out if I'm cooking or ordering in." Although who was he kidding? With the kitchen clean and plans to go out later, he was going to order in and then nap before he had to get dressed.

He showered first, because he hated rushing after a nap, then pulled on an old pair of jeans before heaving the laundry basket on the coffee table, ready to start folding. He'd just queued up the next episode of *Criminal Minds* when someone knocked on his door.

Who the hell could that be?

Riley flung the door open, ready to berate whoever had snuck into the building to tell him he needed Jesus, only to freeze, mouth open.

Tad was here? Why oh why did he never remember to use the stupid peephole?

He stared down at himself, wearing a ratty pair of jeans and pretty much nothing else. This couldn't possibly be how he was arrested, could it? Either way, he wasn't sure he wanted Tad to see him like this.

"Hello."

Tad held up a bulging plastic bag and gave him a killer smile designed to disarm. Which it did, if disarm also meant *melt into a puddle on the floor*. "I brought Chinese, if you aren't doing anything for dinner."

So… not getting arrested, but what the ever-loving fuck was going on? He wanted to ask, and yet he was afraid asking would make the nice pretty man with dinner go away. Then again, how sustaining could a mirage truly be? Because this had all the earmarks of one.

"Uh, no. I was just starting to think about what I was going to do."

Another killer smile, slaying Riley right there in his foyer. "Good."

"I am supposed to be meeting some friends later at a club." Not that he expected Tad to be sticking around that long, but then again, he'd have bet his entire life savings against this little scenario occurring at all.

"When?"

"Ten."

"No problem. Plenty of time for dinner before that."

Riley stepped back, and Tad entered his condo. "The kitchen is on the left. Let me just grab a shirt and I can help dish things out."

"Don't go to any extra effort on my account."

No, oh hell no. Although it sounded as though Tad wanted Riley to stay half-naked, he wouldn't be able to relax at all knowing he didn't have the same solid gym body Tad did. Riley had the benefit of natural lankiness and good metabolism, but he didn't pay nearly enough attention to muscle building and toning. Certainly not enough to feel comfortable standing around in daylight in front of one of the hottest men ever to grace his condo.

He grabbed the first T-shirt in the laundry basket and pulled it on. Then he tucked the laundry basket in a closet. He didn't need his Andrew Christians on display either.

Before long, plates were filled and they were sitting at Riley's tiny kitchen table—which he never used for this purpose—ready to eat.

He couldn't remember the last time he'd eaten at home and hadn't sat in front of the television, but Tad simply assumed they'd eat at the table, and Riley wasn't ready to dissuade him of that notion.

"How's work going?" Tad asked before deftly snagging a piece of orange beef with his chopsticks.

"Not terrible. I haven't been too busy, but I might be the only one."

Tad nodded and picked up a piece of sweet-and-sour chicken.

"You're pretty good with those." Tad made him look clumsy and inefficient.

"Yeah, spent a good chunk of my time in uniform in Chinatown. My first partner was Chinese and taught me how to use chopsticks. Then I got tons of practice."

"Well, you make it look easy. How are things with you?"

Tad huffed out an exasperated sigh. "Been busy. Had some good breaks in a couple cases."

Riley took the time to really look at Tad. He definitely looked tired. There were shadows under his eyes, and he had stubble again. Busy wasn't an exaggeration.

"That's good." Did he dare ask? "What about Gabrielle's death?" He couldn't call it a murder, not yet.

That got him another sigh.

"Honestly, it's not going well." Tad leaned in. "You'll keep this quiet, right?"

"Of course." And he would too, but he still didn't understand why Tad would choose him, out of everyone, to reveal confidential information to about an ongoing case. He couldn't tamp down the fear that this was all some elaborate form of entrapment, but he really didn't want to believe Tad would do that. Mostly because he wanted Tad to think well of him, not think he was some creepy boss-hating murderer.

"We've got basic cause of death, which is anaphylactic shock. Definitely penicillin. But we've tested everything we could looking for the source and can't find any traces. The party complicates things because testing the trash from the party is prohibitively expensive and time-consuming."

"Wow. I never thought of it like that."

"Yeah, we've got a lot of technology working for us, but it's not as quick or magical as it is on TV. Besides, the party gave a lot of people access to Gabrielle that they normally didn't have over the course of a day. Even if we can find the source, that may not do anything to narrow down the suspect pool."

Riley blushed just a bit. He'd known, of course, that things couldn't be as simple as television shows portrayed, but he hadn't spent a lot of time applying critical thinking to it.

"Who would even have penicillin? I mean, it's not the sort of thing that's popular with drug dealers, is it?"

"Just about anything's available for a price, but someone looking to score prescription meds is usually looking to get high or get hard. Requests for antibiotics are going to stick out. We've got someone tracking down that angle, but I'd be surprised if it panned out. More likely it's as you were thinking—someone got prescribed penicillin and kept back one or two pills."

"Couldn't you get medical records?"

Tad snorted. "Not enough probable cause to go poking into people's medical records. Even if I narrow down a request for the records of the people most likely to know about her allergy, that's not enough, especially when we're still trying to definitively state it's murder and not death by misadventure. I need a motive. We've already got some information from HR about a couple of disgruntled former employees, and some financial records which we're hoping will reveal some information, but that takes time. I'm inclined to believe most of the employees aren't aware of her allergy—it's not like a peanut or seafood allergy that could easily come up in situations like your launch party or at business lunches or whatever."

That made sense. Riley hadn't known about the allergy, but he could have easily found out about it, because of his proximity. Gossip would be the most likely way for, say, a disgruntled lab tech or pissed-off security guard to find out, but who would gossip about a deadly allergy when Gabrielle and her boy toy Cody would make far more interesting fodder?

"So you're following the money, as they say."

That made Tad laugh, a happy belly laugh complete with crinkles at the corners of his eyes. Riley couldn't help but smile at the sight, even though he knew Tad was likely laughing at him.

"Sorry, sorry. They do say that, even though it's not strictly applicable here. We know where the money's going—it's more a case of who wanted it bad enough to kill for it. And that's assuming the coroner doesn't rule her death accidental."

"Okay, so maybe you can explain something to me." Or maybe he couldn't—Riley didn't know how much information Tad was inclined to divulge. Already it seemed like far too much.

Tad gestured with a piece of broccoli. "If I can, sure."

Riley explained the incident between the three VPs at their inaugural meeting. "Did that have to do with the will?"

Tad nodded. "Yeah, or the lack of one. As I understand it, their marriage invalidated her will. Since she didn't have time to make a new one, Cody's entitled to $200,000, plus a third of whatever's leftover in the estate."

"What? No wonder François and Floriana were so pissed." Riley didn't even comment on the fact that for a lot of ordinary people, that initial payout would leave the kids with nothing.

"Yeah. What's even weirder is that because the company was still owned by Gabrielle—and actually makes up the bulk of her assets—

he's entitled to his share of that as well. Even without the employment contract, he'd be able to influence how the company was run. But with the contract assigning him as VP, he's also got a voice at the table in decision making."

"Jeez." Good for Cody, but Riley had a little more sympathy for the Gautiers. "That's just wild. Floriana said they were going to go to court."

Tad snorted. "They might have some luck cutting Cody out of the business, but for the inheritance? Good fucking luck. This isn't a case of contesting a will made with undue influence or an outright forgery. This is provincial law outlining what happens if there is no will, and the marriage invalidated any previous wills."

"What about proving the marriage false?"

"Nope. Already confirmed it's real. And although the Gautier kids claim their mother would never have left Cody anything if she'd lived long enough to make another will, Cody's saying the opposite—that if Gabrielle had had enough time to make a will, the kids would be getting less than they are now."

"Holy shit, what a mess! I tell you, it's not going to be a bed of roses trying to get anything done in that company with the three of them battling it out. I think they genuinely hate each other."

"Oh?" Tad's ears perked up, and Riley rolled his eyes. Tad just wanted inside info. Riley should probably be upset by that, but he was enjoying Tad's company too much—however foolish that might be.

"What, you think that's new information? I don't think Cody hates them, actually. But he's certainly not going to let them walk all over him."

"Sounds like you admire him." Tad's tone was neutral, and Riley didn't know how he was supposed to respond to that.

"I guess I do. It takes a lot of balls to stand up for himself with no one on his side. But if he killed Gabrielle to get there, then there would be nothing left to admire."

"Enough depressing talk. Tell me more about this club. Who are you going with?"

If Tad had sounded anything other than interested and engaged, Riley would have changed the topic, but instead he talked a bit about Alisha and Shaun, which went on long enough for them to finish eating.

Then Riley didn't know what to do. He still had to get ready, but not for a couple of hours. He didn't want to kick Tad out, but Tad's agendas were wrapped in mystery and obfuscation. He could ask questions, but he wasn't sure he'd like the answers, and so he again chose silence.

What would he do if this were Shaun or Alisha? He had laundry to fold, but that was hardly urgent. He could easily put it off until tomorrow. The nap wasn't necessary either.

"If you want, we could watch a movie. I don't have to get ready for a couple of hours yet." Riley leaped up to start putting away the leftovers, afraid to look at Tad.

"Yeah, sounds good."

Riley glanced up and smiled. "Why don't you go pick one while I finish up? Did you want some popcorn?"

Tad patted his stomach. "Nah, I'm stuffed. And let me help."

Instead of following Riley's suggestion, Tad helped tidy up from dinner, making him better than just about any date Riley had brought home before.

RILEY SPENT the entire movie tense and unable to pay attention to anything besides the giant furnace sprawled beside him on the couch. Tad wasn't exactly encroaching on his space—not like the thigh-rubbing incident at dinner—but Riley couldn't relax for fear of relaxing too much. What if he accidentally snuggled? Between the spicy scent of Tad's cologne and the sidelong—and hopefully unnoticed—glances where Riley wallowed in Tad's strong profile, Riley had spent the past hour and a half trying to control his dick.

But dammit, Tad smelled so fucking good, and Riley just wanted to pounce. It would be a tragedy of epic proportions if Riley never found out the taste of Tad's skin. He'd already been consumed by his kiss and wanted to experience that again and again. This infatuation might even be worse than the fantasies he'd had in high school, because he had an adult's dreams and an adult's perception of exactly what kind of relationship he'd be missing out on. Although he'd offered a purely sexual relationship, he wanted more, but he couldn't tell if Tad wanted anything at all from him.

The long and short of it was that Tad was driving him right out of his mind.

As the credits rolled, Riley could take it no longer. He twisted his knees up on the couch so he could face Tad easier.

"Tad." Riley cleared his throat. Not only had his voice sounded too seductive by far, but he'd almost slipped and called him Tadeo. Even knowing there could be nothing between them, Riley didn't want Tad to remember him as he'd been. He'd spent too much money on highlights and blue contacts, spent too much time trying to distance himself from the bullied nerd he'd been in high school.

Tad shifted to mimic Riley's pose but left his head resting on the couch. His eyes were hooded and sleepy-looking, much like Riley imagined he'd look in bed, right after a good orgasm.

Fuck. He had to stop thinking about that.

"Yes, Riley?" Tad's voice was also low and growly, and Riley wanted to offer himself up. But that would only end in pain—emotional if not physical. Or both.

"Why are you…?" Here? That sounded awful. But he wasn't sure how to articulate what he wanted to know without sounding like he didn't enjoy Tad's company.

If Tad wanted to be friends—however far-fetched that was—Riley would metaphorically suck it up and resign himself to many a lonely release after spending time together. And yet a part of him couldn't forget the kid he'd been, the kid Tad took no notice of. Whatever changes he'd made to his appearance, he wasn't fundamentally different. There was no reason Tad would want to hang around him, especially if sex wasn't on the table.

"Why am I what?" Tad smiled gently, his voice still low, pupils dilated in the dim evening light.

Riley blushed, thankful the growing dark would hide it. He'd just been staring at Tad like a besotted fool.

"Why are you sharing all this information with me? I mean, it's fascinating, getting this inside look at an investigation, but it seems…." Riley chewed on his lip as he searched for the right words.

Tad lifted his head, but his languid pose didn't change—he was a lot more flexible than his musculature would suggest.

"Seems like what?" Tad prompted.

Riley blushed harder. "Obviously I don't know anything about police investigations besides what I see on TV." His gaming group had once taken a break from D&D to run a generic campaign that revolved around crime solving, but there was no reason to believe that would be any more accurate than *CSI*. "But the stuff you've told me… I worry that you're giving me this information to, I don't know… set me up. Or make me slip up so I'll confess. Aren't I a suspect? I was the one who discovered the body."

Tad laughed—a full-on belly laugh complete with eye crinkles that made Riley smile in spite of himself. "Oh, Riley. First off, I haven't told you absolutely everything. Most of it's pretty dull, aside from being extremely confidential. You're also the only one who had access to Gabrielle's inner circle that I don't suspect."

Riley almost wanted to preen, but he was still suspicious. "Why not?"

"Easy. You didn't have a motive, your story as a temp checks out, and your agency confirmed your presence at Gautier was more or less random—you were the first available for the position—and more tellingly, you had no idea about Gabrielle's allergy."

"I could have lied about that."

"Are you trying to convince me you're the murderer?" The idea seemed to amuse Tad, and he chuckled some more. "Remember, I'm a detective. I can usually tell when people are lying to me, and you weren't. You don't strike me as a very good liar."

For a moment it looked like Tad was going to say more, but he closed his mouth and smirked at Riley.

"I could lie if I had to."

"I'm sure you can." Tad was clearly teasing, and Riley didn't take offense. Silly thing to object to anyway.

"That still doesn't explain everything. I'm sure I'm not the only one around who couldn't have done it."

Tad grew a little more serious. "True. But you're also in the unique position to help me. You've got insight that I can't easily get, and you might see or hear something that could give us a break."

Never before had he wished he were wrong. He'd known Tad had an ulterior motive. But Riley couldn't be too upset. Not when it meant potentially aiding the police in catching Gabrielle's murderer.

"I never thought about it like that." It was still weird that they'd spent far more time just hanging out than they'd spent discussing the case. Riley didn't know if that was meant to put him at ease or if they'd end up being friends at the end of all this. Once Gabrielle's killer had been caught, he could reevaluate. "Won't you get in trouble for hanging out with me?"

Tad shrugged. "You qualify as a confidential informant. It's fine."

A confidential informant? That was fucking cool. A nice little consolation prize, since he wouldn't be getting Tad.

If Riley was going to help, he wanted to be more than a sounding board. He had questions. And a discussion of the case would let him drink in the cozy sight of Tad relaxing on his couch.

"So have you been able to narrow down your suspects at all?"

"Yes and no. The killer choosing the launch party to make his move was almost ingenious. According to your invite list, people from the lab were in attendance, and my understanding is that they rarely, if ever, have any contact with Gabrielle. On the other hand, that makes them less likely suspects. I'm concentrating my efforts on the people who would have had a reason to want Gabrielle dead and/or the people who could have known about her allergy."

"Wouldn't that only be Cody and her kids? Oh, and her ex-husband."

Tad lost some of his sleepy laissez-faire. "Her ex-husband? Was he there as well?"

"No, no. Although he was invited to the official public launch party. He's also a chemist. Works for one of our suppliers."

"Did you mention him for a reason?"

Riley really hoped Tad didn't care that most of what he said about the case was bound to be ridiculous or influenced by television. "Just that—he's her ex, you know? Aren't husbands the primary suspect by default? And she'd told me some things about him earlier in the week that, well, a certain type of man would resent."

Tad tapped his chin thoughtfully. Annoyingly, it drew Riley's gaze to Tad's kissable lips. Fucker. That was just mean. "I can look into him, but the divorce was so long ago, and he no longer has any financial responsibility. It would be a bit of a stretch to think he'd waited all this time to do something violent. And by your reasoning, Cody would be my prime suspect, not David Hall."

Riley let out an embarrassed laugh. "I sort of forgot they were married."

"So you had no idea about the marriage?"

"Not at all. She did ask me if I believed in love at first sight. I wonder now if she was wondering if she could trust her feelings for Cody."

Tad shifted closer to him, almost close enough for Riley to sense his exhalations. But that was merely fanciful thinking. "Could be. I wish I knew why she kept the marriage a secret and how she was planning to change her will. That might give me a better direction."

"Maybe they weren't planning it. Getting married in Vegas is fairly uncomplicated. It might have been a spur-of-the-moment decision. But I'm inclined to believe Cody when he says she was going to write him into the will. Whatever else we—or rather you—don't know, Gabrielle positioned him in a place of significant power in her company. She had that much faith in him."

"It's not her faith that's in question. It's whether he betrayed that faith. And I've seen it far too often." A shadow crossed Tad's face, and Riley wanted nothing more than to reach out and comfort him. Despite seeing the absolute worst of humanity, Tad somehow kept his sense of humor and an innate sense of caring. It pleased Riley to see such strong evidence that Tad hadn't grown into an asshole like his friends were in high school.

Tad checked his watch. "Oh shit. It's getting late. I don't want to interfere with your plans."

It *was* getting late—where had the time gone? "Did… uh…. Did you want to come along?"

A heavy pause hung between them. "Maybe another time." That was it, then. The illusion of anything happening between them shattered, surrounding them with the broken shards of hopeless dreams.

Tad shifted on the couch to face him, eyes filled with heat rather than regret. "I wish I'd had the nerve to ask you earlier."

Riley leaned in. "What?"

Instead of answering, Tad cupped the back of his head and drew him closer. Their lips connected without any fumbling, and that simple touch sent electricity streaking through his veins. Riley opened up to Tad's tongue, thrusting into his mouth like a preview of what was to follow. He fucking loved kissing, the heat, the heaving breaths ruffling his hair, the sheer intimacy of it. Tad must love it too, otherwise Riley would have expected no-strings sex to get right to the sex and not involve any kissing.

Although he didn't recall moving, Riley found himself straddling Tad, granting him better access to that hot mouth. Riley jammed his fingers into Tad's hair, gripping tight as he devoured Tad's mouth. In return, Tad massaged his ass, pushing their groins together.

Riley rocked against Tad's thick erection and moaned into Tad's mouth. The heat between them was just as explosive as it had been the other night, and Riley was almost ready to pop, his hair trigger all due to the chemistry between them.

Before he crossed the point of no return, Riley broke the kiss and stared down into Tad's lust-darkened eyes. His lips were plump and wet and he looked fucking edible.

"Bedroom?" Riley asked, his voice so husky he barely sounded like himself.

"I don't want to make you late."

Riley let out a shaky laugh. "You want to send me to a gay club all revved up and ready to fuck?"

The scowl he got in response thrilled the stupid piece of his heart that hoped Tad would be his.

"No." Tad's lips reluctantly shaped the word.

"Then I guess I'll meet my friends a little late."

Tad made to get up, still holding Riley's ass. "What are you doing?"

"Taking you to bed." Like Riley was an idiot for asking. Sure, Riley probably weighed a lot less; it wasn't that he thought Tad couldn't lift him.

But then Tad stood up, and their similarities in height made the gesture ridiculous. With gravity working against his legs, there was no way he'd be able to wrap them around Tad's waist, and his feet dangled mere inches off the ground. Riley caught sight of them in the hall mirror, and it looked a bit like Tad had hoisted up a crane or some other long-legged, skinny bird.

A laugh burbled out of him, and Tad turned to see what he was laughing at. Then they were both laughing as Tad loosed his grip and Riley let his feet find the ground.

"Okay, I have to admit, when I thought about doing that, I'd sort of imagined you were shorter."

With the knowledge Tad had imagined taking him to bed, another piece of his heart succumbed to a fruitless hope.

No matter how much this would hurt later, he wanted to live in the here and now—he wanted Tad, for as long as he could.

"C'mon." He grabbed Tad's hand and led him to the bedroom.

Inside, Tad paused for a moment. "And you know it's only—"

Riley held up a palm to quiet him. "Yes, I know." But he didn't want to think about the lack of strings or talk about the fact that Tad didn't want a relationship. And he understood it needed to be secret. That didn't matter now, when they were about to get naked.

Near the bed, Tad pulled him back into his arms and started kissing his neck. "You smell so fucking good."

Riley shivered and dug his fingers into Tad's shoulders, his libido firing on all cylinders, despite the brief respite. Thank the gods above that he'd showered before Tad showed up.

They pulled each other's shirts off, and Riley nearly combusted at the sight of Tad's chest, broader and more chiseled than it had been those long-ago days on the lacrosse field.

The kissing got more frantic as they skimmed hands over warm skin. The hair on Tad's chest crinkled under his fingers, and when it rubbed against his own it created their own brand of sexy static electricity. Their pants virtually melted away, leaving Riley naked and Tad in a pair of navy boxer briefs.

Tad groaned. "Fuck, Riley, you've been commando all through dinner and the movie?"

Pure accident, but Riley loved those pained sounds Tad made. "Should have suggested this earlier."

"I won't make that mistake again." Tad slid a finger into his crack and rubbed. Riley returned those gruff sounds right back. He scrabbled at Tad's elastic waistband, wanting him naked too.

Tad helped him, and notched their cocks together. They slid heavily against each other, hot, and slicked a little from precum. Tad's hands returned to his ass and they ground together. Riley's pulse raced, and sweat sprang up along his lower back. Dammit, he was getting close and he wanted Tad to fuck him senseless, not frot to orgasm, although that was fun too. Just not what he wanted, what he needed.

The insistent pressure on his hole made him yelp and yank away from Tad's arms.

"I'm sorry, did I hurt you?" Tad frowned.

Riley gulped in a breath. "No, no. Just too close."

That put a feral, predatory look on Tad's face, and he prowled close, herding Riley back onto the bed. Riley stretched out to grab lube and condoms from his nightstand, foolishly taking his attention off Tad.

Warm wet heat engulfed his cock, and he arched up into Tad's mouth with a keening cry.

"Fuck me, Tad. Now. Please."

Tad swiped the supplies from Riley's shaking hands and quickly rolled the condom on, never taking his mouth off Riley's cock, but letting up the pressure just enough to keep Riley on the edge.

While Riley gloried in the carnal attention, Tad slicked up his fingers. The double assault made Riley twist. "Hurry up, dammit. I'm ready. Please." More than ready. It had been so fucking long, and he'd been waiting for Tad for years.

Tad growled around his cock, then moved up on the bed, erection prodding at Riley's hole.

Riley squirmed, trying to coax Tad inside with nothing more than hip swivels, and all it did was intensify the lustful flush on Tad's cheeks.

"You're killing me, Riley." But he didn't make them wait any longer. Tad guided his cock where it needed to be. There was an eternal moment where Riley hung suspended between pain and pleasure; then Tad slid home and only pleasure was left.

Tad held still for a moment, letting Riley get used to the heft of the cock inside him, but he was already so on edge he was almost drunk with lust. Riley thrust down, and Tad got the message.

Each thrust was solid, rhythmic, and hit his prostate like Tad had a tour guide and GPS. This was going to be over far too soon, but he'd already wrangled the explosion back more than once. He wasn't even going to have to touch his dick. He gripped the sheets and tried to lever his hips closer to Tad and that glorious cock.

"Tad, fuck, Tad."

"Come on. Come on." Tad leaned in and bit his neck, tipping Riley over the edge. His vision darkened around the edges as he unloaded between them, slick and hot.

Tad howled into his neck and plunged deep, muscles rock-hard while his cock jerked inside Riley.

Almost blinded by his orgasm, Riley sank back, boneless, into the bed. Tad collapsed on top of him, heedless of the spunk. They spent the next few minutes breathing heavily, like they'd just run a marathon.

That was fucking fantastic.

"Jesus Christ, Riley. Are you trying to kill me?" Tad eased out of him and flipped down beside him while they wound down.

"Mmm." He didn't have enough muscle control for words yet, but he smiled at Tad.

"Gorgeous," Tad whispered and stroked a finger down his jaw. "But I should probably get going. You've got plans tonight."

"Yes. Plans." No strings meant no sleepovers. Right now Riley really wanted to snuggle up beside Tad and fall asleep, but that wasn't on offer.

They both went to the bathroom to clean up, and Riley tried not to imagine doing this in the morning to get ready for work.

Riley followed Tad to the front door. "Thanks for dinner."

Tad placed a hand on his shoulder and squeezed before sliding it down his bicep, every bit a caress. "I will bring you takeout whenever you want."

Riley shivered as his pulse picked up, electricity crackling along the path Tad's hand had taken. "I'll keep that in mind."

Tad let his arm go and let himself out. Riley was going to be late meeting Shaun and Alisha, but it had been so worth it. Now he just had to hope neither of them noticed he was arriving at the club freshly fucked.

Chapter EIGHT

IT WAS a brand-new day, a brand-new week, and Riley was ready to ferret shit out like a truffle-hunting poodle channeling the Hardy boys. He just needed to figure out how to begin.

Riley strode off the elevator like he owned the damned place. It was going to be a good day. After all, he'd been thoroughly laid over the weekend. Not only Saturday, but Tad had shown up Sunday morning before he left for gaming. At this rate, he'd be getting spoiled.

"Good morning, Alisha." At the club, she and Shaun had gotten along great. She was going to fit right in. She'd even asked to join game night one Sunday.

"Win at game night, did you? Or did you actually get laid yesterday?"

"What?" Was there a neon sign on his forehead?

Alisha grinned. "Well something has to account for this days-long good mood. Or did you meet up with your mystery man again?"

If only blushes were under his conscious control, he wouldn't be getting that smug look. "No. There's no mystery man."

Not really. He certainly wasn't about to admit Tad had tapped him as a confidential informant. Even less was he going to admit that Tad had tapped him in other ways and he was full-on in lust with the detective investigating Gabrielle's death.

"Sure, sure. I bet Shaun wouldn't be convinced by that either."

Great. He should never have introduced them. Because already she knew both him and Shaun too well. He might as well accept he'd now have two people meddling in his life.

Riley couldn't help smiling. That actually didn't sound too bad. "I don't care if either of you are convinced. Want to get lunch today?"

"Mmm. Can't. I'm meeting my mom for a pedicure. Summer is coming."

"That's optimistic. It's only April."

"Actually, she's going on a cruise. With her new man." Alisha rolled her eyes.

"Oh good. You can pry into her love life instead."

Alisha grimaced, making Riley laugh. "Get out. And don't suggest such a revolting thing ever again." She shooed him away. "Don't you have a job to do?"

Some of his good mood dimmed when he reached his desk. This corner of the building had never been particularly populated, aside from the steady stream of people in and out of Gabrielle's office. Now that she was dead, it was—fittingly—tomblike. He could barely even hear any chatter or other office noises. Although he admired the incredible layout and construction, he was more than ready to switch desks. If nothing else, he'd at least have Cody around to make some noise.

Unfortunately, once he logged onto his computer, he found IT had rescheduled his move. He also found some actual work Cody had given him, and another—smaller—deluge of messages from people who'd found out about Gabrielle's death over the weekend and wanted information about donations or the funeral. His log of people he needed to follow up with once those details were released had become enormous.

Just before lunchtime, Riley pushed back from his desk, head throbbing. He'd worked for hours without a break, and his body was telling him he needed caffeine. Or maybe hydration. Both, even. And a sandwich.

While he'd worked, he came up with a couple of real work-related reasons he might have to go poking around for… he almost didn't want to think the word, but it was the only applicable one: *clues.* Letting that one word loose in his brain gave him a shiver. He'd always assumed getting involved in a real-life murder investigation would be a thrill, although knowing and respecting the victim muted most of his excitement. But the more information he could bring Tad, the more opportunities he'd have to call Tad. Although after being naked together, he perhaps didn't need to manufacture excuses to see the man.

First things first—hit the coffee shop downstairs for a jolt of caffeine and some lunch that he could eat at his desk.

FIFTEEN MINUTES later Riley brushed a few crumbs from his shirt, took the last sip of his Earl Grey latte, and stood up.

Taking advantage of the empty office, Riley sauntered casually over to the other side of the floor. Cody had gone out for a long lunch, which Riley didn't begrudge him. By rights he should probably still be on bereavement leave, never mind dealing with an incredibly hostile work environment.

His first stop was Floriana's office, the one on this floor. He didn't expect to find much, not even her admin assistant, since she spent most of her time in the lab and expected her assistant to do the same. Without anyone around, Riley slipped into the open door and partially closed it. He didn't want anyone to happen by and be able to easily see him.

Floriana's office was rather tidier than he expected, considering how scattered she was half the time. There were stacks of scientific reports and journals, reminding him that Floriana had scientific training and wasn't just the entitled, angry woman he'd seen. He didn't think there would be much of anything clue-like in either of those, but then again, he didn't know if he'd recognize a clue if it goosed his ass.

A moment later, he noticed the two degrees hanging askew on the wall, a bachelor's and a master's in chemistry.

After listening closely for any sign anyone was approaching, he quickly opened the desk drawers and rummaged through them. Nothing like a bottle of pills or a newly forged will for Gabrielle leaped out. He did discover that she had a disgusting habit of keeping dusty, dried-out condiment packets in her bottom drawer. There was pretty much zero chance he'd accept one of those ratty old ketchup packets for anything besides a science experiment.

He spent almost twenty minutes poking around, and he found exactly dick. No book to indicate she'd been researching poisons, although with her scientific background, a bunch of those chemistry books might easily have the information she'd need and Riley would never know. No wills, no pills, no nothing.

Somewhat disheartened, he made a quick stop in the bathroom to wash his hands. The office wasn't any dustier than anywhere else— the cleaning staff would have seen to that—but the general disarray and randomness seemed a bit filthy after Gabrielle's almost obsessive precision.

Probably he'd find out more just by combing through the shared servers for incriminating documents, but he didn't much relish spending *years* of his life doing that. Those servers were filled with documents, and no one with half a brain would store something too incriminating on a shared server.

Riley squared his shoulders. He had a plan and he was going to stick to it. No one said catching criminals was easy.

Next, he wandered over to François's office.

Shit. Mary, François's admin, either hadn't taken her lunch break, or she was back already. Still, there might be hope. Mary liked him.

"Hello, Mary."

She smiled at him, a pleasant, matronly smile like he imagined a grandmother would give. "Hello, Riley."

"How was your weekend?"

"Not as interesting as yours, I bet. Although my girlfriends and I went to one of those pole-dancing exercise classes."

Riley tried not to stare. Mary was sixty if she was a day, and plump. He'd often wondered how much say Bethany had had in the hiring of François's admin. "Did you have fun?"

"I did, actually."

"I applaud you. That would take more coordination than I have." He got a sudden vision of trying to convince his gaming group to take a pole-dancing class and nearly tied his esophagus in knots trying not to laugh. Shaun would do it, but he was only in the gaming group under duress, as in Riley would never agree to Shaun's more social plans if he didn't cave and attend a couple of game nights a month.

Mary tilted her head. "Wait, you've never done that?"

Riley did his best to keep his face still and nonjudgmental, but seriously, what had she been watching? Did she just assume every gay man could work the pole—stripper pole, that was—like a pro? People had some weird ideas about gay men. Then again, maybe he shouldn't have assumed she *wouldn't* take pole-dancing classes. "Nope. Never."

"So did you do anything interesting this weekend, then?"

"Just went to a club and hung out with friends." Geeked out at Coffee and Conquer, became a confidential informant, had illicit sex twice with a police detective, and dodged drunken oral sex at Anaconda. Details no one truly needed.

"You need to find a nice man to settle down with."

"One day, Mary, one day. Nice men aren't exactly littered around!"

They both laughed, those insincere laughs that indicate engagement and politeness but not necessarily true mirth. Social contract. But her simple acceptance pleased him. He was probably engaging in some sort of reverse judgment, but he often assumed that people of her generation weren't as accepting of his orientation, and that often made him hesitant to say anything. But it had never been in his nature to hide.

"I haven't seen you since you transferred to Cody. How are you finding that?"

That was a loaded question, especially from someone who had François's ear. And more than likely got an earful from François after he found out about Cody's intrusion into the business. But Mary managed to make the question sound completely innocuous.

"It's fine. It'll be a while before he's up to speed, so I expect the work will be very feast or famine."

"I'm sure everything will smooth out sooner or later. Did you need anything, or just visiting?"

He'd been hoping for a chance to poke around François's office, but it would be tricky. Might actually require a bit more planning. For now, he had other unrelated things he wanted to check out.

"Actually, I do need to compile a report about past product launch events. Cost analysis and whatnot. But I don't think the files I have are complete."

"Oh, that Aaron. I don't know what he was about most of the time, but he wasn't the most detail-oriented person I've ever come across."

He didn't feel right about agreeing, but he could certainly understand why she'd think so.

"Can I get copies of your files, or maybe just borrow them if you've got paper versions?"

Riley assumed they had paper versions, since Gabrielle had been old-fashioned enough to prefer paper over computer, although invoicing, payments, and approvals were done online with paper backup. If there were full duplicate files anywhere besides Gabrielle's file cabinets, they'd be in the Finance department.

"Of course you can borrow them, as long as you bring them back. Do you need them right now, or can I dig them out later?"

Riley smiled—his very best smile that usually got him a man for the night. "I wouldn't want to put you out. I don't mind getting them myself." He gave an ingratiating laugh. "After all, it's about the only task on my plate right now."

Mary giggled. "Oh, cry me a river. You'd best enjoy the lull while you can, because it won't last long."

"Don't I know it."

She waved a hand. "Go on, then. Because I've got a ton on my plate."

"Thanks." Riley opened the door to the file room, a repurposed office on the other side of Mary's desk. He'd have to compare what was entered into the invoicing system with the paper files, but Aaron's files had enough errors that he needed to double-check what was correct. If there was an error, and he suspected there were at least two substantial ones, then those funds needed to be reappropriated.

He wasn't sure who'd be responsible for that, though. François as VP of Finance, probably, although he had more than enough things to deal with just now.

By the time he'd selected the files he needed—in between poking around into files that were absolutely none of his business—an hour had passed. He hadn't been kidding, though. His workload under Cody was still quite light. In addition to Cody figuring out his role, he wasn't exactly used to having a full-time executive assistant. At his previous job, Cody had shared one with five other managers. Riley understood François and Floriana's ire a bit more, since Cody's new position gave him quite the boost up the scale, but it wasn't like Gabrielle's kids hadn't gotten appointed to positions they'd never have been hired for in any other company.

"What are you doing in here?"

Riley leaped at the unexpected sound, whirling around and almost toppling his stack of files.

François Gautier stood there, arms akimbo, scowling as though he'd just caught a street urchin stealing his wares. For a moment Riley was again that undersized bully fodder he'd been in high school.

A frisson of fear made everything in his gut feel just a bit liquidy, but Riley stiffened his spine. The project he was working on might be self-assigned, but that didn't change its validity. And François couldn't have seen him "investigating" other files, or he would have said something earlier. He met François's gaze directly, as Riley was equal in height. He might not be equal in rank, but neither was he entirely dependent on François's goodwill to keep his job.

"Oh, now, Mr. François," Mary admonished from outside the file room. "Riley's working on a report about expenditures for launch events. Which means he's borrowing files. That's what they're there for—reference."

François slowly relaxed his stance, but his eyes remained distrustful. He moved back barely enough for Riley to move past.

"Those files better be back here, in good condition, as soon as possible," François growled.

Somehow Riley managed to keep from rolling his eyes. "Of course. As soon as I'm done."

"And don't leave them out where just anyone can see them. Some of that information is undoubtedly confidential."

Questionable, since they were essentially invoices for parties that had already occurred and been paid for, but he wasn't about to antagonize François if he didn't have to.

"Mr. François." Mary sounded almost scandalized. "I realize Riley hasn't been here long, but he's good at his job. You don't have to worry about that."

"Thank you, Mary." Riley nodded brusquely to François and left the room.

"You have a good afternoon, dear."

As soon as he was out of sight, he almost ran for his desk. Despite the tomblike atmosphere, it still represented a haven.

He tossed the files on his desk, dropped into his chair, and started laughing weakly, that one tiny encounter having sent a rush of adrenaline through him. Terrifying and exhilarating. And he hadn't even found out anything good about François, except Riley had thought he didn't share Floriana's hatred of him. Turned out he was wrong about that.

Mindful of François's warning, Riley put the files in the squat filing cabinet beside his desk, then made himself a much-needed cup of tea. It had caffeine, but not enough to make him jittery, and he'd definitely begun to agree with Gabrielle's assertion that it was soothing. Riley needed a bit of soothing just now.

Tea drank, urgent messages dealt with, he set off on his next avenue of exploration: the lab.

If Gabrielle were still alive, she'd expect him to wear his headset wherever he went and answer any phone calls, but as the majority of the calls he'd gotten since her death weren't precisely business related and definitely weren't urgent, he just shunted everything to voicemail. His headset wasn't set to field Cody's calls yet—that was another task

IT would have to do—so those were also set to hit voicemail, which he checked periodically through the day.

But he thought the headset made him look like he was on official business, and he headed for the lab. Gabrielle had taken him inside briefly when he'd been hired, mostly to show him where Floriana's sanctuary was, but he'd not been inside since.

He swiped his card over the reader. Red. Another swipe. More red.

Interesting. As Gabrielle's assistant, he would have expected his card to give him access to everything. He'd never bothered to test it, and Gabrielle had used her own access card to swipe them into the lab.

Backtracking, he slowly approached François's office. Mary was diligently typing away, and François's office door was firmly shut.

Good. He strode up to Mary's desk. "Hello again, Mary."

"Riley! Twice in one day. This is a treat."

Riley laughed. "I was just going to chat with Renee about something, but I think she's in the lab with Floriana, and my card's not working."

"Oh, honey. Not everyone's card works to get into the lab. Most of the office staff can't get in there. Even Renee needs to be swiped in by someone else."

"Really?" That was highly interesting. "No one in the office has access? Gabrielle did."

"Obviously. But there's so much proprietary information there, they locked it down to people who need access. Mr. François has access as a VP, and Mr. Cody should have access as well, but if you need to get in there, you'll need someone to let you in, and once inside, they'll give you a visitor pass. You can call Renee, or you can ask Mr. Cody if you can borrow his card, although they frown upon that."

Not surprising. The whole reason for access cards was to limit access. But it was slightly annoying that he wouldn't have free run of the lab. He was certain there were all kinds of potential clues inside.

First, he needed to get in. If something caught his eye, he'd figure out a way to return. "Thanks, Mary. I'll give Renee a call."

Thoughtful, he wandered back to his desk. He'd figured he could go into the lab on the pretense of finding out if anything about Gabrielle's funeral had been decided, but if he had to call Renee for access, he could just ask her on the phone. But that wasn't the only reason he might have to enter the lab. He picked up his extension and called Renee.

"Floriana Gautier's office, Renee speaking. How can I help you?" Renee's voice was brisk and professional but welcoming in a way Floriana wasn't. Riley wondered sometimes how Renee managed to support Floriana without becoming equally vituperative, but then, perhaps what Floriana needed—what many admins provided—was a foil, not a mirror.

"Hi, Renee, it's Riley."

"Good afternoon, Riley. What can I do for you?"

"Well, when I started here, someone mentioned the possibility of getting a tour of the lab. With Cody still ramping up, my workload isn't quite as hectic, and with the launch of Invigorate complete, I thought maybe this week would be a good time. Do you think you'll have some time this week to show me around?"

"Sure thing, Riley. I won't have time today, but let me put something on your calendar for tomorrow."

"Thanks, I appreciate that. Say, while I have you, do you know if anything's been decided about the funeral?"

Renee lowered her voice, a sure indication that Floriana must be fairly close by. "No. And I'd rather not ask."

Riley understood. Renee had an incredible capacity to deal with the whirlwind Floriana was on a regular basis, but Riley had seen enough of her mood swings since Gabrielle died that he wouldn't be interested in setting her off right now either. "No problem. I'll see you tomorrow."

If everyone was afraid to ask about the arrangements, then Riley was going to have to gird himself and ask the next time he saw Floriana. Or François. This limbo was getting ridiculous, even if the coroner hadn't released Gabrielle's body.

He wished the tiny information about access to the lab was enough to justify calling Tad, because it already felt like a long time since he'd seen him. It wasn't, though, and he didn't want to distract Tad from his actual work.

He crossed his fingers that he'd find something worthwhile tomorrow, after he toured the lab.

TUESDAY MORNING Riley could not get a handle on the launch party invoices. He'd spent the night dreaming about Tad, much like he'd done in high school, with much the same end result. Wasn't he too damned old for wet dreams? Worse, he'd also started dreaming of other things,

things he couldn't have. Not with Tad. He wasn't at his best, and Alisha had teased him about having a work-night date that went late. Right. Riley only wished.

Renee had set up his tour for eleven, and IT was supposed to move his stuff at three—he wasn't holding his breath—so he got to work on his self-assigned project.

He hadn't gotten enough sleep, though, and these invoices were making him crazy. Each launch party had something that seemed off. Cost per person for catering was the most common. Sometimes it was the sheer amount of food ordered, or bizarrely high prices to rent table linens and chairs. Every launch party had bloated pricing, just tipping over into usurious. It didn't seem to include favoritism for any particular vendor, though, and the files combined the planning for both the internal and external launches, which might be the reason the excesses weren't noticed.

They might not even be noticed by someone who hadn't gotten a number of proposals from vendors such as this to plan other parties. Something wasn't right, but Riley was damned if he knew what. He'd never come across anything like this before.

Gabrielle could have had certain favorite vendors who took advantage of her generosity by artificially inflating their invoices. Aaron might not have thought about checking for more competitive prices. It was possible to negotiate with vendors rather than just accepting the first estimate that came along. Next step would be checking the computer to see if everything matched.

The meeting notification on his computer binged. Digging into those invoices was going to have to wait, thankfully. He was starting to get a headache, and he'd been concentrating on the files for the past three hours. A lab tour would make a nice change of pace before lunch. Riley took the elevator down to the lab to meet Renee.

THE LAB was stunning. Renee made a wonderful tour guide, but Riley had been fucking kidding himself if he thought he'd be able to figure out what everyone was doing and if it was suspicious. The lab techs could have been making meth or nuclear bombs right in front of him and Riley wouldn't know squat. He certainly wouldn't be able to recognize penicillin manufacture—unless he saw a fucking piece of bread on a petri dish, growing mold.

Also, no one in their right mind would be illicitly manufacturing penicillin when they had all this at their disposal. If there was illicit manufacture going on, it would be of something that had significant street value.

For the first time, he understood how daunting and stressful Tad's job must be, and that didn't even include having to deal with dead bodies and possibly getting shot at.

After the tour, they ended up at Renee's secondary desk outside Floriana's alternate office, where her door stood ajar. Riley chatted pleasantly with Renee, asking about her kids, keeping one eye on Floriana, who was inside and on the phone.

The moment Floriana disconnected her call, Riley interrupted Renee. "Sorry, Renee, I need to have a quick word with Floriana."

Before he could think better of it, Riley knocked on her door to announce himself, but he walked in without waiting for Floriana to invite him.

"What are you doing here?" Floriana made no attempt to hide her contempt. He only wished he knew why he annoyed her so much.

Unfortunately for Floriana, he'd stood up to scarier bullies than her. He didn't want to confront her, but he was going to. "Cody tells me—"

Floriana snorted and rolled her eyes at the same time. Riley wasn't about to tell her she looked like a fractious bull when she did that, albeit one elegantly draped in Donna Karan under her lab coat.

Nevertheless, Riley pressed on. "Cody tells me that he's left the arrangement for Gabrielle's funeral in your hands, and François's. Do you have any information yet?"

"Why do you care?"

Riley almost took a step back. Could she really be that oblivious? "Why do I care? I have a mountain of people—people you do business with every day, that you rely on for the success of your business—requesting information because they want to pay their respects. Most of your employees would welcome the chance to say goodbye also." Whatever faults Gabrielle had, Gautier had all the earmarks of a great workplace.

Something in Riley's words halted Floriana and made her think rather than react. He waited, half expecting her to try to fire him again. Instead, she crumpled under his regard, and her eyes filled up.

Riley grabbed a nearby box of tissues and offered them up. Whatever issues he had with her, he'd managed to forget that she had lost her mother just days ago. "I'm sorry. I know how much this hurts, how hard it is." His eyes had already begun to burn in sympathy.

Floriana sniffed. "How would you know?"

Riley sat down in the chair opposite her desk, unwilling to loom. "Both my parents died when I was twelve. I bet it's hard at any age."

That only made her start sobbing. "That's awful."

Riley wanted to hug her, but maybe some doubt about how she'd take it held him back. "It was. And it still hurts, but it was also a long time ago. It's more of a dull ache than a gaping wound."

Sniffling, she worked hard to get herself under control, demonstrating an iron will that was every bit as admirable as her mother's.

While she did that, Riley gazed around the office. It was haphazard and filled with books and papers and folders and various samples of Gautier products. There was no sign of a prescription bottle filled with penicillin, but that meant little. Just thinking about his "investigation" sent a stab of guilt through him. He could empathize so well with Floriana, especially right now, but just because she missed her mother didn't mean she hadn't killed her.

"I'm sorry." Floriana's voice sounded strong and almost conciliatory. Aside from red-rimmed eyes and tiny smears of mascara, she looked every inch her mother's daughter. Impressive to be sure. Crying for Riley meant looking like a heroin addict turned zombie—all the hair color in the world couldn't change his fair complexion, and the ravages lasted for hours.

"I understand."

Floriana nodded. "I also hadn't quite thought of the funeral… the situation… from that perspective. The coroner still—" Her voice broke slightly, but she quickly recovered. "We don't know when they're going to release Mother. And Cody was right. He agreed to let us honor the wishes she'd outlined in her invalid will. When the coroner allows, we're going to return to Montreal and have a funeral there. Bury her there, with her family."

Shit. Riley had never even considered that possibility, but it made sense. Gabrielle had built up a formidable life here in Toronto, but her roots were in Quebec. It even made sense that they'd chosen to continue working—bereavement leave could be taken when they took Gabrielle to her final rest.

"Many people, including your employees, won't be able to travel that far, even if they'd like to. What about a memorial service of some kind? Something where people can pay their respects, but it wouldn't rely on whatever schedule the coroner's office has."

"Yes, that's a lovely idea. Thank you."

Riley didn't know how long reasonable and mild-mannered Floriana was going to last, but he'd be sad when she went back to hating him.

She blinked and dabbed at her eyes a little. "Right before... um... my mother passed, we'd agreed to move forward aggressively with another new product to capitalize on the momentum from Invigorate. Renee and I both have our hands full with that—do you think you could organize the service? Maybe for this week, because our lawyers think we'll be able to head out to Montreal early next week."

Would Tad have anything to say about that? Could he even legally insist murder suspects not leave the province? That was a concern for another time. Because Floriana had just asked him to do an important job, and he hadn't been prepared—not at all—to be trusted with it.

"Of course. Are there any special requests? Did you want a church service? What about a reception afterward?"

Floriana sighed, and Riley wanted to get out of there and give her some alone time, but pulling together a memorial service this quickly would be a challenge. He needed a few answers, and he needed them now.

"She attended St. Stephen's in Forest Hill. If we can get a service there, that would make her happy. I'll host a reception or whatever is necessary at my house afterward. Mother did not approve of church basements, and that's where the reception rooms are at St. Stephen's."

"Perfect, thank you."

"You weren't issued a corporate credit card, were you?"

"No, no, I wasn't." They'd hardly do that for a temp, although it seemed likely that the other admins at his level might have their own.

"Get my card information from Renee. If there's anything you can't set up with our regular vendors, you can use my card to charge things."

"Thank you, Floriana. I'll get right on it." He wasn't aware company funds could be spent in such a way, but they certainly had discretionary funds for launch parties and holiday parties; from a taxation perspective, maybe a funeral wasn't much different.

"Just make sure you give my cleaning service a heads-up."

With that, there was no doubt in his mind that he'd been dismissed. He presumed he could also get the cleaning service contact information from Renee.

Stunned, he got up and left Floriana's office, making sure he stopped at Renee's desk first. His afternoon had just become incredibly busy, and he hoped Alisha wouldn't mind grabbing him some lunch when she went out. He rather thought he wouldn't be eating out again for the rest of the week.

As he made his way back to the sixteenth floor, he groaned. He was going to have to postpone IT again, or he might not be able to get everything done.

Chapter NINE

BEFORE HE did anything, he needed to talk to HR about a memorial service, and Mattie had already gone to lunch by the time he left the lab. He asked Heather, leaning heavily on their friendship with Alisha, about finding time to chat with Mattie as soon as possible. She squeezed him in for the first fifteen minutes after Mattie was due back in the office. Alisha agreed to get him lunch. While he waited, he fired off an email to IT postponing his computer move and then began compiling lists of potential caterers.

It would certainly be interesting to compare this experience with the information he was compiling on the launch parties. Perhaps he ought to expand his search to include holiday parties as well, since it might be the unfamiliar nuances of launch parties that were causing his misgivings.

When his meeting notification dinged, he leaped up and strode toward HR. Mattie was just getting in as he arrived, and Heather let her know Riley was there to see her.

She didn't look enthused. She took off her rain-speckled jacket and stood her damp umbrella in the corner before sitting down. "Riley. You've got an urgent issue? Are things not going well with Cody?"

He almost cracked a smile. Poor Mattie. She must be dealing with all sorts of complaints, with the management in such volatile emotional positions and Cody an unknown entity.

"We're getting along fine. Don't worry about that."

Mattie smiled in relief, the tense set to her shoulders relaxing. "Then what's so urgent?"

"Floriana put me in charge of setting up a memorial service and reception afterward."

"Oh, that's good. I was hoping to hear about one soon. What's the problem?"

"I have no idea how many employees would be likely to attend, and I wouldn't want to schedule it at a time when people who wanted to pay their respects couldn't attend, but I'm not sure an evening memorial service is customary."

"No, no. Schedule it during the day. Whether it's morning or afternoon, I'll authorize minimal staffing for that half day. Once the notice goes out, I'll let team leaders know that if their entire team intends to be away, they'll need to run that by me, but I'd be surprised if every single person would attend. My guess is you'll get more upper management and lab technicians, since they were the people who had the most contact with Gabrielle."

"Thank you. I appreciate it."

Mattie smiled. "I appreciate you getting the ball rolling on this."

"What?" Riley frowned. He could swear he hadn't mentioned his part about taking Floriana to task—he sure didn't want to admit to HR that he'd made a VP cry, however unintentionally.

"Oh, I know Floriana. She wouldn't have come up with this on her own, nor would she have thought to hand this over to you. I'd have done it myself, but I'm definitely in her bad books after my part in bringing Cody on board. But I wasn't going to let the issue fester much longer. So thank you. Make sure you get me the details—I'll draft up an appropriate notice to be emailed to all employees."

Riley nodded his assent and returned to his desk.

"WHERE THE fuck is my computer?" He clapped a hand over his mouth. This might be an unusual situation, but he was normally very good at filtering swear words out of his vocabulary at work.

His notes and files had been shuffled around, but not badly. He opened his desk drawers, but a glance didn't reveal anything amiss except for the glaring absence of his computer and monitor. His heart started racing. Had someone seriously come in and stolen it?

Cody needed to be informed; then they'd have to contact the police. Not Tad, unfortunately. Floriana and François might never forgive him for bringing the cops into their business for the second time in as many weeks.

Walking as quickly as he could without drawing attention—not that there were many people nearby—he arrived at Cody's office almost breathless with upset.

Only to find an IT tech hooking up his computer on the desk outside Cody's office.

"What are you doing here? I emailed this morning that I'd have to postpone this move."

The tech, a guy who looked fresh out of high school, with a complexion that probably never saw the sun, looked at him balefully. "Guess you didn't send it in time. I'm almost done with the computer; then I'll start reprogramming your phone. If you need it moved back, you'll need to submit another requisition."

Riley gritted his teeth against an annoyed reply. IT techs were the same all over, and he'd seen a number of situations that might or might not be IT fucking around behind the scenes, making things difficult for people who were rude or unreasonable.

Seriously, though, the last thing he needed right now was to move his desk. "How long do you think you'll be?"

"Dunno."

So fucking helpful. "Okay, thanks. I guess I'll go pack up the rest of my stuff."

"I already swapped the file cabinets."

He had? Riley moved around Mr. IT Man and pulled open the top drawer. It was filled with the burgundy files he'd borrowed from Finance, stuffed in front of his other files. The little swipe of pink, which Riley assumed was nail polish, still graced the top of the file cabinet. It was usually easier to just move the cabinets than move the contents from one cabinet to the other, but he didn't have many files to worry about, and he certainly hadn't expected that to be part of IT's service.

"Oh. Thank you. I appreciate that."

Maybe he didn't hate the tech quite as much now. But this was a delay he didn't really need.

On the way back to his desk, he scrounged up a few file boxes, then made some tea before settling in to shift the contents of his desk. As long as he got a call into St. Stephen's in the next hour or so, he could still pull this off. Maybe. Getting a date and time for the memorial service was paramount, because he couldn't even start to get catering estimates until he knew that and could at least rule out the caterers who were already booked.

HE OPENED his top drawer, pulled out the teas and honeys he'd collected from Gabrielle's tea caddy, and put them into a box. Behind those was the gift set he'd forgotten to ask Aaron about, but since Aaron had served him tea and hadn't sounded as though he hated Gabrielle, Riley might just take it over to him soon anyway. Be a nice keepsake, although it wouldn't make up for the radical changes in the workplace that Aaron would be returning to.

The gift set went in the box with pens, pencils, pushpins, paper clips, and various other accouterments. On top of that, he piled everything that had graced the top of his desk, which was primarily the notes and files related to his "project." Aaron's personal things were tucked away in a box in the bottom drawer of the filing cabinet. Maybe if Riley had a boyfriend or husband or kids he might consider bringing in a photo. His own personalization included a few geeky toys and action figures— nothing expensive, though, because they'd occasionally disappear, even when he was openly mocked for having them.

He grabbed the second box and started loading files in from the bottom drawer. Right at the back in the corner was a glint of something short and squat, but the drawer didn't open all the way, and he couldn't tell what it was. It wasn't his, but it might be something he'd need. Lips pursed, he considered his next course of action. He'd already gotten grease on his hands from an innocent brush with the side of the drawer. Reaching into the back of the drawer would undoubtedly get grease all over his brand-new powder blue shirt, the one that complemented his eyes, especially with his blue contacts in.

Shit. He already had a tiny smear of yellow grease on his cuff. That was going to be a bitch to get out.

Instead of getting on his knees and scrabbling for the mystery object, Riley grabbed his mobile and flicked on the flashlight app.

What was one of Gabrielle's teas doing back there? He was almost certain he'd already packed all the ones he'd allocated for himself. Twisting just a little more, he was able to see the label. Lapsang souchong.

Adrenaline spiked hard and fast in his blood, and he fell back, sucking in air. Glancing guiltily about, he slammed the drawer shut, then got to his feet. No one was around, but that didn't calm the racing of his heart. A clammy sweat sprang up under his arms as he paced.

This was bad. Bad, bad, bad.

He stared at his mobile, clenched tightly in his hand. He had an excellent fucking reason to call Tad, but it wasn't fun, and there wouldn't be any cutesy dates or, indeed, excellent fucking.

Another glance verified that he was alone. He didn't want to have this phone call out in the open, even if he couldn't see anyone. After slipping into Gabrielle's office, he shut the door gently behind him, walked over to the window, and stared out at the downtown core as he waited for his call to connect.

"Detective Tad Martin."

"Tad, oh shit, I've found something." He'd rather not sound so breathless and scared while talking to Tad, but he was freaked the fuck out.

"Riley? It'll be fine. I can meet you for dinner later."

Was Tad high? This wasn't anything like the other things he'd discovered. "No, you have to come here. Now."

Wait. Riley didn't know who'd put the tea in his drawer, but what if they came and took it away? He strode back to the office door and opened it a crack so he could keep an eye on his desk.

"This isn't really a good time. Are you sure it can't wait until tonight? I've been wanting to try out that new Thai place on Church Street. I can be there for six thirty."

Another fucking date restaurant? Riley was losing his mind while Tad was focused on his stomach. "You don't understand. I found the tea in my desk."

"What tea?"

"Remember I told you one was missing? I found it in my drawer, right at the back, and I didn't put it there."

He'd read about hammering hearts, but he'd never experienced anything like the ruckus going on in his chest right now.

"Shit. Really?"

"Tad, please, I'm freaking the fuck out."

"Hey, hey. Calm down. I'll be there in under ten minutes."

Riley didn't even care that thirty seconds ago, Tad wasn't going to be able to make time for him until early evening, just so long as Tad got here and helped him figure out what was going on.

"Okay. Okay. What should I do?"

"Do what you can to pretend everything is normal. But don't let anyone in your desk drawer, no matter what they say. Try not to touch anything more than you have to. And let Alisha know we're coming. Maybe we can do this fairly low-key, slip in without any fanfare."

"I can do that. Thanks."

"Of course." Tad's voice dropped into his sexy register. "See you soon."

How did his partner even stand it? Riley wouldn't be able to work with Tad being so sexy all the time. Even as scared as he was, he was still so painfully aware of Tad's appeal.

The call disconnected, and Riley returned to his desk. He pulled out a file from the box so he could pretend to be actually working, even though he could barely concentrate on the few commands Tad had given him. With shaking fingers, he put on his headset and dialed the extension for the reception desk.

"Alisha, you have to do something for me," Riley said as soon as she answered, not even giving her a chance to get out her customary welcome greeting.

"Sure, what's up?"

"In a couple of minutes, a detective, maybe two, will be arriving. Can you send them back to Gabrielle's office with a minimum of fuss?"

"Riley." Alisha sounded worried. "What's going on? Is everything okay?"

"Yeah, it's fine, I just... I just found something that might be pertinent to the investigation is all. But if we can get them in and out without any disruption, that would be perfect."

"I'll do what I can. As long as there aren't any uniforms, it'll probably be easy. The ones with the heavy commute are going to be heading out soon."

Shit. Was it already that late? He hadn't even started on the memorial service planning. He was going to be here all fucking night.

TWELVE MINUTES later—because he'd been obsessively checking the time—footsteps warned him to look up. Tad's partner, Detective Wilson, led the way, scowling, followed closely by Tad and a woman with a ponytail carrying a case.

Tad's simple presence was enough to calm Riley's racing heart. The knowledge that someone, just days after Gabrielle had been murdered, had planted something in his desk terrified him. Those other lovely teas and honey he'd liberated? The ones that were unsealed? There was no fucking way he'd be using them. The only reason they weren't in the garbage already was that he was worried the police might need them.

During a brief moment when both Detective Wilson and the crime scene technician turned away, Tad gripped Riley's shoulder, reducing his upset even further. The touch was innocuous enough but showed he cared that Riley was upset, and wanted to help.

Like he was prescient, Tad let his hand fall away fractions of a second before Emma straightened up and turned their way.

"Thanks for calling us." She didn't sound any happier than the first time Riley had encountered her, but quitting smoking was hard.

Within a surprisingly short time, the CSI tech had claimed the container of tea for testing and dusted the drawer for fingerprints again. If Riley was hoping for unobtrusive, he was going to have to clean up the mess. Again.

Tad let the two women get several steps toward the exit before he spoke. "Do you want to meet up tonight? I could bring dinner over."

Riley didn't know what he wanted right now. He still had a number of tasks to accomplish before he left the office, and although he already knew he didn't want to do anything besides hibernate in his condo, he probably ought to eat something. "Can I let you know later? I'm not sure what time I'll be able to get out of here."

"Yep. I could come over later than six thirty if that's easier for you."

"I'll think about it." He wasn't sure he wanted to be alone either.

"Text me and let me know. Be careful." Tad glanced furtively around before planting a quick kiss on Riley's temple; then he turned on his heel and strode after his partner.

Riley collapsed in his chair. What the *actual* fuck had just happened?

But the ticking clock in his head wouldn't stop. He cleaned up as quickly as he could. Thankfully, that errant tin of tea was the last thing in his desk. As soon as all evidence of the CSIs had been erased, Riley moved his boxes to his new desk. Unsurprisingly, the IT guy was long gone, and Riley had messages from Alisha.

First things first. He pulled out his notes for the memorial service, called St. Stephen's, and nailed down a time for the memorial—early Thursday afternoon. He fired off an email to Mattie in HR with the information and emailed requests for quotes to the four caterers used most recently for launch parties. He didn't expect answers from any of them today, since it was so close to the end of business hours.

When Alisha called again, he answered.

"Come out here now."

Did he dare? He never thought he'd be the sort to need hugs, but he could really use one right now. And if he couldn't get hugs from Tad,

Alisha's would be warm and comforting. He wondered what he could tell her, though. He wasn't sure what was confidential, nor did he want anything weird to happen to her.

"I'll be out in a few minutes." Alisha was only on the clock for another thirty minutes or so.

He quickly gathered his files and considered locking them in the cabinet, but most of the file cabinets' locks could be jimmied with a hairpin. They weren't exactly secure. Then again, the tin of tea hadn't necessarily been placed in his desk today. For all Riley knew, that tea had been lurking in his drawer mere moments after Gabrielle had died, and wasn't some malicious response to his lame attempts at investigating. He'd learned nothing, for fuck's sake.

But he didn't have any other options at the moment, so he piled the files inside. Normally he wouldn't even bother locking the cabinet, but that small precaution seemed necessary now.

Taking the long route to the reception desk, he passed by François's office. It had just occurred to him that depending on Floriana's mood, François might first hear about the memorial service from Mattie's company-wide email blast, and that didn't seem appropriate.

Both Mary and François were nowhere to be seen, although François's door was open. Riley took advantage and stepped inside. He could always claim to be waiting for François, because he did have legitimate business.

Probably he should be scared shitless of trying to find more information, but his logic had begun to reassert itself. Even if the tin of tea was the murder weapon, there wasn't any reason to think Riley himself was in danger. It didn't even mean anyone was worried about Riley. He was merely background noise—no one noticed the admins.

François's office was the polar opposite of Floriana's, and far more similar to Gabrielle's "everything in its place" methodology. Books on business administration, finances, economy, and taxes lined his bookshelves. There were a couple of typical pictures of him with Bethany, on vacation and on their wedding day. François was certainly less somber than he was on the average day, but Riley couldn't exactly call his expression happy. Bethany smiled brightly, but none of the skin from her cheekbones up crinkled in any way. Apparently she'd started the Botox way early.

Two degrees hung on François's wall: a Bachelor of Science in chemistry, and an MBA in finance. Unlike the ones in Floriana's office, they both hung with ruler-like precision. Riley hadn't realized both of the Gautier kids had taken chemistry as undergrads. He'd be willing to bet his entire life savings that Mama Gautier had had a heavy hand in that decision. He'd bet Gabrielle absolutely hated visiting Floriana's office. Although, like a queen bee, Gabrielle almost never gave up home-turf advantage. For all Riley knew, Gabrielle hadn't even known the state of Floriana's office, or François's, for that matter.

Before he had a chance to rethink it or overthink it, Riley popped around the other side of François's desk. The top drawer was unlocked, but there didn't seem to be anything of interest, like a random bottle of penicillin tablets, inside.

The bottom drawer was locked, and despite Riley's deep-seated belief that the locks could be picked with a hairpin, he didn't even know where to get a hairpin, much less what he'd do with it. He wasn't going to risk getting caught for no good reason.

He waited a few more minutes, but there was no sign of either of them. Well, he'd tried. If he waited any longer, Alisha would be done for the day and be free to come seeking him.

With minutes to spare, he skidded to a stop by the reception desk.

"What was that all about?" Alisha whispered, even though there was no one within earshot.

"I found something."

"Oh my God, do I need to tickle you or something to get you to spit out your secrets? You can't just leave me hanging. Was it a bomb or another murder victim or the murder weapon?"

He wanted to trust Alisha implicitly and tell her everything, but he couldn't. Maybe one day, but not today. Stupidly, he didn't want Tad to be disappointed in him if he found out Riley had blabbed all over the place.

"It wasn't anything, just a misplaced tin of Gabrielle's tea. I know they took samples of all the teas in her caddy, so it seemed reasonable that they would want samples of this one as well." Alisha didn't need to know that Riley hadn't actually watched the police take samples.

Alisha tilted her head to the side and narrowed her eyes as she inspected Riley. "Mostly true. And maybe you can't actually tell me everything. This isn't exactly a who's-sleeping-with-who situation. But when this is all over? You owe me dinner and the full story. Got it?"

Now that Riley could agree to. "Absolutely."

She wagged a finger in his face. "Now, that was a simply prime specimen of man that came in here. If he was here the night Gabrielle died, I must have been in shock not to notice. There's a man you need to ask out."

The comment, completely out of left field, sent blood boiling into his cheeks. "I'm sure there are regulations about that. And he might not be gay."

"Are you sure about that? Maybe your gaydar is on the fritz."

Riley let out a strangled laugh. "Maybe."

"Hmph."

"Maybe you should have asked him out." His throat nearly choked as he uttered the sacrilegious thought. If Alisha took up with Tad, the green-eyed monster would simply slay him where he stood.

"Please. Do you see the neckline I'm wearing today?"

Riley made himself focus below her neck. "Yes. You're looking… quite exposed today."

She rolled her eyes. "Booby. I'm looking particularly booby today. I forgot to do laundry this weekend, so I got stuck wearing my third-date 'you're getting lucky' shirt. It doesn't get into rotation very much, and sometimes I think it gets lonely, so it's not entirely a bad thing. Anyway, the V on this shirt got more attention from each of those women with him than it got from that gorgeous hunk of a man. And if he ends up playing for your team, you're taking me someplace *nice* for dinner. With champagne. Secrets and champagne. It'll be great."

"Did you miss the fact that I'm the admin for executives, not an actual executive myself?"

"Ha. That question alone indicates you're expecting to have to pay up."

He'd take her out for a nice dinner—it was the least he could do for a friend who had consistently proven to have his back. "I'd be happy to pay up, but don't be too disappointed if our dinner is secrets and Sprite at the Keg."

"I'd take the Keg. They make a damn fine steak."

"It's a date."

"With that very fine cop? Yes, I think it will be."

Riley chuckled at her stubbornness.

Alisha glanced at her computer. "I'm shutting down now. You ready to go? We can walk out together."

There wasn't much more he could do tonight, not without quotes from caterers or the email from Mattie about the memorial service. In the morning he could send out a mass email to most of the people in his log. Some of them required a personal touch, including the one to Aaron, and he could attend to those tonight, but the thought of sticking around by himself as the office workers trickled out made him jittery as hell. A good night's sleep and a decent meal would help.

"Yeah, let me just swing back to my desk and shut down my computer. In case you're looking for me, IT moved me to outside Cody's office today."

"Wow, that was fast."

That made Riley laugh. He wasn't the only one who'd had bad experiences with them.

As he walked back to his desk, he wondered if he'd just rationalized his way into clearing his evening so Tad could come over as offered. Whether he had or not, the reality was that he was free tonight and he did not want to be alone.

He shut his computer down, but before he grabbed his coat, he sent Tad a quick text.

6:30 is good. Bring whatever for dinner.

Living in downtown Toronto had given him a taste for just about any cuisine takeout could offer.

RILEY HELD his lockbox tightly under his arm. There was plenty of room to keep snacks and tea safe under lock and key. Or well, just lock. It would easily fit in one of his drawers at work, and it would take a fairly determined person to break into it—no one could just walk by and jiggle a handle.

When he'd left work with Alisha at his normal time, he'd gone shopping instead of getting on the streetcar right away. The whole wandering-tea incident still unnerved him, and although penicillin wouldn't adversely affect Riley, the idea that there was a killer running loose in Gautier had to stay in the forefront of his mind. A killer who could easily stoop to poison, given the mostly easy access to a damned laboratory.

It was only prudent that he protect himself.

Partway to the streetcar stop, Riley passed a Shoppers Drug Mart. Then he stopped and did a one-eighty back to the entrance.

A quick perusal of the shelves netted him a couple of boxes of tea bags. Maybe not quite the quality of Gabrielle's, but at least he'd be able to keep them in his lockbox and make himself a cup of tea without worrying he'd be fatally poisoned. Or even nonfatally poisoned. That didn't sound like fun either.

On impulse, Riley went to the back of the store. There wasn't a lineup for the pharmacist. A couple of days ago, he'd looked up stuff about penicillin online, but it hadn't really been all that helpful. A pharmacist might not help either, but asking couldn't hurt. He walked up to the counter and waited.

"Can I help you?"

"Are you a pharmacist?"

"I am. Do you need a prescription filled?"

"No, I had a question about penicillin. I, uh, have a friend who's allergic, and I was wondering if you could tell me... I don't know. Is it still used? People talk about it, but it often sounds like a catchall phrase to encompass a lot of antibiotics."

"Yes, it's still used. Some bacteria have developed a resistance, and it shouldn't be prescribed for viruses as it won't do anything to help cure those, but it still gets the job done in a lot of cases. Granted, amoxicillin, which is in the penicillin family but broader spectrum, is more often prescribed, but that could still trigger an allergic reaction. You're talking about penicillin proper?"

Riley considered that for a moment. He thought it likely Tad would have mentioned amoxicillin if that was what had poisoned Gabrielle. "Definitely penicillin." Didn't they prescribe it for certain sexually transmitted diseases, like syphilis or something?

"It's occasionally prescribed for a number of different infections, but most often I see it for dental procedures. As a prophylactic."

Riley almost let out a laugh like he was a teenager instead of an adult man. He knew, of course, that *prophylactic* had applications outside of condoms and merely meant *preventative*, but it gave his inner potty-humor-loving kid a tiny slice of funny. "Dental procedures. Is it expensive?"

"Nope. Not at all. The prescription filling fee is more expensive than the drug itself."

"Thanks."

Riley made his way out of the store, wondering if he'd learned anything. Even though Tad had been thwarted at getting medical records, it didn't seem likely that a potential murderer would use pills he'd been prescribed, especially if it was recently. And he didn't think any of Tad's "people of interest" were stupid.

Maybe Alisha would know if anyone had been out recently for dental surgery, but this didn't feel like a worthwhile lead.

Riley bought his tea and hurried to the streetcar and smiled for the first time in hours. Soon he'd be home and Tad would arrive. He just knew Tad could soothe this jittery, unsettled feeling. The last thing he wanted was to go home and not feel safe, even there.

IN EXACTLY twenty minutes, about ten minutes after Riley got home, Tad knocked on Riley's door.

He didn't exactly spring up and sprint for the door, because the day had definitely dampened his spirits, but Tad's presence was like the first shoots of spring, a promise of better things to come.

"You doing okay?" Tad asked when he opened the door.

Riley shrugged. "Better now."

After kissing him—sweet and almost chaste—Tad took the bags into the kitchen.

"Just sit down, relax. I've got this."

Riley slumped at his kitchen table and waited. He wasn't even sure he wanted to eat. Tad clattered around for a moment before presenting him with a heaping plate of fish and chips. The salty, greasy smell started him salivating, and his mood perked up a bit more. Maybe he could eat some. Tad had a matching plate, and he slapped his phone down on the table.

"Vinegar?" Riley asked.

"Of course. Wouldn't be fish and chips without it." Tad laid out an assortment of packets, malt and white, as well as more salt. Smart man.

Riley didn't eat like this often, but the occasional indulgence didn't hurt.

Not much interested in conversation, Riley dug into the food, thankful Tad picked up his cues and ate steadily without trying to engage Riley. It was enough that Tad was there, his presence warding away the gloom.

The sheer amount of food would have defeated Riley even if he'd had a normal appetite, and he slowed down before Tad. Just as Tad finished, his phone buzzed angrily, and Tad swiped it up, quickly reading the message.

"Huh."

Riley lifted a brow but waited. Even if the message pertained to Gabrielle's case—and there was no reason to assume Tad didn't have other murders—it might be confidential.

But when Tad pressed his lips together and gazed intently at Riley, his stomach roiled.

"What?"

"They determined penicillin had been added to the tin of tea."

Riley gasped. "So she was poisoned with the tea."

Tad shook his head. "No, the coroner determined she hadn't ingested the penicillin. I think we were meant to believe the tea had been poisoned. I think we were meant to believe you had poisoned the tea. Someone is trying to frame you."

Subzero temperatures swept through his kitchen, making him shiver and constricting his lungs. "How… I mean…. Frame me?"

Tad grabbed his hand and twined their fingers together. "Calm down. Deep breaths. In and out. It's fine, you're fine."

The initial panic receded some. "I'm glad you believe I didn't do it."

"No. I don't believe it, Emma doesn't believe it. You're not a suspect."

While he didn't think Tad would be above blatantly lying to someone in the hopes they'd incriminate themselves, he didn't think Tad would be sleeping and eating with him as some sort of elaborate honey trap.

"C'mon. Let's watch TV." Tad guided him to the couch.

They found a station running *Galaxy Quest* and left it on that. Tad spent the entire time rubbing absently on Riley's leg or back. All of his touches were soothing and comforting, not an attempt at foreplay. He seemed to know exactly what Riley needed.

"Can you stay tonight?" Riley didn't want Tad to leave, but he braced himself for a wince or a rejection.

"Of course. Ready to sleep now?" Tad dropped a quick kiss on his temple.

Riley assented, and they shared the bathroom again to get ready for bed.

Naked in the dark, cozy comfort of Riley's bed, Tad held him close. Tad smelled faintly of grease from the fish and chip shop where he'd gotten their dinner, but underneath that were the enticing scents of man and sweat. Riley shifted to press his face against Tad's neck, making sure every possible inch of skin touched this man. He rubbed his nose against the stubble that told him Tad hadn't shaved that day. Then he started licking. Tad groaned beneath his lips, a sound he felt more than heard. The salt of Tad's skin was far different than the salt from the fries, but delicious in its own intoxicating way.

Slow and gentle, he slid a leg between Tad's, the sensation of hairy skin against hairy skin giving him goose bumps in the best way.

When Tad's cock nudged Riley's hip with growing insistence, his own cock woke up and started taking interest in the situation.

They writhed sinuously together, slow and sensuous rather than the frenetic pace they'd set previously. Every moment made Riley harder and more eager, but he didn't have the energy for fucking. He slithered around on the bed, and Tad quickly figured out what he was about. They fitted themselves together, cock to mouth, and Riley sucked in Tad's solid shaft while Tad's skilled mouth wrapped around his own cock.

He groaned around his mouthful, the salt leaking from the slit in Tad's cock sharper still, and he swirled his tongue around the head.

Perfection in his mouth, perfection enveloping his cock, and all with minimum energy expenditure.

Within a few minutes, Tad's hips started thrusting, sending his cock deeper down Riley's throat, and Tad's sucking got a little sloppy, a little more desperate, and a whole lot hotter. Then Tad stiffened and moaned, filling Riley's mouth.

Riley swallowed, then gentled his ministrations, resigned to the likelihood he'd have to finish himself off. Then Tad growled around his cock and sucked it deep while cupping his balls, the sudden intense sensation enough to send Riley rocketing into climax. He let Tad's cock slip from his lips while the orgasm whited out his senses.

Limbs limp as wet noodles, Riley let Tad shift him back around so they were both lying on the pillows. Tad kissed him gently, and the taste of himself in Tad's mouth might have revved him into a second round if he wasn't so fucking exhausted.

Riley let Tad's overactive heat generation and the comfort of his arms lull him into a deep, undisturbed sleep.

Chapter TEN

THE DAY dawned dark and dreary, as though the weather were affecting a somber mood, but by the time the memorial service at St. Stephen's was over, the sun was out and beaming brightly, the damp in the cracks of sidewalks and asphalt the only reminder of the morning's rain.

The service was well attended. Tad and his partner had chosen to stand at the side of the church, gazes flicking over everyone who arrived. Riley had gotten one quick smile from Tad before his stern police mien returned. Tad had come over last night as well, and they'd ended up sleeping through the night together. Even though they'd had to scramble for them to both get to work in time, after some spectacular oral sex, almost getting into work late hadn't bothered Riley a bit. It was almost sacrilegious to be as happy as he was today, considering where he was.

Riley made sure to sit at the back of the church and scamper out as soon as was polite in order to make sure he was at Floriana's in time to deal with any issues the caterers had. One of the many people Floriana hired to do various things for her had let the caterers into the house, freeing Riley to attend the service, which was nice. Still, he expected he'd be playing the role of butler and general gofer for the entirety of the reception.

He took advantage of the calm before the storm—excluding the chaos in the kitchen as the caterers set up—to poke around the cupboards in the kitchen. There was no evidence of any sort of pills, much less penicillin.

A glance at his watch revealed he had at most ten minutes before the mourners hit the house. The family would probably be some of the last to arrive, since they'd be accepting condolences at the church from anyone who wasn't coming back to the house to eat.

There would be no point in checking medicine cabinets in any of the "public" guest bathrooms. Riley headed straight upstairs, looking for the master bedroom.

The pale blue interior with diaphanous sheers and silky bedspread surprised him a little. It was a dreamlike atmosphere for a woman who mostly seemed cold and uncaring.

A full en suite matched the color scheme with navy and silver accents, but Riley didn't have the time to admire her decorator's taste. He flipped open the medicine cabinet. The haphazard organization made him wonder what lay behind the closet door in the bedroom. There were a number of prescription bottles, old and new, from a nearby Shoppers Drug Mart. The most recent prescription, dated the day after Gabrielle's death, was Valium. Understandable.

The others Riley recognized were a couple of additional antianxiety meds, an antidepressant, and some prescription-strength muscle relaxants. Nothing in the cabinet was penicillin or amoxicillin or any other kind of -cillin.

He supposed she could be carrying it with her, or keep it in her car or even somewhere in the lab. This certainly wasn't conclusive evidence of anything. Huffing out a sigh, he rushed back downstairs. This detecting thing was not nearly as clear-cut as it was in fiction.

Just in time too. The doorbell rang as soon as he hit the living room.

RILEY HAD spent the past two hours circulating and making sure everything went without a hitch, much like he'd done at the launch party.

No one had better die, or Riley would end up a pariah at all social events for some time.

Tad and his partner hadn't shown up, which indicated they had some sense of what Floriana would accept. She'd glared at them periodically during the service but hadn't given in to an outburst. That would not be the case in her own home.

Aaron had shown up. Riley kept an eye on him, as he'd never seen Aaron interact with his coworkers. Riley's deduction that Aaron was isolated from just about everybody was borne out in his interactions with the other guests. Many of them greeted him politely, but he didn't stick with any one social cluster and finally ended up sitting on the side of the couch, plate of food in hand, people watching.

It was possible, of course, that Aaron suffered from some sort of social anxiety. That could make it difficult for him to develop many interpersonal relationships. But unlike most of their colleagues, he didn't stare in amazement at Floriana's beautiful house, the likes of which most of them would never be able to afford if they lived a thousand years.

So many explanations for that, but he wondered. Could Aaron have had anything to do with Gabrielle's death? Being on medical leave would be a hell of an alibi. And if the penicillin had indeed been in one of Gabrielle's tea things, he might have found a way to poison something before he left, knowing the average person probably wouldn't even notice the addition.

Riley wasn't sure that made any more sense than suspecting the three people who profited from Gabrielle's death. Aaron certainly didn't profit and might end up in a worse situation than he'd been before. Riley couldn't speak to Gabrielle's treatment of Aaron. For all he knew, Aaron had taken medical leave due to some sort of mental breakdown. He might have lied when he said he loved working with Gabrielle, and maybe he hated her enough to plan her death. Aaron had been her assistant for two years. He could have easily known about her allergy.

"What's got you gnashing your teeth over here in the corner?" Alisha's sudden appearance nearly made him cry out.

"You startled the fuck out of me."

"Which wouldn't have happened if you weren't trying to stare holes in Aaron's clothes."

"What? No."

"He's not bad-looking, but he is definitely straight. Unlike your detective."

Alisha had taken to calling Tad Riley's detective after she'd figured out Riley was in possession of Tad's business card, and therefore had the ability to call him whenever he wanted.

"Not my detective. And are you sure?"

Alisha discreetly waved at her chest. "Um, yeah, pretty sure. There was also a rumor going around that he and Floriana were involved."

Riley's ears perked up. "Really? Are they?"

"Nah. Can you imagine Gabrielle allowing that? I bet she had some son of a robber baron all lined up, ready to welcome more wealth to the family."

Yet Riley couldn't quite shake the notion that when he'd visited Aaron there had been a woman there. Aside from the incongruity of the idea of Floriana becoming enamored of an admin—and based entirely on his own interactions with her—there wasn't any real evidence that they weren't involved. Would Tad be interested in such idle speculation? Probably not "date"-worthy, but Riley would try to remember to mention it.

His head was spinning from the possibilities. He had no idea how Tad kept it all in his head and teased out the tangles to lead to a particular person. Then again, perhaps many of his cases were a little more straightforward or included video or other types of direct evidence.

No matter what Tad said, Riley had a vested interest in figuring out who was behind Gabrielle's death, since either by accident or intent, he or she had almost implicated Riley as a murderer.

If only the asshole had left more obvious clues.

FRIDAY MORNING was almost anticlimactic. Riley was exhausted—between the memorial service, his raging allergies, and Tad keeping him up nights, he'd stopped at a Starbucks and loaded up on caffeine. A giant latte with an extra four shots of espresso. At his desk, he chugged it, hoping it would kick in soon. Tea couldn't quite compare.

Riley logged on but didn't really start anything. Cody was late, so there were no tasks forthcoming yet. Riley also hadn't gotten used to the location of his new desk. Almost everything was reversed, like he was trapped in a mirror, with the exception that Cody didn't have a kitchenette. The executive conference room took its place. Considering a giant part of Riley's job consisted of diving right in, in unfamiliar environments, he was a little surprised that he was having a hard time. This side of the floor was busier too. Gabrielle had done a good job of setting things up so that her office was apart from the hoi polloi.

There were good things about being on this side, though. It was easier to chat with the other admins, and many of them he could see from his desk. This side of the floor didn't seem quite so isolated and quiet. Made him feel safer, although maybe it shouldn't. The shared kitchen was a pleasant bustle, and while making tea from his carefully protected hoard of tea bags, he'd heard more gossip in the past week than he'd heard since he started with Gautier. No wonder Alisha had her finger on most of the little scandals. Riley was kind of glad she saw fit to filter that sheer amount of information.

Exactly what positions Ginny had been using to try to get pregnant, and vivid descriptions of Amir's three kids and their battle with a virulent stomach flu, were things Riley didn't need in his brain. His very first foray into the communal kitchen the morning after he'd switched desks had exposed him to the information that Martina's two boys had come home with lice, and the measures taken to prevent further spread... well, he'd itched all day Tuesday and taken a very long, very hot shower when he got home.

Coming in to work this morning had been a little surreal, since having Thursday afternoon off just messed with his mental schedule, even without the memorial service. A tiny part of him had expected Tad to come barging into Floriana's house and seclude all the potential suspects in a room, seated in a loose circle, then elucidate his conclusions until one of them confessed, lured into Tad's trap by a bait-and-switch argument. But that only happened in fiction.

One time, his gaming group had had a lively debate on a meme Raj had seen postulating that Jessica Fletcher in *Murder, She Wrote* was probably the most successful and prolific serial killer the fictional world had ever seen, given how many times she "accidentally" stumbled over a murder victim and somehow managed to "discover" evidence that implicated someone else. The end result was the lot of them had agreed that would have made a kickass mind fuck of a series finale.

By virtue of his position as Gabrielle's admin, most of upper management had shared their online calendars with him to make meeting scheduling easier. He'd even been desperate enough to start checking back for dental appointments, although preparations for the memorial service had taken up most of his time.

Scrolling through calendars didn't seem like an activity that had much return on investment, but with one full event for Gautier under his belt Riley could dig into the mystery of the event invoices, a mystery he was moderately more capable of solving. Maybe.

He'd no sooner pulled out the files than Cody rolled up, looking the roughest Riley had ever seen him, although in Cody's case that still meant he was better-looking than 80 percent of the male population.

"Are you okay?"

Cody shrugged. "A little hungover. Yesterday was tougher than I thought."

"I'm so sorry." He really hoped Cody hadn't murdered Gabrielle. He was starting to like Cody. Dammit, he was starting to like all of the likely suspects, and it would pain him to find out any of them was a murderer.

"No help for it. Can you get me some coffee?"

"Caffeine today?" Cody had yet to ask for anything but decaf, but then, this was the first time Riley had seen him hungover.

"Ugh. No, I'd better not. I already drank a small cup of regular coffee on the way in."

It was probably an irrational fear, but Riley avoided the kitchenette off Gabrielle's office. Grabbing coffee from a shared carafe seemed safer than trusting anything that could have been tampered with in the kitchenette. There was something so incredibly malicious about poisoning, making Riley uncomfortably aware how vulnerable everyone was, every day.

Riley shook off his morbid musings as he poured Cody's coffee, then added double cream, double sugar. Friday mornings were supposed to be cheery and upbeat, only hours away from the weekend. Tad might randomly decide to drop by again. And then Sunday was gaming day.

He forced a smile and returned to Cody's office.

When he turned to leave, Cody stopped him. "Shut the door, would you? I want to talk to you about something."

Any other time and under any other circumstances, those words might make him wary, but as soon as Tad caught the killer, Riley was calling his agency to pull the plug on this contract. There was no way he wanted to continue on here after this. He was keeping Alisha, so he wouldn't be leaving anything or anyone important to him.

He did his best to radiate interest and unconcern as he waited for Cody to begin.

Riley did not expect him to reach into his desk drawer and pull out one of the Invigorate gift packs containing five different Invigorate products.

Cody held the gift pack and stared down at it. "Floriana came to me and made a *suggestion*."

"A suggestion made with a sledgehammer?"

That prompted a chuckle from Cody, who then groaned and pressed his fingers to his temples. "Yes, definitely a sledgehammer. Or maybe even C-4. But the thing is, I agree with her. The product is doing well, but the launch has definitely been tainted by the police and their murder investigation. Every review, every mention, ties Gabby's death to the product, keeping it fresh in the minds of our consumers, even if the media has moved on to more sensational news. She thinks, and I agree, that we need to rebrand and relaunch as soon as possible."

Riley relaxed fractionally. This meeting had nothing to do with his performance, and he hadn't been caught snooping by anyone. Even though he planned to shake Gautier off as soon as possible, he didn't welcome any tarnish to his thus far sterling reputation. "That makes sense, but when you say rebrand, surely you don't mean change the color scheme and images and bottle shapes, do you?" The cost to change already produced product would be staggering.

Cody grimaced. "I hope it doesn't come to that. I'm hoping a simple change of messaging, a different focus for targeted advertising, will be enough, but we're going to change the outer packaging as well and test it out on some focus groups."

"What can I do to help?" He didn't think Cody had kept him in here just to shoot the shit about future plans for Invigorate.

"I have a problem." Cody sighed. "You know how I always have decaf?"

"Sure. Although you said you had regular this morning."

"And I really shouldn't have. I had a severe reaction to caffeine not too long ago. First time Gabby introduced me to her kids, as a matter of fact, although they were under the impression they were meeting their new account manager from Treyhorn Associates."

Right. Riley remembered Alisha telling him Cody had been an up-and-comer who'd been given the Gautier account when the previous account manager had retired.

"Okay. What kind of reaction?"

"Arrhythmia. Bad enough they had to call 911 because they thought I was having a heart attack. So I have to avoid caffeine." He stared down at the packaging. "Normally I start all marketing campaigns by personally trying the product so I know what it is, what it does, and if there are any glaring issues that need to be minimized. The reports say caffeine absorption through the skin is far less than a cup of coffee, but in this case, I don't dare test this out myself."

Uh-oh. Riley knew damn well what was coming out of Cody's mouth next.

"Can you test it? Let me know what you like and what you don't? It would be a great help. Gabby mentioned a couple of times she liked that you used her products."

Gabrielle had been pleased when he'd told her, but he hadn't realized she'd retained that tidbit long enough to pass it on to anyone else. Riley picked up the gift set and turned it over in his hands, surreptitiously checking that the box ends were sealed. Then again, it was basically just moisturizing creams and soap. And if Cody were trying to kill him, there were less elaborate and simpler ways to do so.

"Yeah, I can do that."

"Thanks. I appreciate it." Cody smiled and shook his hand.

Riley's boss looked positively every shade of gray. "You should probably go home. Get some sleep."

"I'll be fine. Home is… too quiet right now, but I may take off early. Start the weekend sooner rather than later. You ought to leave too. Don't think I don't know that this has been hard for you too."

"Compared to what you and François and Floriana are going through, it's been nothing. I'm just glad I could help."

Riley slipped out of Cody's office and closed the door behind him. If Cody wasn't going to take the day off, Riley would at least make sure he wasn't disturbed, and maybe Cody would take advantage of the quiet to catch a couple of winks.

At his desk, Riley read the back of the gift set, which explained the purpose of each item and how best to use it. A quick snap of his wrist with the letter opener broke through the clear round seal on the box.

He pulled out the inner plastic container and frowned. First off, this particular style of presenting a gift set seemed rather old-fashioned. That might actually be Gabrielle's influence. But it made for a lot of unnecessary packaging, not all of it environmentally friendly, and created extra garbage.

After pulling out the notebook where he'd started jotting comparisons of the different event invoices, he flipped to a new page and started making notes.

The packaging of each individual product was, however, pleasing to the touch and had a nice heft to it. Just holding it almost felt decadent, and for top-level products like this, decadence was part of the experience.

Cheap plastic and readily visible seams didn't say what Gautier wanted. Changing the name or color scheme of the outer box might be helpful from a rebranding perspective, but he didn't think the bottles and jars should change. He even liked the abstract leaf shape of everything.

All the paper he touched every day and the lingering effects of Toronto's cold, dry winter meant his skin got dry. Also, he'd been washing his hands a little more obsessively since his first encounter with fingerprint powder. No time like the present.

There wasn't any hand cream in the gift box, so he chose the small tub of body cream, opened it, and sniffed. The cream had a fresh herb-and-mint scent that managed to smell invigorating. Since the added boost of caffeine was intended to be exactly that, Riley could only applaud Floriana's team. He added a quick note about choosing color schemes that would make the product more gender-neutral, because the scent wouldn't need to change to appeal to both men and women.

He scooped out a dollop and rubbed it well into his hands. It was smooth, creamy, and absorbed instantly. Riley smiled. This might be one of the easiest tasks he'd ever undertaken.

Another scent began to overtake the fresh herbal scent of Invigorate. Garlic? Who the hell would be eating something so garlicky first thing in the morning?

As he craned his head around, trying to find the source of the smell, one pointed memory came back. One that he had dismissed as absolutely nothing at the time. A few minutes before she died, Gabrielle had complained of the scent of garlic. And she'd probably retreated to her office because she'd started feeling badly, perhaps not knowing why. Not making the connection between her symptoms and her allergy, because why would she? It wasn't easy to accidentally come in contact with penicillin.

Riley's heart started racing and his mouth dried out. It could be fear, or it could be the onset of… something. Not penicillin, because he wasn't allergic, but the garlic scent was too specific to ignore. He ran for the executive bathroom, only a few feet away from his new desk, and furiously washed his hands, but the garlic odor didn't abate. Hands still damp, he rushed back to his desk.

With a shaking hand, he grabbed his phone and called Tad.

"Morning, Riley. We're actually on our way over—finally got one of the warrants we were waiting for."

"I think I've been poisoned," Riley whispered into the phone.

"What? Are you at work? I'm on my way. What are your symptoms?"

His eyes started burning. He didn't want to die. "Only the smell of garlic. So far." He thought. He wasn't sure if the other symptoms were incipient panic.

"Garlic? I... don't understand."

Tad's voice got quieter, and Riley assumed he'd turned away or covered his phone with his hand. "Emma, get Medical over to Gautier Cosmetics. Possible poison.

"Okay, Riley. Tell me what's going on. Why is garlic important?"

"I don't know." Riley almost wailed, but he didn't want Cody to hear him. Cody had given him the cream. "But Cody asked me to test out a new cream, and as soon as I did, I started to smell garlic, and then I remembered that was the last thing Gabrielle said before she left the party. The caterers had used too much garlic."

"Fuck, fuck, fuck. And you're definitely not allergic to penicillin."

Riley wondered if that meant Tad didn't know what he'd been poisoned with either. Tad had told him the coroner suspected Gabrielle hadn't ingested the penicillin, it was likely a contact issue, but maybe the penicillin had been incidental and whatever was causing the garlic smell was the true murder weapon.

"Tad, I'm scared."

"Hey, hey. I'm here, Riley. I'm here. I'll stay on the line. We're almost there. Don't do anything."

Riley waited, letting Tad's comforting tone wash over him, although he couldn't focus enough to listen.

After what seemed like an eternity, feet pounded right to him. He had a moment to be thankful he'd already told Tad about his move in location, because otherwise Tad might have had to look for him.

Tad crouched in front of him, face pale, and grabbed for his hands, but Riley pulled them back. "It had to be in the lotion."

"Are you sure?" Tad narrowed his eyes, taking in the array of small bottles on the desk, including the open jar. Emma snapped on a pair of gloves and started bagging bottles into evidence bags.

"Sure." Was a heart supposed to beat this fast? "Running late this morning. Bought a latte from my regular place. But that's it."

"We're going to wash your hands while we wait for the EMTs. They were only a few minutes behind."

Riley didn't bother to say what they were both thinking. Without knowing what poison he'd been given, the hope of getting correct treatment wasn't good. Tad pulled a pair of gloves out of his pocket and put them on. "If nothing else, we can minimize contaminating anyone else."

"I already did that," Riley rasped. "But... the executive bathroom. I touched things in there."

Tad pulled out another pair of gloves and helped Riley slip them on.

"We'll make sure no one goes in there." Emma nodded, apparently half listening to him and half listening to a radio, before saying something into it that Riley didn't have the energy to try to decipher.

Tad squeezed Riley's gloved hand in his. It wasn't the same as skin to skin, but the heat and strength in Tad's grip was enough for him to cling to for now. "And you said Cody gave this to you?"

Riley nodded, afraid if he spoke he'd throw up.

"Where is he now?"

Riley pointed to the office. Tad's expression darkened, and he stood and slammed the door open. Cody squawked as Tad dragged him out. Cody's eyes were heavy and his hair was in disarray.

"What the fuck did you give him?"

Cody flicked his gaze nervously between Tad and Riley. "I don't understand."

"What. Did. You. Put. In. The. Cream." Tad shoved Cody up against the wall, his voice modulated and harsh but not loud. Riley had never seen Tad angry and intimidating. He was good at it, and Riley would be fucking impressed if it didn't feel like his heart was going to explode.

"What are you talking about?"

Riley almost let out a nervous burst of laughter. Tad might have actually woken Cody up. He couldn't believe Cody would do that to him.

"What poison did you put in that cream?" Tad pointed at the desk, and Cody paled.

"Nothing, I swear. Riley, are you okay?" Cody tried to approach, but Tad still had ahold of his shirt.

"No," Riley whispered. "I don't think I am."

"Cody Rosenberg, you're under arrest for attempted murder."

Cody's face whitened even further, stark against his crimson dress shirt. "No! I didn't. I swear. Floriana gave me the cream. I was the one who was supposed to test this. Not Riley. Whatever is going on, it was supposed to be me." He sagged in Tad's grip and turned pleading eyes on Riley. "I'm so fucking sorry."

"Riley, can you verify that?" Tad snapped.

"He said it was her idea to rebrand. I don't know if she brought the cream, but I wasn't at my desk much yesterday." It was believable, though. Riley might have done some gentle poking and prodding, but Cody was the one who'd thrown a wrench in the whole inheritance machine. If Cody wasn't the murderer, it was perfectly reasonable that the poison had indeed been meant for him.

Four uniformed officers headed in at a run.

Detective Wilson instructed one uniformed officer to guard the bathroom and not to let anyone touch anything. Tad told two others to bring Floriana Gautier in for questioning. Cody offered his access card, and they pounded toward the lab.

"Let me send that cream to the lab."

"Oh, I don't think so," Tad growled. "That's evidence."

Cody wrenched himself out of Tad's grip. "And if you want to save Riley's life, you'll let me help. We're almost standing in a world-class laboratory, with topflight chemists. You're a fool if you don't take advantage of that. How long will you wait for a criminal lab to do the work?"

"Where the fuck are the EMTs?" Tad huffed, but he turned to look at Detective Wilson, who gave him a quick nod. "Make the call, Cody."

Cody lunged for Riley's phone, but Tad put his arm out, fast, like a striking snake, preventing Cody from touching the phone. He handed Cody a pair of gloves. "Just in case. And put the phone on speaker."

Looking utterly freaked, Cody nodded and dialed an internal extension.

"Trix Henderson speaking."

"Trix, it's Cody. I need you up at my office immediately. Bring a sterile sample bottle."

"Be right there."

"It's an emergency. Run." Trix let out a little gasp, and there was a clatter before the line disconnected.

Tad moved back to Riley and grasped his hands again. "Try to breathe, slow and deep and even."

Riley tried to mimic Tad, hoping to slow his racing heart and counteract the light-headedness, but so far to no avail.

His sense of time was all messed up, because before he knew it, Trix was there, snapping on a pair of her own gloves.

"Riley, what's going on?"

A pair of EMTs showed up before anyone could answer her, with Alisha behind them.

That was enough to garner the attention of the entire office. Tad barked a command for everyone to stay back.

"Riley, oh my God, Riley, what happened?" Alisha sounded distraught, but the EMTs were already checking him out, and he didn't have the strength to reassure her.

EMT Number One, a large black man, squatted in front of him as Tad moved out of the way, glancing curiously at his gloved hands. "It's fine. You're going to be fine. But I need to know what you took."

Tad spoke up before Riley could. "Contact poison in hand cream. We don't know what it is."

Riley didn't need anyone to interpret the look in EMT Number One's eyes. "Symptoms?"

Tad stepped in again and even mentioned the garlic scent, but it was obvious that no light bulb was pinging for the EMTs. EMT Number Two, a slender auburn-haired woman, was on her radio, asking someone to run a check on the symptoms.

"Did you say garlic?" Trix asked. Everyone turned their attention to her.

"Yes." Tad spat out the word.

"Oh shit."

"What is it?"

Trix waved a hand. "It's not a poison itself. It's a way to allow a chemical to cross the dermal layer. Called DMSO. Dimethyl sulfoxide. There's a possibility of using it for cancer drugs, and we tested with it initially for this product, but aside from a few other issues, we couldn't get around the garlic scent as a side effect. The DMSO is probably acting as a way to get whatever it is into his bloodstream faster."

"Then what was he poisoned with?" Tad sounded more desperate than Riley would have thought, but at least he was no longer expected to talk.

"I don't know."

Cody stepped in. "Can you test it now? Fast?"

Trix looked unsure, but her voice was steady when she replied. "I'll do my best."

She opened a specimen bottle and stepped toward the small pile of evidence bags on Riley's desk, but Detective Wilson stopped her. The detective opened the bag with the body cream, took the specimen bottle from Trix, and poured about half of the cream inside. She then returned the original packaging and cream to the evidence bag and handed the specimen bottle to Trix.

Detective Wilson pointed at the remaining uniformed officer. "Go with her. Report to me as soon as you know anything." The officer nodded, and the two of them disappeared.

EMT Number One held Riley's gaze. "Until we know exactly what to treat, we're going to focus on symptoms as we get you to the hospital. Right now, the most aggressive issues are cardiac-related, so we're going to deal with those first." He readied a syringe. "I've got something here to help you relax."

In seconds, chemicals forced a relaxation on Riley, despite an awareness that his symptoms had not abated.

A third EMT rattled up with a gurney, and during the process of lifting Riley onto it, blackness overcame him.

Chapter ELEVEN

RILEY BLINKED awake. Everything was stiff, sore, and his mouth was as dry as British humor. His eyes slowly focused, hospital monitors coming into view.

Another few moments and he remembered being poisoned. He tried to sit up but groaned as his head swam.

"Hey. It's okay. Relax." Tad leaned over him with a tender smile and this time held his hand while neither of them was wearing gloves.

"Tadeo?" Wait. He wasn't supposed to use Tad's full name for some reason. Judging from Tad's smile, he didn't seem to mind. "Are you really here?"

"Yes, I am."

"Can I have some water?"

Tad grabbed a cup with a bendy straw. "Here. Drink slowly, just in case."

The cool water flowed like a miracle across his parched tongue.

"Am I okay? What time is it?" It had been a few minutes after nine when he'd called Tad. He had no idea how long he'd been out. Tad looked tired; maybe he'd been working late. Or maybe Riley just hadn't noticed details like that while he was in the middle of being poisoned.

"You're fine. Now, anyway. Trix was able to figure out pretty fast that the amount of caffeine in the cream was well above safe levels, and mixed in with that chemical, DMSO, to increase its absorption. Once they knew what to look for, our lab was able to confirm. Which makes a lot of sense, since we'd already determined that Gabrielle hadn't ingested the penicillin."

"But I'm fine now?"

Tad pressed his lips together and glanced away, but his grip on Riley's hand tightened. "It was touch and go for a while. It's Saturday afternoon and they just moved you out of Intensive Care."

Saturday afternoon? He'd lost more than a whole day. He didn't know what to think about that. Nor did he know why Tad was at his bedside, but he wasn't going to knock it.

"What happened after I passed out?"

The grim smile Tad wore promised retribution, but somehow Riley knew Tad meant to protect him from anything bad. How he knew that, he had no idea.

"We arrested Floriana for murder and attempted murder."

"Oh my God. I can't believe she was behind it all. All for a stake in her mother's company. I guess Cody's secret marriage was the reason Cody was a target."

Tad nodded. "Looks like. She's not talking, and her lawyer will probably have her out on bail by tomorrow, but yeah. That's what we think."

Imagine having all that expertise in chemistry and using it to kill. She was such an angry woman, but Riley never would have imagined her grief was false. Showed what he knew about murderers.

It was a relief, though, knowing it was all over.

Tad stroked the hair away from Riley's face. "So, you called me Tadeo when you woke up."

Under the unflinching fluorescent hospital lighting, there was no hiding his blush. Tad smiled widely and cupped Riley's face. "I knew you remembered me."

"How could I forget…." Riley sat up. "Wait. What do you mean, you knew I remembered you? I… you… you mean you remember me?" Riley's voice cracked as incredulity sent his voice into an unaccustomed high register.

"Yeah. I do. Nosy Parker, alive and well."

Riley swatted Tad away, but he just grabbed Riley's hand instead, holding it tight, but like a lover, not like a cop restraining a suspect.

"Fucking hell. How? When? You never even knew I was alive in high school."

Some of Tad's mirth disappeared, replaced by an intense stare. "I knew you were alive. I was so fucking impressed by the way you never hid, never lied about who you were. True, I didn't know who you were until that last year. And maybe if Lisa hadn't hurt herself, had been able to continue on as head cheerleader senior year, maybe I wouldn't have known. But when she needed another extracurricular activity for university and dragged all of us into the drama department, well, I think we all sort of realized we were invading your turf. And you never backed down. Never let us push the hard-core drama people out. Never let anyone intimidate you."

Riley frowned. "And you never stopped your friends from trying to intimidate me."

"I will regret that for as long as I live. I wasn't as brave as you were in high school. If I were, I would have admitted then what I didn't until I got to university."

"Admit what?" Riley asked, a dark suspicion blooming in his chest.

"Obviously that I'm gay too. But back then, I was also in awe of you. Maybe even crushing a little."

"Shut up! You did not." Just hearing those words made Riley soften.

"Did too." Tad moved in closer, lowered his voice intimately. "They took out your contacts. I much prefer this color to the blue. Your eyes have always reminded me of river rocks in the spring. Greenish gray and vibrant as hell. I mean, I guess you chose the contacts over glasses, and I can understand that, but that boring blue? Why that?" He brushed his hand through Riley's hair. "And why the bottle-blonding?"

It wasn't exactly fair for Tad to ask him such uncomfortable questions while he was trapped in the hospital, also not looking his best.

"I wanted a makeover after high school. I hated being bullied, so with a friend's help, I remade myself into a twink. Everyone liked the blond-haired, blue-eyed boys. I wanted to be someone people liked."

Tad looked pained. "I am so fucking sorry I never stood up for you. Because I liked you. I still do." Tad stroked a finger along Riley's jaw. "I lo… I like you a lot."

Tad's words were killing him dead, right there in the hospital. His feelings for Tad ran much deeper than like, and it sounded as though Tad reciprocated. But Riley could understand being afraid. He'd been afraid too, back in the day. If Tad had actively bullied him, Riley didn't think he'd be attracted to him now and didn't know if he'd be able to forgive him. Neutral wasn't great, but for just about everyone Riley had come across since, high school had been a trial by fire. No one escaped unscathed. And if Riley had scars, so did Tad.

"Thank you for that." A sincere apology was better than he could have hoped for. "I still don't understand why you didn't say anything that first day. I…." So embarrassing to say, and yet, Tad had been the trailblazer this time. "I had a crush on you in high school, and seeing you again flustered me. Enormously. I was afraid my stupid reaction would get me arrested."

He wasn't ready to admit to deeper feelings either. Not yet.

"Oh. Er." Tad glanced around, and this time the pink was in his cheeks. "So, that first day, I knew you looked familiar. And I'm a detective and all. I was able to recognize straight off you were wearing colored contacts and dyed your hair. But I couldn't place you."

"You couldn't place me? I told you my name."

The ruddiness in Tad's cheeks intensified. "Uh, well, I'm not entirely sure I even knew your first name was Riley. Everyone always called you Parker. Or, well, Nosy Parker."

Riley rolled his eyes.

Now here he was, in a hospital gown, messy, unshowered, and in desperate need of a toothbrush, having a discussion about mutual admiration with his high school crush. After seeing each other naked, it shouldn't be so awkward, but maybe it was because they were both avoiding the truth about their feelings.

"Uh. Do you know when I can leave? And have a shower?"

Tad smiled. "Soon, I think. The general consensus seemed to be once you were transferred out of Intensive Care, you'd be going home in short order."

The curtain around Riley's bed fluttered, and Riley's brother appeared at the foot. Tad slipped his hand out of Riley's and shifted his chair back slightly.

"What are you doing here, Jonathan?"

"What am I doing here? You were poisoned, for fuck's sake. I'm your brother. Why wouldn't I be here?"

Riley didn't quite know how to respond to that. It had been literally years since he'd laid eyes on his brother.

Jonathan came to the other side of his bed. "How are you feeling? The doctors said I could take you home with me in an hour or so."

"Home with you? Are you crazy?"

Riley could see Tad trying to figure out what was going on, but he didn't have the energy to throw him an assist. Not with Jonathan showing up and pretending they were some sort of happy family that did things like spend time with each other.

"Why would you say such a thing? You'll probably need some help for a day or so."

"And you're the one who'd help?" Riley snorted out a bitter laugh. "Did you run this plan by Meredith yet?"

"No, but I know she'd feel the same."

"Right. This is the same woman who's done her best to carve me out of your life."

Just like that, Jonathan's affable expression turned to exasperation. "Not this again, Riley. Grow up. My wife doesn't hate you."

"Whatever. I'm not going home with you either way, but maybe you just ought to check Meredith's reaction. For shits and giggles."

"Riley, you're being ridiculous."

"I don't even know who would have called you."

"I'm your emergency contact."

"Oh. Sorry about that. I'll make sure I change it."

Those words acted like a slap in Jonathan's face, although Riley didn't know if even a physical slap would make his brother wake up. "I can't believe you feel that way."

The last thing he needed on top of being poisoned was family drama. It was far too exhausting. He slumped back on the bed, the head of which had miraculously been maneuvered upward, so he didn't have far to go. Had to have been Tad's handiwork.

"Just go, Jonathan. You can tell yourself you did your duty. It's fine. I'll be fine."

His brother looked like a perfect cross between a kicked puppy and a person witnessing a puppy being kicked, but he turned on his heel and left.

"Wasn't that a little harsh?"

"Didn't I tell you about my brother?"

"No. I mean, you told me you had one and you weren't close, but he was trying."

"Pfft. Trying because I nearly died. It has literally been years since I've seen him. There's always some excuse. His wife lied to keep me away from his fortieth birthday party, which was the weekend before I met you. Do you know where he lives? Close to Sunnybrook Hospital. If I were inclined for a hike, I could walk to his place, and I don't think he knows where I live."

Tad frowned. "Wait. Years? What about Christmas?"

"Last year Meredith insisted on spending it in the Maldives. Which I couldn't afford. The year before was Portugal. Also too expensive."

Tad picked up Riley's hand again. "I'm so sorry."

Whatever. He'd just as soon sit here and wallow in the knowledge Tad was gay and holding his hand. It was like he was a teenager all over again, although he'd much rather explore some of these feelings while naked together in bed. Because they were grown-ups, and whether Tad liked it or not, they were already in a relationship. Revealing it to their friends and family was all that remained.

With a gentle hand, Tad brushed his fingers along Riley's. "Alisha and your friend Shaun have been haunting the place."

More than his brother, he'd wager. "Yeah? I'd like to see them."

"They actually just went down to the cafeteria. They'll be back soon. Cody also came by, but the doctors were still working on you. He feels pretty bad about what happened."

Riley shrugged. "I'm not gonna lie. It sucked." And it was fucking weird to spend an hour or so at work Friday morning and then lose several hours, the intervening time a giant blank. "But if he'd actually been the one to use that cream, he'd probably be dead. The whole reason he didn't test it out was because he'd had a bad reaction to caffeine."

One that Floriana had probably been relying on.

"More susceptible. Yeah, I can see that. Because it's unlikely they could cram a fatal dose of caffeine for a typically healthy person into lotion. The only reason you had such a bad reaction was the addition of your allergy meds, particularly the decongestant, and the huge amount of caffeine already in your system."

"And he wouldn't have known what the garlic meant, so we'd probably have called 911 too late, and they wouldn't have known what the issue was anyway."

Now that he thought about it, it gave him a warm fuzzy feeling. He'd saved Cody's life. Maybe not intentionally, but he had, and it was because he'd pieced together different bits of information. Maybe there was something to this detecting thing after all, and he didn't completely suck at it.

Tad heaved out a sigh. "I need to get going. But I'm so glad you're okay."

"Wait, when can we meet up again?" What he really wanted was for Tad to crawl into the bed with him and hold him close, but he'd settle for some alone time once he got out of the hospital.

That expression. Oh fuck, Riley knew that expression, even if it was filled with more remorse than the last time he'd gotten dumped. So much for Tad's stupid "admiration" speech.

"I can't." Tad rubbed his thumb along Riley's jaw.

"Yeah. Of course. I get it. All those times we hung. Just for work, right?" He shouldn't be mad. They'd agreed to no-strings sex, and super temporary. But he didn't want it to end, and he wanted a string or three.

"No, Christ, no." Tad's vehemence made him blink. "That was me skirting the edge of ethics and risking tanking the case because I wanted you. Wanted to spend time with you. Find out if and how you'd changed. Besides the eyes and hair and height." Tad gave him a sad little smile.

"And what? You didn't like how I'd changed?" This was a little more direct than most times he'd been dumped, and it hurt worse. Did the truth hurt, or was it because he was already more invested in Tad than he'd been with any other man, however dangerous that was to his emotional well-being?

Tad huffed. "You're still as prickly as ever, but fuck, I like that about you. Except when I'm trying to explain something to you."

Riley crossed his arms over his chest. "So talk."

"I loved spending time with you." His eyes darkened as they did right before he kissed Riley. "And the sex was spectacular, but so far over the fucking line it's not funny. As long as no one knows about the sex, I could explain our time as me getting information from a confidential informant should the powers that be ask. Yes, you're a witness, but you weren't a suspect. Regardless, now that we've made an arrest, I can't see you. Not until the case is over. Otherwise we risk compromising the conviction. And this is going to go to trial—Floriana isn't accepting any deals."

"Couldn't we wait until the trial is over?" Prickly or not, Riley didn't want to lose Tad, not when he was so damned close to having him. Damn the consequences.

"We could, but it might be years, especially if there are appeals."

It was like the light had drained out of the room, leaving only gray fog. The universe couldn't be so unfair.

"Then I guess you'd better go." Riley wanted to latch on, yell at him to stay, but maybe it was better now, before they got even more attached. However much it hurt.

Tad nodded and then leaned over, capturing Riley's lips in a sweet kiss. Firm, possessive, and so fucking hot Riley might spontaneously combust. And then, in a flash, it was over. Tad's eyes looked wet and anguished, and Riley's burned with unshed tears.

"Goodbye."

"Yeah." Riley wanted to tell him to have a good life but couldn't figure out how to say it without sounding like a douche.

Then Tad was gone, taking all the hope and promise with him. Riley let out a sob and curled into a ball, trying not to cry for a future that would never be.

WHEN HE was all cried out, Alisha was gently rubbing his back while Shaun paced nervously at the foot of the bed.

"Oh. Hi. Sorry about that. Guess I'm just emotional. Must be the drugs." If they were any sort of friends at all, they'd take that explanation at face value.

"Sure, sure. You almost died, Riley." Alisha sniffed. "You're entitled to feel however you want."

Shaun turned back and smiled. He wasn't any better with comforting people than Riley, but Riley could see the last few days had been difficult on him too.

"That's a bit of an exaggeration, isn't it?" He probably wouldn't be chugging any more dirty lattes any time soon, but it hadn't sounded too dire after the fact. No matter how fucking scared he'd been at the time.

Alisha glared. "Come on. Shaun grabbed some clothes for you. Once you get changed, you can get going."

The two of them helped him out of bed, and Alisha squeezed him near to death with a hug. Riley almost started crying again, but his head was already throbbing from the last bout. In a shocking move that nearly finished him off, Shaun hugged him tight when Alisha let go. Riley hugged him back. This man had been his best friend for over ten years. It was about time they did more of this.

Shaun gave him a wet, smacking kiss on the cheek. "Never again. Understand? No more of this almost dying shit. Got it?"

Riley smiled. "Got it."

It took longer than he'd have liked, but eventually he ended up at home, Shaun sacking out on the couch just in case he needed something.

The next morning Shaun shook him awake far too early. "What's up?"

"I need you to get up and moving around. Resettled on the couch."

"The fuck why?"

"Because then you can tell me if I need to call out of work today."

For that consideration, Riley could maybe forgive being woken up at what-the-fuck o'clock. "I'll be fine. Go to work."

"Nope. I need you up and mostly coherent before I'm leaving you alone."

An hour later Riley was on the couch, wrapped in blankets in front of the television, toast and fruit nestled beside him in easy reach.

Five hours later Riley was losing his mind from boredom. Or at least that's what he told himself. Every single show he flipped to reminded him of Tad. His bed was too empty, his kitchen too quiet. Even the wretched couch was made of memories that were too fresh, the wounds too gaping. He wasn't sure if the scent of Tad's cologne lingered in the air or if it had simply infected his mind. No promises had been made, no feelings explored, only shared experiences built on trading information in a murder investigation and some mind-blowing sex. And yet he mourned this loss more than any other romantic entanglement. It wasn't fucking fair.

MONDAY AFTERNOON on the King streetcar was a very different crowd. Also much sparser, aside from a strange abundance of baby strollers. Riley didn't know if this was the regular state of affairs or a one-off. Shaun had called him in sick to Gautier and let his agency know at least some of what had happened. Gautier was under the impression that Riley was going to return and finish out his contract.

He hadn't told anyone otherwise, but he was done. Done. He had a few things he wanted from his desk, though, and he'd left a jacket he'd rather not lose. When the boredom set in, he got dressed and shuffled out to the transit stop. A quick in and out to grab his stuff; then he'd let his agency know to cancel his contract.

Floriana. What a great fucking actress. They'd commiserated together about losing their mothers, and all the while she'd been planning how to take out her new stepdad. Riley wondered if she even cared that he'd been the one to almost die, or if she was only upset she'd failed to kill Cody. If Aaron truly had been having an affair with her, Riley wanted to let him know he'd dodged a bullet—like the kind they used to take down elephants. A woman who knocked off her own mother wouldn't hesitate to see murder as a convenient solution to an inconvenient husband.

Since he'd woken up, he'd tried not to think about Floriana and how her role as a murderer fit so poorly into his worldview. He tried to pretend his near-death experience hadn't shaken him up. Maybe going into Gautier to get his stuff wasn't smart. Alisha would be happy to box up his stuff and bring it to him, but as wobbly as he was, he also felt he needed this. One last time into the jaws of the demon, just to prove he had the guts. He wasn't running scared with his tail between his legs, or at least, not that anyone else could see.

If he didn't do it now, he'd never do it, and that knowledge would fester like a pocket of gangrene under his skin. But he could no longer block out thoughts of Floriana.

Then he remembered. Tad hadn't actually told him why they'd arrested Floriana. They must have had some other evidence besides Cody's assertion that Floriana had given him the poisoned cream.

After taking out his phone, he absently stroked it. Tad had said no contact, but Riley wouldn't be able to rest until he knew. Hearing Tad's voice might make him break down and beg, which wouldn't do either of them any good. Nor did he want his fellow commuters to hear him being pathetic. Texting would have to do.

You never said—maybe you can't. What prompted Floriana's arrest? Did you find evidence?

A reply came quickly. *Your poisoning and Cody's statement were enough to get a warrant to search Floriana's house. The penicillin was right there. In her medicine cabinet. Hidden at the back, but it was there.*

Riley straightened up in his seat. Not possible.

What? Are you sure? The medicine cabinet in her bedroom?

He waited for a reply, but nothing came before his stop, so he pocketed his phone. It was unclear if Tad was just busy or if he thought he'd already provided more than enough information to a guy who had no right to it.

With all the energy and speed of a ninety-year-old with severe arthritis, Riley stumbled off the streetcar and walked the block to Gautier, an empty backpack hanging limply from his shoulder. A wild spring wind whipped through the streets, swirling old leaves and garbage finally released from the last of winter's grip. Grit hit his face, and he covered his eyes with his arm as he battled into the building. His access card got him past security, and as he waited for the elevator, the brassy reflection showed his pallor and the tumbleweed currently masquerading as his hair.

No, he hadn't thought this plan out well at all.

His phone buzzed. Tad had replied, but with a photo. A photo of a prescription bottle sitting on a shelf. With other prescription bottles. With Floriana's name on them. There were only two things wrong. One, that bottle had definitely not been there when he'd rummaged through the cabinet the day of the funeral—he'd looked at every one. Two, the "smoking gun" had a label with different colors than all the other prescription bottles—it came from a different pharmacy, Rexall.

The elevator doors opened and Riley got in, still staring at the image. Zooming in confirmed the penicillin not only came from a different pharmacy, but it was one closer to the office than it was to Floriana's house. There was a Shoppers Drug Mart location closer to the office than the Rexall was, so hitting the Rexall for the sake of expedience didn't make sense. If Floriana needed a prescription desperately, it would make more sense for her to stick with a Shoppers Drug Mart, which would have all her insurance information. It didn't make any sense for Floriana to go to a different pharmacy for penicillin.

He tapped out another text to Tad.

Something's wrong. I looked through that medicine cabinet after the memorial service. NO PENICILLIN. Filled at different pharmacy. Proof = my fingerprints on ALL other bottles.

That last bit might convince Tad, but in retrospect it maybe demonstrated he hadn't properly thought out his supersleuthing. What if he'd made himself look guilty by touching the wrong thing? Like if that pill bottle *had* been there on Thursday, he could have been in deep, deep, Marianas-Trench-deep shit.

???

Great. That was a helpful reply. And here he was at the damned office again, with a potential murderer. The only thing he knew was that Floriana *probably* hadn't killed her mother and *probably* hadn't had anything to do with Riley being poisoned, whether she was a scientist or not. A frisson of fear twisted his stomach. He was going to be here thirty minutes, tops. Nothing was going to happen.

The elevator doors opened, and he hung back a moment, seriously considering just going back home and forgetting all about proving something to himself. No one was going to be impressed.

Nothing is going to happen. That was his new mantra of hope going out to the universe. He wasn't even going to need thirty minutes. Ten, maybe.

He stepped out, and Alisha immediately squealed, rushing him with her arms open. "What are you doing here? How do you feel?"

Riley let himself get enveloped by her hug. "I feel okay, thanks. And I'm just here to pick up my stuff."

Alisha stepped back and frowned. "You're not staying?"

His laugh was bitter. "Would you?"

"Fine. I guess I wouldn't. But... but...."

Riley smiled. "I'm not leaving you behind. I'm probably going to take this week to rest, but if you're up for it, come to game night on Sunday. It'll be fun." Partly because they hadn't had a girl there in ages—not since Holly got married and moved to Niagara Falls—but mostly because he thought Alisha would fit in and have a good time.

Her eyes shone with tears. "It's a date, Riley. No backing out—you're stuck with me."

"I'm okay with that." Riley's eyes burned just a bit. "I'm heading in. I'll be back in a few minutes."

Making the conscious choice to take the path past Gabrielle's office, he arrived at his desk without anyone actually noticing he was there. Cody's door was shut, and Riley didn't know if he was trying to keep Gautier hobbling along after Floriana's arrest or if he'd taken a much-needed mental health day.

He scooped out his lockbox but opened it and dumped out the contents, just in case. There wasn't anything from this place he wanted to put in his mouth. His Star Wars Pop! figures went into his bag. It took all of about two minutes.

If Floriana wasn't the murderer, did that mean Cody was still in danger? The question was so absorbing, he didn't realize he'd started walking toward Mary's desk.

"Riley, oh you poor dear." Mary leaped out of her chair and bustled around her desk to give him a warm, motherly hug. Okay, he might miss Mary just a bit. "How are you feeling?" She peered at his face and tapped his cheek with her palm.

"I'm fine, Mary. Just need some more sleep."

She clucked her tongue. "Make sure you eat too. You're too thin."

Ha. Not hardly. But he did have a tendency to avoid food when stressed, unlike many other people he knew. "I will, Mary, I promise."

Be easier if he had a boyfriend to lean on, but at least he had good friends.

"Since you're here, let me ask you a question?"

"Sure, Mary." Did she even have a clue this would be the last time she'd see Riley? He didn't much feel like enlightening her, though.

"Do you know of a good dry cleaner around here?"

Since she'd dropped a handful of plastic-sheeted shirts when she'd seen him, he had to assume she knew of at least one.

"Which one is that?" Riley didn't wait for her to respond; he just reached out and smoothed the receipt stapled to the front of the stack. "Sorry. This is the one I use. Never had a reason to find another one. What's wrong?"

She let out a great gusty sigh. "They just delivered Mr. François's shirts, and this one…." She grabbed one of the shirts and shifted it to display the arm. "See? This yellow grease stain? I specifically told them it needed to be taken care of, and you can see it looks almost untouched."

The air around him got suddenly thin, like he'd been rocketed to the top of Kilimanjaro. He had a grease stain that looked almost exactly the same, on the cuff of the shirt he'd been wearing when he'd found the penicillin-spiked tea container in his desk drawer. The same one he chose not to pull out for fear of completely ruining the shirt with grease stains.

His breath got shallow and his heartbeat galumphed. The last thing he needed was to panic—he'd already had enough cardiac incidents for one lifetime—but he couldn't help it. The coincidence was too much. Too much.

"Hey, Mary, did François recently have a dental procedure or surgery maybe?"

"Oh, no. That Mr. François. He keeps postponing his root canal. I keep telling him it's nothing to be scared of. I think we rescheduled it for next month." She shook her head, exasperated, and completely oblivious to the fact that Riley was just about ready to pass out. Or scream. It had never occurred to him to check everyone's calendar for future dental appointments.

"What does that have to do with the dry cleaning?"

"I have to go, Mary, thanks."

Adrenaline in his system demanded he run, and run as fast as he could. Somehow he kept his exit to a controlled fast walk.

"Call me later, Riley," Alisha said as he passed the reception desk.

He waved a hand at her but didn't stop. Too jittery to even wait for the elevator, he slammed open the door to the stairs and started down. Everything in him demanded *out, out, out, fast as you can.*

Running down fifteen flights of stairs wasn't nearly as physically demanding as going up them, but it was enough to burn off some of the adrenaline, enough to smooth out some of the shaking. He burst out into the windy gray day and walked to the side of the building, then slipped into the alleyway there. Backing away from the street might be silly, because no one had followed him.

His fingers trembled as he initiated a call to Tad. And got his voicemail. No, this was too important to leave on voicemail—people never checked the damn thing right away. And his fingers weren't going to work well enough to text it all out. He tried again. Then a third time. The fourth attempt connected.

"Detective Tad Martin." There was a trace of exasperation in his tone, but Riley ignored it.

"It's not Floriana. It's François."

"Riley, is that you? Where are you?"

"At Gautier. But you're wrong. About Floriana. It was never Floriana."

Something heavy slammed into him from behind, and he fell to his knees, phone skittering away. "Tad," he yelled before he twisted around to face his attacker.

Stupidly, he hadn't bothered paying attention to the other end of the alley.

Rage twisted François's face, and he brandished his briefcase in a threatening manner. Riley had a moment to be thankful they didn't work at a baseball-bat factory as he scrambled away from the next blow.

However ludicrous trying to beat him to death with a briefcase was, François had already committed murder once and tried for a second one. He wasn't to be dismissed, and he was desperate.

François loomed over him, and Riley managed to get to his feet and run for the street. A cracking sound informed him of his phone's demise, but all he needed was the street, and people. A taxi.

The briefcase came low and hard, getting tangled in his feet. Riley went down, hitting his head.

He rolled over, vision swimming, feeling like he was trapped on a tugboat on the lake. "Help! Help!"

He tried to block François, who was attempting to wrap his hands around Riley's neck.

"Help me," he tried again, but it wasn't as loud this time. He was going to die in this alley, strangled by an asshole accountant.

Weakened by one poisoning attempt and the knock on his head, he didn't have the strength to get the upper hand with a man who outweighed him by at least thirty pounds.

He scrabbled at François's fingers, digging in his nails, trying to loosen his grip, but it was a losing battle. His vision blackened at the edges. He had another second or two.

"Hands up!"

Everything held still for a moment, hanging in limbo. Then a dark blur moved over him. François jerked, his hands opened, and he went down, Tad on top of him.

Riley sucked in great heaving breaths and twisted his head around. Detective Wilson held a gun in the direction of Tad and François, but François was no challenge for a trained police detective, and he was already facedown on the ground, cuffed.

Sirens blared, getting closer, and Riley tried to haul himself up, but he couldn't manage more than a bleat of distress. Detective Wilson moved closer to François while Tad gathered Riley into his arms and rocked him while Riley clung to him and cried.

"It's okay, it's okay," Tad whispered into his hair.

Riley had never been so scared, not even when he'd been poisoned. He'd thought he was brave for standing up to bullies, but those had only been bruises. He'd never had anyone want him dead before. Brave he wasn't.

Then EMTs pried him from Tad's arms, and in the ensuing medical attention, he lost track of Tad.

ANOTHER DAY, another hospital room. This time the drugs were a bit better. His throat and head were still painful, but the pain was muted, buried.

The curtain rustled and Jonathan appeared, looking wan, worried, and ruffled. Riley stifled a groan. It hadn't even been a week since his last hospital visit—he hadn't had time to change his emergency contact information.

"Riley." His tone was conciliatory, but Riley wasn't buying.

"What?"

"I'm worried about you. This... I don't want to lose you."

If he died, Jonathan's life wouldn't materially change. Sure, he'd miss the occasional phone call, but before long, Jonathan wouldn't even notice the lack.

"You're the only family I have left. I want to make a point of making more time for you. For us to spend together."

Riley would believe it when he saw it, but he could at least believe his brother believed what he said. In no time at all, they'd be back to brief phone calls on birthdays and holidays, and all plans to get together would keep getting postponed.

"Fine. We can try." He was a lying liar. He was all out of trying. If his brother was serious about this, he was going to have to do more than meet Riley halfway.

The deep discomfort on Jonathan's face didn't fade.

"I'm so sorry I didn't listen to you."

Riley frowned in confusion. His brother didn't apologize. Not since that fateful day when he'd had to break the news about their parents. "What?"

Jonathan scrubbed his hands over his face, mussing up his hair. "You were right. Merry admitted she'd lied, and more than once, to keep us apart. And I'm so fucking sorry, Riley."

Holy shit. He'd never expected those words in a million years.

"We're going to... take a break, spend some time apart."

"I'm sorry, Jonathan."

"No." His brother practically glared. "This is not on you, this is on me. Things will be different from now on, whether or not my marriage survives. I was blind and I... want you and I to rebuild, if we can."

"I think we can do that." Riley didn't know if he had blind faith ready for his brother, but he'd be willing to see how it went. He hadn't wanted to cut ties.

"Good." Jonathan smiled and patted his arm.

"Excuse me." Tad's voice was stern. "We'll need to ask Riley some questions."

Jonathan looked slightly startled, but he acquiesced, and in the blink of an eye, Tad stood at the foot of his bed.

"We?" Riley croaked.

Tad gave him a sheepish smile. "It serves a useful purpose, but at the moment, it's just me. Emma will be along in a few minutes."

In an uncomfortably poignant déjà vu, Tad sat down in the seat beside Riley's bed and grabbed his hand.

"You have to stop scaring me like that. I thought… I thought…." Tad's voice broke. Yeah, Riley had thought that too. "If I hadn't heard you call out, I might have just gone in the building and gone upstairs and been too fucking late. Thank God I was already in the area."

"I'm fine." Concussion, and massively inflamed tissues in his neck, but mostly he was fine. Or he would be eventually. He understood his phone had not been nearly so lucky.

Tad threaded his fingers through Riley's and squeezed. "I'm so sorry. Those penicillin tablets were the first piece of real evidence we had, and because this case has gone on too long and you'd been poisoned, I leaped on that bottle too fast. What tipped you off?"

Riley explained how he'd asked a pharmacist about penicillin and found out it was sometimes taken before dental procedures as a safeguard against infection, and the grease on François's sleeve, and his upcoming root canal. Take that, Jessica Fletcher.

"Incredible. When you called, Emma got on the horn and hounded the lab. She was able to confirm pretty quick that your fingerprints were on all the bottles in the cabinet, and there was a suspicious lack of prints on the penicillin bottle. And I have to say that was incredibly dangerous. Snooping can get you in a lot of trouble, you know."

Whatever. He hadn't been poisoned for snooping, and he didn't think that even this would deter him in the future, although he might reconsider it if there was another murderer involved.

"Do you have enough evidence now? Especially if you get the shirt? I bet Mary still has it; François wouldn't have had time to destroy it. What about following up on the prescription? I bet you'll find the name is illegible or was written out to an F. Gautier."

"We'll get the shirt. As for evidence, Floriana's and Cody's fingerprints were all over the outside of the gift box with poison, but all of the vials were wiped clean. Except for a partial on the inside of the body cream lid. And that belonged to none other than François.

We also tracked down the prescription. You're right, it was made out for an F. Gautier, and the pharmacist identified François as the person who brought in the prescription and said it was for Floriana. He'd been planning to frame her all along and take over the company."

"Shit. I can't... no, I guess I can believe it. But it's still weird that I know a murderer."

"And with your suggestion about the prescription, we should be able to tie François to Gabrielle's murder as well."

Riley smiled and rubbed Tad's thumb with his own. Now he could finally relax. All the pieces made sense.

"Do you know why? I mean, obviously he wanted the money, but that's a big step. It's not like the whole family isn't well-off."

"There was a mountain of financial data, and we're not all the way through it, but it's starting to look like François and Bethany were living beyond their means, with a significant amount of gambling debts. It was one of the leads we'd been pursuing until you got poisoned."

"I can't even conceive of being able to spend that much money, never mind that money not being enough to live on."

Tad snorted. "Ain't that the truth."

"You might want to check the launch events and holiday parties first. I noticed something weird with the amounts, but I never got a chance to track it down."

Shaking his head, Tad chuckled. "You trying to get a recommendation to the police academy?"

"Uh, no. I think maybe I've had enough sleuthing." Although it was still so fucking cool that he'd contributed to the whole thing—found out who was behind it all before the police. Not bad for a nerdy gamer. "What happens now?"

"We've got him dead to rights on assault and attempted murder, and it'll only be a matter of time before we get the proof for Gabrielle's murder too."

"Good."

Tad cleared his throat. "Uh. So, I have to be going. Thank you for your help."

Riley's jubilant mood splattered all over the floor. "You're leaving." Again.

To be fair, Tad looked stricken. Torn. But it didn't help. Their situation wasn't any different from when Floriana was arrested and Tad had outlined why they couldn't be together. It still fucking hurt, and it was going to take a hell of a lot longer to heal than his concussion.

"I'm sorry." Tad leaned over and kissed him, heat and love and want all there for Riley to taste in a fraction of a second, but it didn't belong to him. It would never be his. His sinuses burned with the sudden onslaught of tears, and he struggled to hold them back. His control over his emotions was nonexistent, and he didn't want Tad to see him cry again.

Although it was almost physically painful to draw away, Riley did so nonetheless. He couldn't prolong the agony any longer.

Tad stroked his cheek one last time, and he turned away.

Hot tears leaked from Riley's eyes, soaking the pancake of a pillow beneath his head as he listened to the squeak of Tad's shoes recede.

ALTHOUGH RILEY could have cried all day, he just didn't have that much moisture left in him, and he was already feeling achy and his head was throbbing. The curtain jangled, and he sniffed before daring a look.

Floriana and Aaron stood together, carrying a teddy bear holding a box of chocolates. Riley blinked at them. They were literally the last people on earth he'd expected to see, and he was including Elvis and the queen on his list.

Floriana smiled, more warmth in her gaze than Riley had ever seen. "I'm so sorry, Riley."

Aaron set the bear down on the table by Riley's head.

"Sorry for what?"

Floriana flapped her hands. "For François, mostly."

"Not your fault."

Aaron murmured agreement.

"I know, I know. Aaron keeps trying to tell me. I just wanted…. I'm also sorry for how I treated you."

"Um. Okay." Was this some sort of misguided attempt to get him to come back and work at Gautier? Because Hell would have to reach absolute zero—none of that sissy freezing bullshit—before Riley would step back in that place.

"No, really." She sat in the chair Tad had so recently occupied, and took his hand in hers. Her hands were too small, too chilly, to provide the same comfort Tad could. It struck him that he should probably be nervous, but the drugs kept him from freaking out too badly.

Floriana's smile wobbled as though she was going to start crying again.

"Aaron and I have been seeing each other for a while. Mother absolutely hated that. Thought I was lowering myself. She did everything she could within the letter of the law to convince Aaron to quit, and it got so stressful he needed to take some time off, at the advice of his physician. When she hired you, and I kept hearing about how much she liked you and how she wanted to keep you on…. She never said, but I knew she meant she wanted to get rid of Aaron. I hated you for taking his place, for being someone my mother liked. It wasn't your fault at all, and I shouldn't have taken out my problems with my mother on you."

That explained why people were careful not to talk too much about Floriana's love life and why no one really mentioned Aaron.

"Thank you. So what happens now? For you and the company."

Floriana shrugged. "Cody said he'd keep Aaron on, and we're going to do our best to work together. It's… the hate… it's not good."

Uh, no. Too bad it took her brother killing her mother to figure that out.

"Best of luck to you."

"Get better soon." Aaron clapped his shoulder gently, and they left, Aaron's arm around Floriana's waist.

Chapter TWELVE

"So what did you guys want to play?" Riley didn't want to talk about the murder anymore. Mostly he wanted to forget, and it had been fucking hard while sitting alone in his condo all week recuperating from his injuries. He had a new contract coming up, but with his bruising still visible, he'd asked the agency if it could be postponed another week. As much as he'd like to start work again on Monday, he'd be verbally biting and stabbing if he had to explain the still-obvious finger marks around his throat.

"I think our resident hero ought to choose." Shaun cuffed his shoulder while Riley rolled his eyes.

"I don't know. Something good for five."

"I hate to break this to you, sweetie, but I think maybe that concussion isn't better. There's only four of us today." Shaun smirked at him. It was nice to get back to something resembling normalcy.

"Yes, but I invited someone."

Just like that, Shaun's expression turned disapproving. "Not Tad, for fuck's sake." Riley had kept his silence about his involvement with Tad, but in the hospital it hadn't been hard for Shaun and Alisha to see something was wrong, that Riley had been devastated all out of proportion after Tad had left that last time. They'd come to mostly the right conclusion, but Riley didn't confirm. Talking about it would only make it harder to get over.

Riley rolled his eyes. "Of course not Tad. I told you, nothing's happening on that front. What about Betrayal at House on the Hill? That's a good one to get beginners started." Riley redirected. If they were going to offer him the choice, then he was going to take it. He'd already pulled it from the wall of games, just in case.

"Oh. You invited a newbie, did you?"

"Yes, I...." Riley glanced up. "There she is now."

Alisha blew through the door of the café, wearing jeans and a low-cut T-shirt. Across the table, Ozzy craned his neck to see who Riley was talking about. As he twisted back to stare fixedly at the table, he made a strangled sound that might have been *meep*.

She saw Riley immediately and gave him a hug and kiss, and hugged Shaun before moving a chair beside Ozzy.

Riley introduced her to Raj and Ozzy, although Ozzy had a hard time looking her in the face.

"So, lay it on me, kids. What are we playing?"

Ozzy glanced at her, face flushed, before looking back at the table. "Betrayal at House on the Hill." There was a throaty, gravelly sound to Ozzy's voice that Riley had never heard. He stared at his friend, but Ozzy resolutely wasn't catching anyone's gaze as he reached over to grab the box.

Alisha clearly saw something that no one else did. She shifted just enough so that her breasts brushed Ozzy's arm. "Can you help me out, teach me what I need to do?" Alisha was almost purring, and Riley shifted in his seat, just a little uncomfortable at the display. A glance at Raj and Shaun confirmed they were as confused as he was.

He expected Ozzy to move away, or hand her the instructions, or something. Instead, his ears turned almost purple as he replied, "Of course, Alisha."

The way Ozzy said her name told Riley everything. Something had clicked between them, right here in front of the gaming group. Love at first sight. Maybe this was what it looked like.

Riley smiled, even as it hurt inside. He wanted that for himself. If Riley was going to find a happy ever after, he'd need to work through his feelings for Tad, but it wasn't going to be any time soon.

One day.

AMAZINGLY, ALISHA and Ozzy stayed to game, despite some incredibly heated looks. Ozzy even went so far as to help her when she'd randomly been chosen as the traitor. Normally Ozzy was a stickler for rules, but almost like he was a different person, he helped her well enough that she managed to beat the rest of them.

They were partway through the second game when Shaun poked Riley in the side.

"What?"

Shaun gestured at the door, and Riley looked up.

And nearly melted into his chair. Tad stood just inside the café, smiling hesitantly. He had chosen to wear jeans and a tight T-shirt, and although Riley could objectively admit Alisha looked great, seeing Tad in similar casual clothes turned him on and made him squirm.

"Well, go talk to him," Shaun whispered.

"You owe me a nice dinner," Alisha added.

Shaun hadn't been too impressed with Tad's actions up to now—Riley hadn't been able to keep all of that pain inside, and he'd told Shaun almost everything. In light of that, Riley wasn't sure why Shaun was encouraging him to talk to Tad. Hell, he wasn't even sure his legs would hold him.

The rest of the group had glanced to where he and Shaun were staring, and Alisha spoke up. "I told you that man was hot. And I know he's not here for me, so get your ass over there and see what he wants."

Tad had already ripped his heart to shreds far too many times, and Riley was afraid. If Tad was here to tell him François had escaped or something, he was going to lose his mind.

But there wasn't any possibility that Riley could ignore Tad standing there, looking sheepish and oddly awkward.

He got up and walked slowly to the door.

"Hey."

Tad was going to have to do better than that. "What's up?"

"Can we talk?"

Riley sighed. Admittedly, he'd learned he was an emotional masochist, and the only way to keep his sanity would be to refuse. Tad's no-contact rule needed to be enforced. After today. Riley needed one more day, one more moment to wallow in what might have been.

The only thing was, he knew how much it sucked to have a game interrupted, and he was worried whatever Tad needed to talk about would upset him enough that he wouldn't want to continue.

"We're halfway through a game. Can it wait until we're done?"

Tad shrugged. "Sure. Can I hang out and watch?"

Shaun was going to kick his ass—if Riley didn't beat him to it. This was the ultimate stupid idea in the history of stupid ideas. But it was easier to be strong when Tad wasn't standing right in front of him, smelling so fucking good and looking like an underwear model.

"C'mon, pull up a chair."

Tad followed him to the table. He greeted Alisha and Shaun, who both said hello with some suspicion. Riley introduced Tad to Raj and Ozzy as a guy he went to high school with who he'd recently crossed paths with. Alisha and Shaun rolled their eyes.

Ozzy and Alisha were especially anxious to finish the game. Riley might have teased them about it, but he was a little anxious to be done with the game too and make his excuses to leave. The sooner he found out what Tad wanted, the sooner he could hide in his condo and try to knit his shredded heart back together.

THE SECOND half of the game was possibly the most fun Riley had had in a long time. Tad picked up the game mechanics quickly, but Riley didn't mind answering his questions. And whenever Riley picked up a spooky event card, Tad gleefully read it aloud in an appropriately spooky voice. This time Riley ended up the traitor, and he had his own backup this time, Tad's ability to strategize making him a natural at the game.

Every so often, Tad would stroke Riley's back, making him shiver. He wanted to turn his nose into Tad's neck, drink in that spicy scent that drove him wild, and then lick and bite at that strong neck to his heart's content. But he had no right, and he suspected Tad's touch might be more absentminded than intentional.

When they finally won after whittling down the opposition, Riley was laughing along with Tad. All too soon, he remembered that Tad wasn't part of his life, and he probably had some sort of bad news for Riley.

They called it a night, and after saying his goodbyes, Riley followed Tad outside.

He was going to kill Tad for giving him a taste of what they could have together. None of his previous boyfriends had had any interest in getting to know his gaming group, never mind interest in the games themselves.

"Can I drive you home?"

Great. They were going to have this talk on Riley's turf. That wasn't going to suck one bit. Oh wait….

"Sure." At least on his home turf he could kick Tad out and have a mini breakdown immediately, rather than trying to hold it together on public transit before he got home.

The car ride covered banal pleasantries, and the elevator ride up to his place was spent in silence.

Inside, Riley turned to Tad. "Did you want a drink? Coffee or tea?" He had a lot of bad memories to deal with after his experience at Gautier Cosmetics, but he'd also come away with tea and Alisha, so he couldn't regret it.

"Water's fine, thanks."

Riley could have used some soothing, but he'd make a pot of tea after Tad left and find some sappy romcom to sob over while he drank it. He got a couple of bottles out of the fridge and handed one to Tad.

"What's up?"

Tad bit his lip. "I don't know if you'll think this is good news or not."

Riley rolled his eyes. "Just tell me. Imagining things is going to make me lose my shit."

"François pleaded guilty."

Riley waited, wondering if there was more, but Tad just stared at him, gaze hot and intense. "What does that mean, exactly?"

"It means he's forgoing a trial. Going to jail. Admitted to killing his mother and trying to kill both you and Cody."

That made no sense. François was an arrogant son of a bitch. "Why would he do that?"

Tad smiled at Riley like he was proud of him. "Those events you told us to look at? Yeah, he was definitely embezzling from the company to pay gambling debts. He had nothing—his place was mortgaged to the hilt. His wife, Bethany? She comes from money—more money than the Gautiers, if you can believe it. Anyway, they had a prenup covering a number of situations, one of which was François getting arrested. She filed for divorce within an hour after his arrest, and that divorce would leave him with nothing but debt, and a lot of it."

"Okay, that's sad, I guess, that Bethany wouldn't even wait to see how things went, but why are you telling me this?"

"Because the highbrow lawyer François called when he got arrested didn't stick around very long once it became clear there was no way for François to even cover his retainer, and his sister wasn't going to front him any money, not after he tried to frame her. I guess François didn't think he'd fare too well with a public defender, and he'd have nothing to return to even if he did win."

Riley downed half his water in one gulp. "I appreciate you telling me this."

They stood there, staring at each other. Then Riley realized that buried in all that information was possibly the most important, pertinent nugget. "No trial?"

Tad smiled wide. "No trial."

Then that might mean…. "I'm not a witness."

That smile stretched even wider. "You're not a witness." Tad took a couple of steps closer, and Riley mimicked him until there were mere inches between them.

Tad stared into his eyes. "No contacts?"

"No. I got Lasik after high school. I only wore the contacts for the color." Riley's breath hitched. "But someone told me they liked the real color of my eyes."

A rumble shook Tad's chest, and he cupped Riley's cheeks in his hands. "Can we try and make a go of this? Please say I didn't fuck up my only chance with you."

Riley stared into the warm depths of Tad's brown eyes. "You didn't."

A tremble shook Tad before he leaned in that last bit to press their lips together. For a few seconds, Riley savored the gentle sweetness of lips he'd missed kissing more than he'd missed anything else in his life. Seconds later, the kiss went from virginal to voracious. Tad slid his hands down Riley's body and brought him tight against Tad's chest.

Breath coming fast and hard, Riley pulled away. "Not that I'm not loving this, but… I'd been thinking I might never see you again, you know? This is a little much to wrap my head around here."

"I know. It was shitty the way I left things, and I wouldn't blame you if you hated me, but Riley…." Tad buried his head in Riley's neck. "I love you."

The words were muffled, but Riley heard them loud and clear. And they shook him to his core. "Did you… just…."

Tad took a deep breath and stared him straight in the face. "I don't deserve another chance, but please take pity on me. I'm lost without you. I want to watch TV with you in your sweet little condo. I want to hang out with your friends, learn how to play games."

Riley cupped his cheeks. "I want to brighten your day when you've endured the worst humanity can offer. I want to brush my teeth side by side with you. I want to meet your family. Spend weekends in bed together."

A tear slipped down Tad's cheek. "So you'll give me another chance?"

"How could I not? I love you too, and missing you has been painful."

Another tear spilled over Tad's cheek, making Riley's eyes burn in sympathy, but they were both grinning like fools.

Tad kissed his nose. "Want to watch a movie? Did you eat dinner?"

"Actually, no." The guys had ordered food shortly before Tad had shown up, but Riley hadn't been too interested in eating at that point. "I could order pizza?"

"Sounds good." Tad stroked his face gently, lovingly, before stepping back, then followed Riley to his couch, hopefully for the rest of his life.

KC BURN has been writing for as long as she can remember and is a sucker for happy endings (of all kinds). After moving from Toronto to Florida for her husband to take a dream job, she discovered a love of gay romance and fulfilled a dream of her own—getting published. After a few years of editing web content by day, and neglecting her supportive, understanding hubby and needy cat at night to write stories about men loving men, she was uprooted yet again and now resides in California. Writing is always fun and rewarding, but writing about her guys is the most fun she's had in a long time, and she hopes you'll enjoy them as much as she does.

Website: kcburn.com
Twitter: @authorkcburn
Facebook: www.facebook.com/kcburn

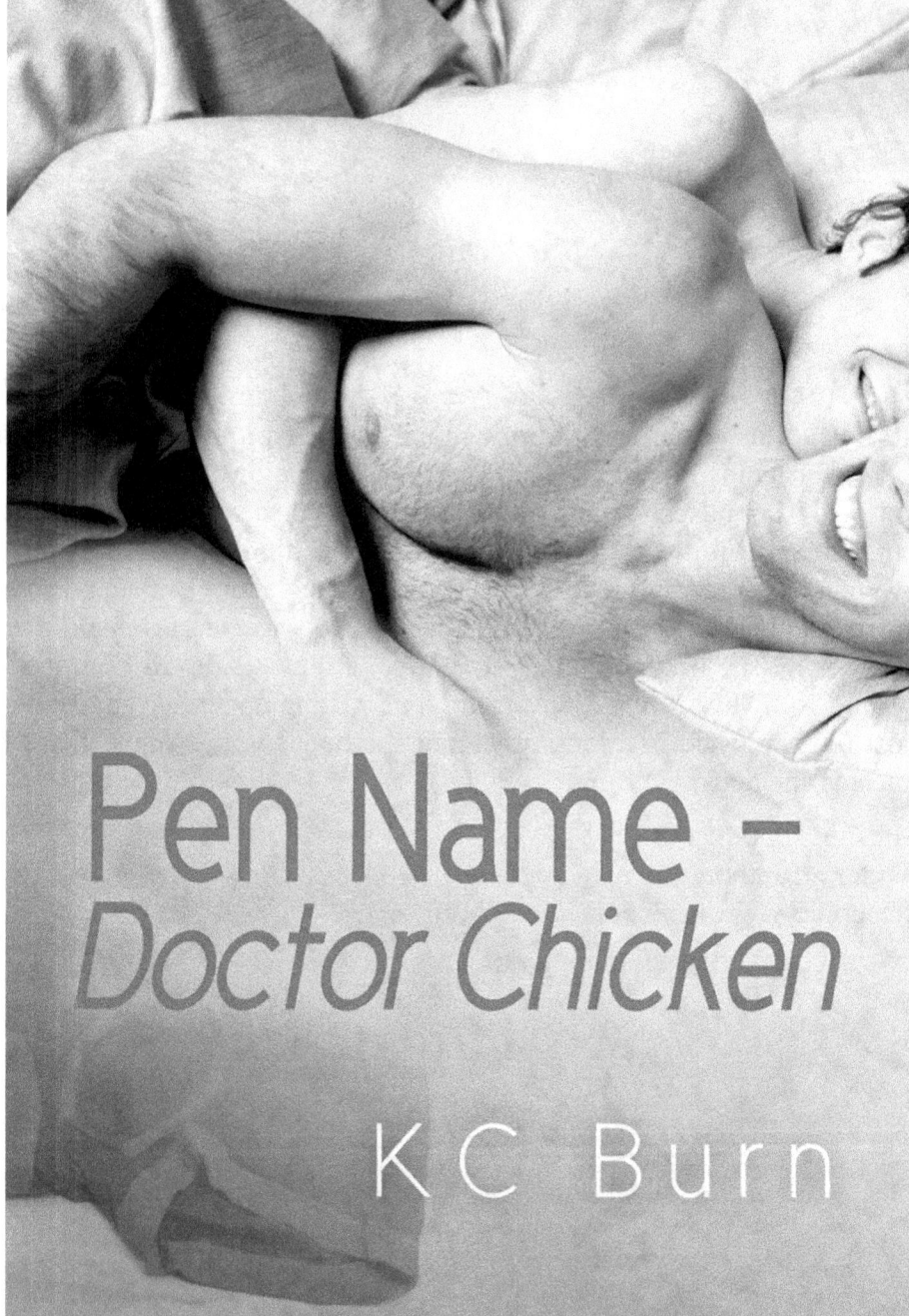

Pen Name –
Doctor Chicken

KC Burn

Sometimes Stratford Dale feels like Doctor Chicken consumes his life. It's his pen name for a series of wildly popular children's books. They were his brainchild; he meant for them to be a way to pay his many bills while he pursued his dream of publishing graphic novels. But the Doctor Chicken contract was a raw deal. Instead, he churns out book after book for a pittance, leaving him broke and no closer to his dreams.

Stratford's dreams of love have fared no better, but he's still trying. After yet another disastrous date, he's intrigued by a man going into a cooking class—so he takes the class too. Vinnie Giani is a successful, self-made man who is charmed by Stratford's bow ties, sharp humor, and clumsiness—which leads to an opportunity to take Stratford in for stitches. Vinnie is, above all, responsible, having taken on the care of his mother and sisters from a young age. Perhaps it's natural when he begins to treat Stratford more as a child who needs a parent than as an equal partner. But when Vinnie tries to "fix" Stratford's career woes—including the Doctor Chicken problem—and ends up making the situation worse, their fledgling relationship may not withstand the strain created by blame and lies.

www.dreamspninerpress.com

RAINBOW BLUES

KC Burn

Having come out late in life, forty-three-year-old Luke Jordan is at a loss about how to conduct himself as a gay man. As a construction manager, he's not interested in being out at work, but he'd like to find a boyfriend or at least some gay friends. Two years after his wife got all their friends in the divorce, he's no closer to the life he wants.

Zach, Luke's adult son, takes charge and signs him up for the Rainbow Blues, a social group for gay blue-collar workers. At an event, he not only finds friends but meets Jimmy Alexander, part-time stage actor and full-time high school biology teacher. Jimmy loves the stage but wishes potential boyfriends weren't so jealous of the time he devotes to it. When he meets Luke and finds him accepting of his many facets, he thinks it's a dream come true.

Their relationship quickly moves into serious territory, but their connection is tested to its breaking point by the offer of a juicy movie role that takes Jimmy to the opposite coast and into the path of a very sexy costar.

www.dreamspinnerpress.com

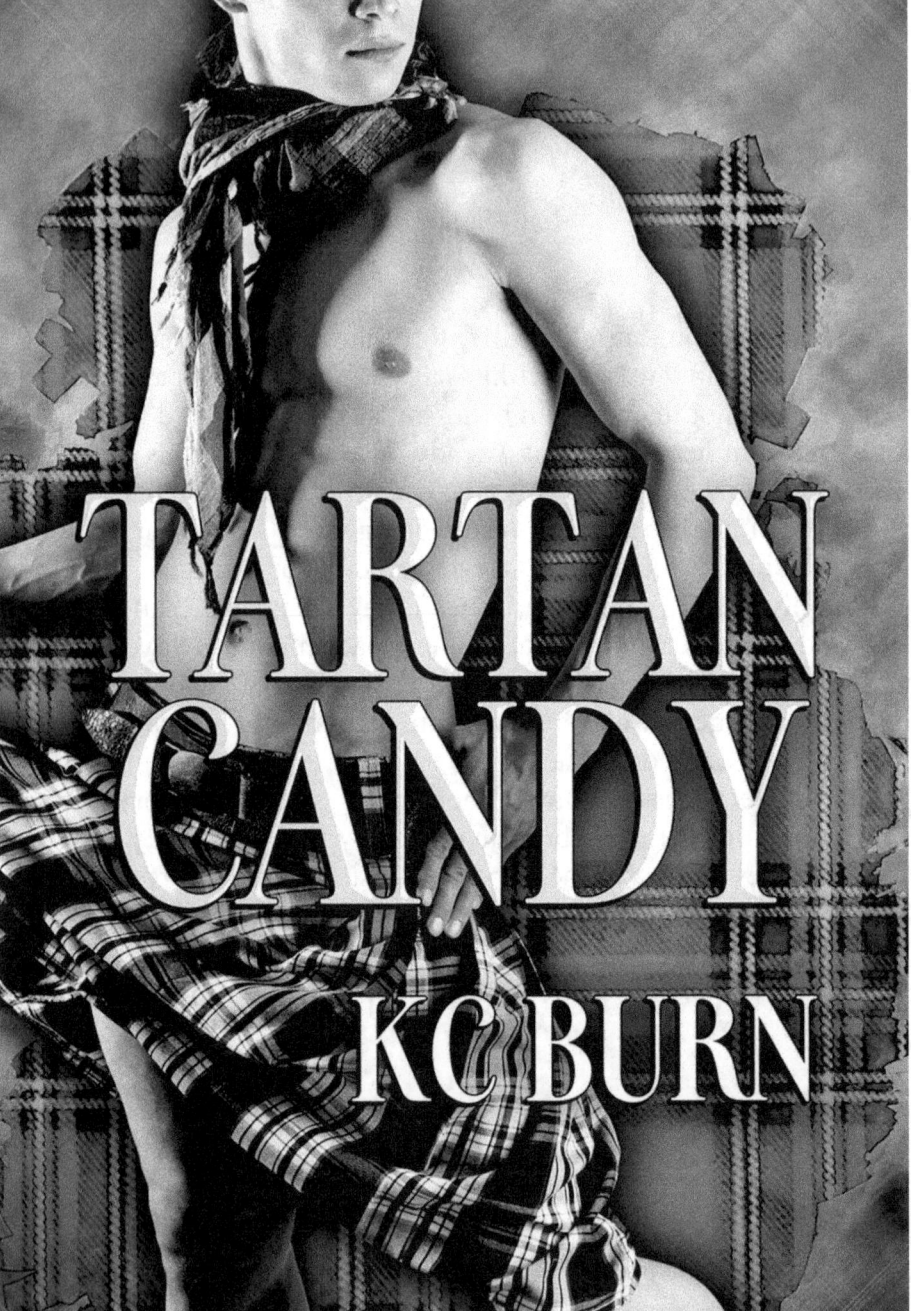

TARTAN
CANDY

KC BURN

A Fabric Hearts Story

Finlay McIntyre (aka Raven) is a successful adult film star with a penchant for kilts, until an accident cuts short his stardom and leaves him with zero sexual desire, lowered self-esteem, and no job. He knew his porn career wouldn't last forever, but he wasn't prepared for retirement at twenty-eight. While trying to figure out the rest of his life, Raven agrees to attend a high school reunion. That's when a malfunctioning AC unit in his hotel room changes everything.

Caleb Sanderson, an entrepreneur with his own HVAC business, has no idea what to expect when he steps into Raven's hotel room to fix his AC unit. They're attracted to each other, but Caleb, closeted, can't afford a gay relationship, not with his mom pressuring him to produce grandchildren. If he wants to keep Raven—who no closet could hold—he'll need to tell his family the truth. But Raven has a few secrets of his own. He refuses to reveal his porn past to Caleb, a past that might be the final obstacle to Caleb and Raven having any kind of relationship.

www.dreamspinnerpress.com

PLAID
VERSUS
PAISLEY

KC BURN

A Fabric Hearts Story

Two years after his life fell apart, Will Dawson moved to Florida to start over. His job in the tech department of Idyll Fling, a gay porn studio, is ideal for him. When his boss forces him to take on a new hire, the last person he expects is Dallas Greene—the man who cost him his job and his boyfriend back in Connecticut. He doesn't know what's on Dallas's agenda, but he won't be blindsided by a wolf masquerading as a runway model. Not again.

Dallas might have thrown himself on his brother's mercy, but his skills are needed at Idyll Fling. Working with Will is a bonus, since Dallas has never forgotten the man. A good working relationship is only the beginning of what Dallas wants with Will.

But Dallas doesn't realize how deep Will's distrust runs, and Will doesn't know that the man he's torn between loving and hating is the boss's brother. When all truths are revealed, how can a relationship built on lies still stand?

www.dreamspinnerpress.com

JUST ADD ARGYLE

KC BURN

A Fabric Hearts Story

Tate Buchanan is a troublemaker who can't keep a job, no matter how many times his lucky argyle sweater gets him hired. Add to that a learning disability and an impetuous nature that sends him into altercations to protect the defenseless, and he hardly manages to make friends, let alone find a man who's interested in him for more than one night.

Most people think EMT Jaime Escobar is a player, but the truth is he wants a serious partner—he just can't justify wasting time on guys he knows aren't a match. But when he treats a gorgeous redhead after a fight, he finds the spark he's spent so many years looking for.

Jaime wants to take the next step with Tate, but it's clear Tate's not going to curb his impulsive behavior—his next fight sends him to the hospital. Jaime's relationship with a near criminal isn't something his family is ready to accept, not any more than Tate is willing to be kept a secret. Jaime will need a lot of understanding—and some luck of his own—to keep them both. But this is one fight he's going to see through to the end.

www.dreamspinnerpress.com

KC Burn
COP OUT

Toronto Tales: Book One

Detective Kurt O'Donnell is used to digging up other people's secrets, but when he discovers his slain partner was married to another man, it shakes him. Determined to do the right thing, Kurt offers the mourning Davy his assistance. Helping Davy through his grief helps Kurt deal with the guilt that his partner didn't trust him enough to tell him the truth, and somewhere along the way Davy stops being an obligation and becomes a friend, the closest friend Kurt has ever had.

His growing attraction to Davy complicates matters, leaving Kurt struggling to reevaluate his sexuality. Then a sensual encounter neither man is ready for confuses them further. To be with Davy, Kurt must face the prospect of coming out, but his job and his relationship with his Catholic family are on the line. Can he risk destroying his life for the uncertain possibility of a relationship with a newly widowed man?

www.dreamspinnerpress.com

Toronto Tales

COVER UP

KC Burn

Sequel to *Cop Out*
Toronto Tales: Book Two

Detective Ivan Bekker has hit rock bottom. Not only is he recovering
from a bad breakup with a cheating boyfriend, he's also involved in a
drug bust gone bad. Ivan had to kill a man, and his friend was shot and
is now fighting for his life. Though Ivan is under investigation for his
part in the shooting, his boss sends him on an off-the-books undercover
operation to close the case. The timing is critical—this could be their
chance to plug a leak in the department.

Off-balance and without backup, Ivan finds himself playing a
recent divorcé and becoming Parker Wakefield's roommate. He finds it
hard to believe that sweet Parker could possibly be a criminal, much less
have ties to a Russian mafia drug-trafficking operation, and Ivan lets
down his guard. His affection is unprofessional, but Parker is irresistible.

When Ivan comes across clear evidence of Parker's criminal
involvement, he has to choose: protect their relationship, regardless of
the consequences, or save his career and arrest the man he loves.

www.dreamspinnerpress.com